D0182405

ZAFFRE

First published in the UK in 2022 by
ZAFFRE
An imprint of Bonnier Books UK
4th Floor, Victoria House, Bloomsbury Square, London, WC1B 4DA
Owned by Bonnier Books
Sveavägen 56, Stockholm, Sweden

A CIP catalogue record for this book is
available from the British Library.

Hardback ISBN: 978-1-83877-726-5
Trade paperback ISBN: 978-1-83877-761-6

Also available as an ebook and an audiobook

1 3 5 7 9 10 8 6 4 2

Typeset by IDSUK (Data Connection) Ltd
Printed and bound in Great Britain by Clays Ltd, Elcograf S.p.A.

Zaffre is an imprint of Bonnier Books UK
www.bonnierbooks.co.uk

One

Santiago, Chile

Warrant Officer Jamie Carter stood at the edge of the training range, the stiff afternoon breeze scraping through his dark hair, and wished to fuck he was somewhere else.

A few paces away, the last soldiers were piling out of the assault vehicles that had ferried them over from the main compound two kilometres away. There were twenty guys in total. Recruits to the Pumas, the newest addition to Chile's Special Forces brigade.

The cream of the crop, Carter had to remind himself. The country's finest warriors. Though some of them didn't act much like it.

Every day for the last month, Carter had been reporting to the camp shortly after dawn to oversee a training package for the soldiers. Under his guidance, the lads had spent hours on the ranges and in the lecture rooms, practising shooting drills, doing range work, studying navigation techniques and fieldcraft, intermingled with gruelling fitness sessions.

Now they were about to undertake their latest exercise.

They had gathered at the edge of a wide parcel of land the approximate size of a football field. A hundred metres away, in the middle of the field, piles of car tyres had been arranged in two-metre-high stacks, filled with sand and laid out in the shape of a hedge maze, with doors hanging from wooden frames denoting the various entry points.

Tyre Village was part of a wider military training area. Beyond the maze there were separate zones for shooting ranges, grenade and mortar practice, fields for conducting physical drills and digging hides and murder holes. Everything the soldiers needed to know to transform them into a decent SF outfit.

The camp was set on the floor of an arid valley, surrounded by a patchwork of scrubland, bare hills and irrigated fields. Shreds of tissue-like cloud clung to the peaks of the distant mountains. They were eight kilometres from the nearest small town, fifty kilometres north of Santiago.

More like the bloody arse end of the world.

He had arrived several weeks ago, on a two-year posting. Continuation training, they called it in the Regiment. Overseas instruction for friendly SF units.

Carter had another name for it: purgatory. Send over a Blade to spend a couple of years in-country, overseeing a programme for a bunch of sub-level operators. Train one section of soldiers for six months, get them up to scratch, pass them out, then move on to the next intake.

Rinse and repeat.

No one liked continuation jobs. Fact. The work was lonely and dull, and it was hard to stay motivated when you knew that most of the students would let their standards drop as soon as you left. But it was big business for the British government, Carter knew. Foreign countries were willing to pay a small fortune for the privilege of having their troops schooled by a Regiment man. More importantly, the programmes had the Whitehall seal of approval: the prestige of the SAS was a useful tool for currying favour with tinpot dictators and foreign rulers.

No one seemed to give a shit that the guys you were educating might end up facing you on the battlefield one day.

Some years ago, a bright spark had changed the rules so that the money from these contracts went straight back to the Hereford coffers instead of the government. Now roughly fifty per cent of the work done by the lads involved training packages for foreign armies.

But it was still a crap assignment.

Carter knew he was in Chile for purely political reasons. The British government leased a base in the south of the country, which was critical for mounting airborne operations around the Falklands if things ever kicked off there again. In return for the lease, Whitehall had agreed that 22 SAS would help to train up a new covert SF unit, drawn from the ranks of the Chilean armed forces.

Another twenty-three months of this shite, Carter reminded himself.

And all because I pissed off the wrong people.

Carter shoved aside his anger as he marched over to the soldiers.

They were decked out in their standard-issue camo uniforms – no one wore black kit to conduct house assaults these days, not even the lads back home in Hereford. Fifteen of the Pumas had M4 assault rifles slung over their shoulders. The others carried PGM 338 French-manufactured sniper rifles, chambered for the .338 Lapua Magnum round. All of them were equipped with leg-holstered Beretta Px4 Storm semi-automatic pistols as their side-arms. Each man also had a swept-back ballistic helmet, tactical plate carrier with front and rear armour, knee and elbow pads. Plus L2 grenades and flashbangs stowed in the pouches on the front of their vests, spare mags for their primary weapon systems, tactical radio sets, throat mics and headphones.

Carter wore the same uniform as the rest of the lads, but a rank above. The Regiment liked its instructors to keep a low profile while they were on the job. For security reasons, mainly. Better to have the trainers blend in with the regular troops, especially if Whitehall didn't want to advertise its relationship with the domestic government. Having to put on a foreign uniform every day only added to Carter's foul mood.

This isn't why I joined the Regiment, he thought. *Dressing up in the gear of some second-rate military and lecturing a bunch of amateurs.*

I shouldn't be here.

Carter had nothing against these lads personally. They were no different from the soldiers he'd trained in a bunch of other countries during his nine years in the Regiment. But he knew how these units operated. Often, the training programmes were a waste of everyone's time. Whether a student passed or failed had little to do with his capabilities as a warfighter, and a lot to do with politics.

In theory, Carter was there to develop a highly disciplined elite fighting unit.

But in reality, he was more like a glorified range safety officer.

It was like asking a World Cup-winning coach to manage a pub team.

'Right, lads,' he began. 'This is the situation.'

The soldiers listened keenly as he briefed them on the mission background. Painting a picture for them. Carter spoke in a deliberate, slow tone. Although these guys were reasonably fluent in English, some of them struggled to understand his Geordie accent.

'Terrorists have taken over the Japanese embassy in Santiago,' he went on, waving a hand in the direction of Tyre Village. 'All attempts to negotiate a peaceful resolution have failed. An hour ago, the terrorists executed one of the hostages. They're now threatening to kill one civilian every hour unless their demands are met in full. The President has been updated and has authorised the use of violence to resolve the situation. This is where you come in, fellas.'

He paused as he glanced round the sea of faces in front of him. Carter had spent the past few weeks assessing the students and he'd swiftly identified those who were up to the job. There were a few of them, he reflected. Dedicated professionals. Guys who trained hard and took themselves seriously in spite of the crap pay and the political bullshit. Lads who were keen to learn from their mistakes.

Most of the others were willing but limited. Honest soldiers, but not up to scratch as elite operators. Carter had no problem with them, as long as they put in a shift, did what they were told and didn't pull the piss.

But several of them had no business being anywhere near a Special Forces unit.

Upon his arrival Carter had been dismayed by the poor quality of some of the recruits on the training ranges. He'd seen soldiers getting panicky when handling grenades, dropping them by accident at their feet instead of hurling them at their targets. A few students had failed to cover their flanks or raced too far ahead of their colleagues during fire-and-movement drills. Lectures on navigation and map-reading had fallen flat. Some of their weapon-handling skills were slack.

In the Regiment, you'd weed out the bad apples early on in the selection process. Time-wasters didn't last long.

Here, Carter had no choice but to grit his teeth and get on with it.

He said, 'Snipers have been observing the stronghold for the past twenty-four hours. We know that there are sixteen embassy staff and civilians being held hostage inside, and eight X-rays. They have to be dealt with now, to prevent any further loss of life.'

He looked towards the unit commander. Captain Carlos Medel was a single bloke in his early thirties, tall and lean, with a chin so prominent you could hang a coat from it. He was a fundamentally decent soldier who, rather unusually, appeared to have earned his rank on merit. He was diplomatic, disliked small talk and bluster. He was also one of the few friends Carter had made since he'd arrived in Chile. They often enjoyed a few jars in one of the bars in Santiago, shooting the breeze.

'Captain, I want you to plan a multi-entry assault,' Carter said. 'You've got thirty minutes. Then I want you to prosecute an attack on the stronghold. Understood?'

'Yes, Jamie,' Medel said. 'No problem.'

'I should lead the main assault group, Captain,' one of the soldiers cut in.

Carter slanted his gaze towards the guy who'd spoken. Fabian Vargas. One of the bad apples. A doughy-faced fat kid in his early twenties. Carter had taken one look at the guy and wondered how the hell he had managed to get selected for SF duty. When he'd put the question to Medel, the captain had merely shaken his head and muttered something about the kid's father, a general who had recently been appointed as the President's chief of staff. Carter had disliked Vargas on first sight, and nothing he'd seen since had changed his opinion.

The previous day they had been practising a Man Down drill. A straightforward exercise. A couple of guys run over to a soldier pretending to be wounded, lift him up and carry him to safety while their colleagues put down suppressive fire to cover them. Vargas had even managed to cock that one up, dropping the injured lad as they legged it from the kill zone. The guy was a walking disaster.

'Put me in charge,' Vargas carried on. 'I'll cut those bitches down, Captain. Show the gringos how we do things here.'

Carter laughed. 'The only thing you should be leading is the line at the camp cookhouse, you fat fuck.'

A handful of the other students chuckled among themselves. Vargas stared at the instructor, jaw clenched tightly with rage. Carter wasn't bothered by his reaction. He wasn't here to throw an arm around the soldiers and make them feel good about themselves. Then he noticed something, and his expression shifted.

'Where the fuck is your rifle?' he demanded.

The soldiers instantly fell silent, sensing their instructor's bad temper. Vargas flushed and rubbed the nape of his neck.

'I asked you a question,' Carter growled.

'In the truck,' Vargas replied. 'I forgot it. No big deal.'

'That's "sir" to you.' Carter jabbed a finger at his flabby chest. 'Rule number one. Your weapon doesn't leave your side. It should never be more than arm's length away from your person. That's basic.'

'It was a mistake . . . sir,' Vargas replied defensively.

'I don't give a shit.' Carter stepped closer, moving into the Chilean's personal space. 'Start taking this exercise seriously or do us all a favour and fuck off.'

Vargas stared back at him, lips pressed into a hard line. He said nothing.

'I didn't hear you,' Carter said.

'Yes, *sir*.'

'Fuck's sake. Hurry up and get your weapon.' Carter watched Vargas hurry over to the truck, then turned to the others. 'What are you lot waiting for, a bloody invitation? Get a move on. Clock's ticking.'

Medel turned and barked orders at one of his subordinates. Victor Ramirez was a stocky bloke with short-cropped hair, eyes that were too close together and a nose so wide it looked as if he'd snorted a golf ball. He was the team's Method of Entry expert. The demolitions guy. He was also a moody fucker. Carter liked him about as much as he liked tofu and low-alcohol beverages.

The soldiers hastily gathered around a patch of dirt on the periphery of the range while their captain took a knee in the middle of the semicircle. Like footballers getting a pep talk from the coach before the big match. Carter looked on from a distance as Medel fashioned a crude map of Tyre Village on the ground, laying out sticks for the walls, rocks to mark the entry points. Then he divided his men into five three-man assault groups and started delegating. Telling the guys who would go where.

Although the soldiers were familiar with the range, they didn't know the precise layout waiting for them inside. To add to the element of surprise Carter had spent the morning on the range with a pair of staff helpers, laying traps. Targets depicting masked gunmen and hostages had been pasted onto strips of plywood and strategically placed around the rooms, with some hidden behind bits of furniture, or sited inches from the hostages. Booby traps had been planted: smoke grenades triggered by tripwires, some of them strung out at ankle level, others at chest or head height, because guys conducting an assault tended to focus on the ground and often missed the threats closer to eye level.

An instinct thing, Carter guessed.

Medel continued briefing the team.

Carter checked his G-Shock. Counting down the minutes.

As he watched and waited, the hot anger flared up in his chest again. The same rage he'd felt back at Hereford a couple of months ago, when they had told him about his next job.

The head shed had stitched him up. He was certain of it. There had been no good reason to fly him out to South America on a training stint. They had stuck Carter on a shite posting as punishment.

Eleven months earlier, things had been different. He had been the toast of the Regiment back then. Hero of the Bamako siege.

Carter had been posted to Mali to run a training package for the security forces while the rest of the country went to hell. A bullshit job, but he'd accepted it without complaint.

Until one morning, five months into the rotation, his phone had vibrated with an incoming call from a voice he didn't recognise. Which turned out to belong to the defence minister.

There had been a terrorist attack, the minister had said. Gunmen from a breakaway faction of Islamic State were laying siege to one of the city's most popular hotels. Dozens of Western aid workers, businessfolk and embassy staff were bottled up inside. The security forces were struggling to coordinate their response and the minister wanted Carter to help organise the assault.

At that particular moment, Carter had been working on the ranges several miles outside of the city. He'd hastily grabbed his gear, bundled it into his civvy vehicle and raced over to the scene. Then he'd thrown on his plate armour, grabbed his suppressed M4 rifle and flashed his military ID at the cops manning the cordon, telling them to point him in the direction of the terrorist attack.

Within minutes, he'd cleared the hotel lobby, dropping three targets.

Carter had then turned his attention to securing the upper floors of the hotel, where the rest of the gunmen were holed up with the hostages. He had been rapidly organising the security forces when he'd received a hostile call from Nigel Brathwaite, the British ambassador, ordering him to back down.

'This isn't your job,' Brathwaite had thundered down the line. 'You're here in a strictly advisory capacity. Leave it to the domestic forces to resolve. That's a fucking order.'

Carter had ignored him. A no-brainer. Lives were at risk. He was in a position to do something about it. He wasn't going to walk away.

The assault on the hotel complex had been a textbook deliberate action plan. A swift coordinated attack to neutralise the gunmen without having to gamble away the lives of innocent civilians. Carter had directed the security forces every step of the way.

The desperate firefight inside the building had lasted for less than four minutes. By the time it was over, twelve terrorists had been killed for the loss of one hotel security guard. Fifty-eight hostages had been rescued, including the British chargé d'affaires and several American citizens.

If Carter hadn't formulated the plan of attack, he doubted many of them would have survived. Maybe none.

Although his picture and name had been withheld from the media on the orders of the Regiment, everyone at Hereford knew him as the guy who had done the business on the ground in Mali.

Slotting the enemy. Saving lives.

In the aftermath of the attack, the President of the United States had privately met with Carter to express his gratitude. Later, there had been a discreet medal ceremony behind closed doors in Washington, attended by a coterie of high-ranking generals and members of Congress. There Carter had been presented with the Medal of Honor, the highest award the US can bestow on a warrior. The decoration was traditionally reserved only for American service personnel, but the President had personally insisted that Carter should receive it.

The head shed had been uncomfortable with a Hereford man accepting such a rare distinction and had only grudgingly agreed on condition that the ceremony remained a private affair, withheld entirely from news outlets. That had been fine by Carter. He didn't want the publicity anyway. He was a quiet man by nature. Happiest in his own company, walking the hills around his home in Credenhill.

For a while, he had been a living legend at Hereford.

Then it had all gone south. Big time.

Brathwaite had given Carter a bollocking for his refusal to follow orders. Soon after his return to Hereford, Carter had realised the extent of his mistake: he'd made a powerful enemy for life. The ambassador had used his clout in Whitehall to make Carter's life in the Regiment a misery. Turned him into an outcast. Hence the bullshit job in Chile. Punishment, for failing to follow orders.

Now I'm babysitting a batch of second-rate troops.

One thing was sure. He was finished with the Regiment after this posting. No doubt about it.

Carter figured he'd keep his head down, serve his time. See out this gig. Then he'd return to Hereford and tell the top brass he was finished. The Circuit was not as lucrative as it had been at the height of the wars in the Middle East, when there were fortunes to be made for those with the right skill sets, but Carter would find something. An ex-Blade with his credentials would have admirers in the world of private contractors. It wouldn't be the best-paid job in the world, maybe. Dull work, but steady.

Better than staying at Hereford and being treated like a pariah.

Carter glanced at his watch again.

Two minutes later, he strode over to the soldiers.

'That's it. Time's up.' He cocked his chin at Medel. 'Captain. Who's leading the front assault team?'

The captain gestured to Vargas. 'Fabian will take the lead.'

From the sheepish look on the commander's face, Carter had the impression the decision was a political one. The kid had no doubt insisted on being the first man in, and Medel had decided not to argue with him.

A grin stretched across Vargas's mug. 'I'm gonna teach these fuckers a lesson,' he said. 'Drop them like a bad habit. Just you see.'

'Right.' Carter suppressed his anger and nodded at Medel. 'I'll be following the main assault group inside.'

'You will come with us, sir?' Vargas frowned. 'Why?'

'Because I fucking said so,' Carter growled. 'Do you have a problem with that?'

'No, sir,' Vargas replied icily.

'Stay alert,' Carter said. 'Remember the drills.'

He had a good reason for tagging along with Vargas and his mates. He wanted to make sure the drill went smoothly. Which meant walking in behind the main assault group, following them from room to room. CQB exercises could get tasty, bullets might be flying past you, but Carter regarded it a vital part of his job. These lads were going into a situation with live rounds and live bodies. Multiple teams were going to be pouring into the structure from different directions, looking to maintain the momentum of the attack, pushing forward aggressively and at speed. There was going to be a lot of kinetic action. People running around all over the place. Things could get confusing. That's when mistakes happened.

It was the job of each individual assault group to clear the rooms in their sector, engaging targets without shooting hostages or accidentally hitting their mates. In that situation, it was vital that everyone knew what they were doing and coordinated the attack properly. Otherwise there was a risk of ending up with a blue-on-blue.

While Vargas wandered off to check his kit, Carter took Medel to one side.

'Are you sure about letting him lead the attack?' he asked in an undertone. 'He's hardly a model operator.'

Medel shrugged his shoulders. 'Vargas has friends. It is better not to make trouble,' he said under his breath.

'It's your call,' Carter muttered. 'Get the lads ready.'

There was a sudden flurry of activity as Ramirez dished out orders. The snipers snatched up their weapons and quickly fanned out across the range, dropping to prone firing positions to cover the various approaches to the stronghold. Then the five three-man assault groups made for their respective entry points around the tyre maze.

One of the teams hooked round to the far side of the structure. Two more teams made for the entrances on the left; a fourth bee-lined towards the breaching point on the right. At around the same time Vargas set off with the fifth assault group.

Carter broke into a quick jog as he followed the main assault team across the training ground. Vargas led the way, hurrying towards the entry door on the southern side of the stronghold.

The two other guys on the team ran close behind.

The second guy, Ivan Garrido, was a mean-looking soldier with more muscle than brains. His calves looked like somebody had strapped a couple of sandbags around his legs. His biceps were the size of medicine balls. Too many hours in the gym, probably. Dead-lifting heavy weights and pumping himself full of steroids. The third man on the team, Carlos Zamorano, was a lanky streak of piss. He brought up the rear.

After fifty metres Carter breezed past Vargas. He ran on and reached the entry point a couple of beats after Garrido and Zamorano. Then he glanced back and saw Vargas twenty metres away, face locked in a grimace as he struggled to catch up with his muckers.

'Get a fucking move on!' Carter shouted at him.

Vargas staggered on, then reached the pile of car tyres to the right of the door frame, gasping for breath. Sweat glossed his brow and ran down his face in rivulets.

Christ, thought Carter. *We've only just started the drill, and this idiot looks like he's about to have a heart attack.*

He trained his attention on Garrido as the latter hustled over to the door. Zamorano circled round, reached into a pouch on the back of his colleague's vest and pulled out a pre-assembled breaching charge. Which was essentially a spool of det cord, about as thick as a clothes line, packed with explosive material, fixed to a strip of double-sided sticky tape and rigged up to a length of electrical wire.

Garrido peeled off the backing tape and applied it vertically to the middle of the door panel, making sure it was firmly stuck down. Then he removed a chunky handheld firing device from his pocket with a lever and a safety catch. Garrido took the end of the electrical wire and plugged it into the clacker unit. He eased back the safety clip from the handle and shouted to the others, telling them to get behind cover. Vargas and Zamorano quickly shifted to the opposite sides of the entrance, stepping out of the blast radius.

They were almost ready.

Carter had taken part in hundreds of similar exercises over the years. The assault drill was simple enough. Once the other teams had confirmed that they were in position, Vargas would give the order to go. Then Garrido would fire the clacker, sending an electrical current down the wire to the det cord. The blast would blow apart the door, allowing Vargas's team to swarm inside. In the same beat, the other four groups would simultaneously trigger their charges and rush in through their designated entry points.

Once inside, the assaulters would begin systematically going through each room, putting rounds into the terrorist targets until the entire facility had been cleared.

Except Carter wasn't going to make it that easy for them.

He had a trick up his sleeve.

One more surprise for the team, to keep them on their toes.

Over his personal radio, he heard the other teams checking in as they reached their designated breaching points. The soldiers spoke in English for the benefit of their Brit instructor. Carter needed to hear what they were saying, so he could judge how effectively they were communicating with each other during the chaos and confusion of the attack.

'Charlie One, in position,' Medel said.

Vargas tapped the pressel switch on his radio.

'Alpha One, in position,' he rasped into his throat mic.

The four other teams came over the radio net in quick succession, confirming that they were ready to commence the attack.

As soon as the last team checked in, Carter thrust a hand into one of the pouches on the front of his vest and pulled out an M84 stun grenade.

The three Chileans weren't watching Carter. They had their attention fixed on the door, mentally running through the layout and their responsibilities as they prepared to storm inside. They had no idea what was about to come next.

Carter ripped out the firing pin, pushed away from the tyre wall and hurled the grenade over the top, towards the centre of the maze.

He didn't see the searing flash of light as the grenade detonated, but he caught the ear-splitting bang that followed.

There was a moment of stunned confusion among the soldiers. Just as Carter had expected.

The team hadn't been anticipating the detonation. All of a sudden, their neat plan of assault was in tatters. Now they had to react.

Good SF teams had to be able to act fast when things went sideways.

This wasn't a good team.

Garrido and Zamorano were looking towards their group leader, waiting for him to show some initiative. Vargas simply stood there, staring at the door. Paralysed by indecision.

'The terrorists are on to you!' Carter yelled at him. 'You've got to go, right fucking now! Give the order!'

Then it all kicked off.

A staggered sequence of loud booms ripped across the air as the other groups depressed their clackers, triggering their door charges individually. They would have heard the blast of the grenade from within the structure and assumed that the main assault force had breached their door, signalling the start of the attack.

It was Vargas's fault. He should have alerted the groups as soon as the grenade went off, ordering them not to detonate their charges until he gave the signal. Now, instead of a smoothly coordinated assault, the teams would be clearing the rooms at different times. Which could lead to all kinds of problems.

That was the kid's first mistake.

It wouldn't be his last.

In the next breath, the fat Chilean started screaming frantically at Garrido, 'Go! Go! Get in!'

Carter looked towards the entry point. He saw Garrido sidestepping to the left of the door, clacker in his hand. Electrical wire loosely trailing from the firing device, the other end taped to the strip of det cord.

Garrido squeezed the clacker.

The opening was instantly engulfed by a swirling cloud of smoke and debris as the charge ripped through the door. In the next moment the main assault group broke forward. Vargas led the way inside, charging through the smoke-wreathed void, keen as fuck to start plugging enemies.

From inside the facility, Carter heard a series of sharp cracks. Rifle reports. More than one of them. Coming from the nearest room. Vargas, he thought. The guy must have started letting rip as soon as he'd set foot inside.

Another bad sign.

A couple of metres away, Garrido was darting through the entrance after Vargas. Zamorano hastened after him.

As Carter started to follow, he heard Vargas's breathless voice in his headphones. The kid was yelling above the staccato bursts of gunfire coming from elsewhere in the facility.

'Room X-One clear!'

Carter stepped through the shredded doorway and found himself in the first room, a square-shaped space, four metres by four, sparsely furnished with a table and chairs and a wardrobe shoved against the wall to the left.

In the opposite corner, a pair of Figure 11 targets had been mounted on tripods and placed two or three inches apart. One of the targets depicted the standard terrorist image of a masked gunman wielding a rifle. The second picture showed a woman clutching her child. Carter had deliberately positioned them close together to test the soldiers' accuracy.

Both of them were punched with bullet holes.

Carter moved on, sticking close to the assault group ahead of him. Unlike the students he wasn't carrying an assault rifle; he had his belt-holstered Beretta pistol, but he wouldn't be engaging any X-rays. Not today. He was taking part in a strictly observational capacity.

And trying not to get winged in the process.

Voices crackled over the net as the other groups swept through the rooms in their designated sectors, punctuated with short bursts of gunfire.

'Room X-Seven cleared,' Medel reported.

'Room X-Nine, clear,' Ramirez said.

Carter crossed the room in another quick stride and caught up with Vargas and his two comrades as they prepared to sweep into the next room.

Vargas caught his ragged breath and shouted something at Garrido. The latter retrieved a flashbang from his webbing, depinned it and posted it through the opening.

Standard CQB tactics, intended to temporarily disorientate any X-rays lurking inside. Stepping through the doorway was the point of maximum danger in any attack. Fail to disable the enemy, and you'd end up getting plugged as soon as you charged into the room.

There was a searing flare of light as the flashbang kicked off. Like a million phone torches flicking on and off simultaneously. A thunderous boom pulsed through the room. Then Vargas swept inside, Garrido and Zamorano trailing in his wake.

Carter hurried after the soldiers, keeping a close eye on them as they began clearing their arcs. Vargas was scanning the right side of the room, his rifle raised, index finger feathering the trigger as he searched for hostiles. He was focused entirely on what was going on at eye level. Carter took another step forward, and then he heard a loud bang at his right. He looked back at Vargas and saw the Chilean swathed in a cloud of acrid smoke, realised that he must have blundered into one of the tripwires.

Christ, this guy is a liability.

In his headphones, he heard the four other teams updating Medel on their progress as they pushed on through their individual sectors. Each team had a number of rooms to secure. Once they had cleared the facility the five assault groups would meet in the middle, and Carter would declare the end of the exercise. Then there would be a debrief to run through the mistakes the guys had made.

A violent blast shuddered from the opposite end of the maze, and Carter guessed that someone had hurled a fragmentation grenade into one of the rooms, dispatching the targets inside.

The assault wasn't anywhere near as fast or fluid as the Regiment guys in action, but as far as he could tell Medel was doing his best to coordinate his teams' movements, getting them to maintain a steady flow of information over the net. It wasn't the worst assault he'd ever seen.

But Vargas was doing his best to screw things up.

Carter hurried after the guy as he barrelled into the next room, mindlessly drilling targetry. Vargas brassed up the terrorist behind the sofa and riddled the two civilians either side as well. Carter couldn't believe what he was seeing.

Even the slop jockeys at Hereford could do better than this.

He figured maybe two minutes had passed since the attack began.

Radio chatter confirmed that most of the rooms had now been secured. Vargas stumbled on towards the opening at his twelve o'clock, setting off another smoke grenade as he waded into the path of a tripwire strung along at waist height. The guy was going for the world record of training-ground fuck-ups.

Ramirez's voice hissed over the net, reporting that his group had finished securing their next room.

'Preparing to exit and enter Room X-Four to engage targets,' the dems man added.

Carter saw Vargas two metres away at his twelve o'clock, ploughing on through the grey tendrils of smoke as he led his men towards the adjacent room. He stopped at the side of the entrance and signalled to Garrido. The stocky soldier tossed in a flashbang moments before Vargas barrelled through the opening.

Carter instantly grasped what was happening.

He hurried towards the assault team, shouting over the comms, but no one was listening.

Ahead of him, Garrido and Zamorano were piling into the next room after Vargas. The two soldiers quickly peeled off to the left to clear their arcs while Vargas scanned for targets to the right.

Carter charged through the opening, his heart thumping terrifically. He swept through a curtain of thinning smoke into a rectangular space, substantially larger than the rooms they had previously cleared, with a metal-framed bed next to a desk with a lava lamp on it. He saw Garrido and Zamorano to the left of the entry point, sweeping their weapons across in broad arcs. Looking for hostiles that weren't there.

He saw Vargas to his right. Weapon raised.

Aiming at a paper target on the far side of the room, six metres away.

Right next to Ramirez's assault team.

The three soldiers were stacked up beside a separate exit point leading to another room. Ramirez stood at the rear of the line. One of his colleagues was shaping to chuck a flashbang through the aperture. None of them had noticed Vargas charging in behind them.

Carter's heart stopped.

He had no time to shout a warning at Vargas. The guy was already squeezing the trigger. He didn't appear to have seen the other assault group.

The Chilean was suffering from sensory overload. Carter had seen it happen before. Some guys panicked when they found themselves in a highly stressful situation. They stopped looking at what was in front of them and saw only what they wanted to see. Vargas had obviously caught sight of the paper terrorist in his peripheral vision and decided to engage.

Ramirez was six inches from the target.

Dangerously close.

Rounds flamed out of Vargas's M4.

Three of them.

Vargas's aim was terrible. The bullets missed the Figure 11 target. Two of them thumped into the rubber treads of the tyre directly behind Ramirez, missing him by no more than two or three inches. A third round smacked into a knackered old stereo resting on a table beside the wall, shattering the cassette deck.

Ramirez and the two other guys in his team were already rushing into the next sector, completely unaware of what had happened behind them. None of them would have heard the gunshots over the incessant chatter in their headphones.

Carter snapped his gaze back towards Vargas. The guy didn't seem to realise he'd come close to slotting his muckers. He was already charging headlong through a separate exit point at his twelve o'clock, hard on the heels of Garrido and Zamorano, plugging away with his rifle. Carter clenched his jaw and set off after the soldiers again.

Fifteen seconds later, he heard Ramirez's voice coming over the net, confirming that the final room had been secured.

Carter tapped the pressel switch on his radio.

'Endex! Endex!' he said. 'Weapons safe. Repeat, weapons safe. All groups to Room X-Five for the team debrief.'

He walked back into the large room with the metal-framed bed and the glowing red lava lamp. Vargas stood a few paces away, playfully punching Garrido on the shoulder, the pair of them grinning like idiots.

Celebrating.

Carter felt the rage simmering in his veins once more.

The rest of the assault teams trudged into the room, the selectors on their assault rifles set to 'SAFE' to guard against the possibility of a negligent discharge. After what had happened a few moments earlier, Carter didn't want to take any chances. He waited until the last stragglers had filed inside, then folded his arms and looked round the sea of faces as he prepared to debrief them. The drill had lasted no longer than three or four minutes but the men were drenched in sweat from the exertion and adrenaline rush and the weight of the kit they were carrying.

'That was good shit, boys,' Vargas said. 'Great work, no? That's how we roll in the Pumas.'

He grinned again, bumping fists with Garrido and Zamorano.

Carter fought a powerful desire to punch the kid in the face.

He stared levelly at Vargas and said, 'I'll discuss the other lads in a moment. But you should be ashamed of yourself. I've never seen anyone perform as badly as that.'

Vargas pulled a face. 'Who, me? What did I do?'

'You're a fucking embarrassment. You haven't listened to a thing I've been saying for the past month.'

Carter pointed out the section of the wall Vargas had riddled with bullets.

'See this?' he went on. 'You were a cunt hair away from putting a round in Ramirez's group.'

Ramirez's eyes widened in shock. 'Shit. No way.' He stared at the bullet-studded tyres, then looked round at Vargas. 'What the fuck, man? I could have been killed.'

Carter expected a show of contrition from the kid. An admission of guilt, perhaps. Or a promise to learn from his mistakes. Instead Vargas spread his fat lips into a grin.

'When I come through the door, people better hide, eh?' He chuckled. 'Fabian Vargas don't take no fucking prisoners, bro.'

A few of the other guys burst into laughter. Carter glared at him. 'Make another joke, and I'll knock the taste of blood out of your mouth.'

The smile fell from Vargas's face. 'You can't talk to me like that.'

'I'll talk to you however I bloody want. You almost slotted your own guys, you stupid bastard.'

'Not my problem. They shouldn't have been in my way.'

Carter stepped into the kid's face. 'If you had bothered listening to the radio, you would have realised that Ramirez's team had already secured this area and was about to move on to the next room. Instead of staying put, you stormed in here and started engaging targets without thinking. A couple of inches to the right and them lads would be lying in a pool of blood right now.'

Vargas grunted. 'You told us to clear this place of bad guys. I was doing my job. *Sir*.'

'I told you to pay attention and keep your wits about you,' Carter replied. 'Not ignore the orders from your mates and charge around the place like a maniac.'

'What's the big deal?' Vargas flapped a chunky arm at one of the Figure 11s. 'We nailed the terrorists. Problem solved.'

'Bollocks,' Carter snapped his teeth. 'You've messed up every step of the way on his drill.'

Vargas flushed with anger and shot him a screw-face. Carter counted the kid's mistakes on his fingers as he continued.

'Before we came in, you got flustered by the flashbang going off and failed to coordinate with the other groups. As a result, the teams carried out a staggered entry. That's a fail. In the first room, you shot a hostage. Another fail. In the second room, you killed two more civilians. Then you missed a target hidden in the wardrobe. On top of that, you triggered two tripwires because you didn't look where you were going. Either one of those would have wiped out your entire team.'

'This is bullshit.'

Carter ignored his protest and said, 'Your attitude is pathetic. If it was up to me, you'd be binned. You're more of a threat to your mates than the fucking Taliban.'

A dark look flashed across Vargas's face. He opened his mouth and started to say something, then thought better of it and pressed his lips shut again.

Carter continued with the debrief. For the next half-hour he walked through the stronghold with the other soldiers, pointing out where they had gone wrong and why, commenting on their targeting skills and coordination. Most of them at least made an effort to understand what was required of them. A few of the better-quality recruits even asked questions.

Maybe some of these lads have got potential after all, Carter mused. *Better than the dross served up by Vargas and his mates.*

The sun was already beginning to dip down behind the mountain peaks as the men trooped out of Tyre Village and walked back across the range towards their vehicles. Behind them, the safety officers were busy clearing up the site, removing debris and targetry. Carter made for his Land Cruiser, looking forward to changing into his civvies and getting back to his rental apartment in the city. He had almost reached the driver's side door when Medel called out to him.

'See you at the party tonight, Jamie?' he asked as he trotted over.

Carter gritted his teeth as he remembered. Vargas's father, General Juan Vargas, was hosting a barbecue at his mansion in El Arrayán. The entire SF team had been invited to attend, including Carter, along with the British ambassador and a few other officials involved in the training programme. Carter had been tempted to give it a miss, but the ambassador had insisted that he put in an appearance, implying that there was a lucrative deal in the pipeline involving the British government and they needed to keep the general sweet. A big arms contract, the ambassador had hinted. Worth a few hundred million pounds down the road.

Carter had grudgingly accepted.

'Aye,' he said. 'I'll be there. As long as I don't have to speak to that prick.'

He tipped his head at Vargas. The kid was folding himself into the front of one of the trucks, laughing and joking with his muckers like a bunch of teenagers.

Medel laughed.

'You won't have to,' he said. 'Fabian will be too busy entertaining his friends.' He noticed the uncertain look on Carter's face and smiled. 'Besides, it will be fun. Free drinks, food. Music. What more could you possibly want?'

I can think of one or two things.

A transfer back to Hereford for a start.

He grunted and said, 'I'll not be staying late. We've got a lot of drills to run through tomorrow.'

'As you wish.' Medel hesitated. Then he added, quietly, 'A word of advice, Jamie.'

Carter looked evenly at the captain. Waited for him to continue. Medel glanced over his shoulder, making sure no one else was in earshot before he continued.

'Don't single Fabian out for criticism. Not in front of the other men. It's not a good idea.'

'The kid's an accident waiting to happen,' Carter said testily. 'If you want my opinion, he shouldn't be within ten miles of this unit. He could have killed someone today.'

'Maybe so. But his father is Chief of Staff,' Medel reminded him. 'Which makes him one of the most powerful men in the country. General Vargas has lots of friends in high places.'

'He'll need them,' Carter said acidly. 'When his son accidentally plugs one of his mates in training, he's going to need all the help he can muster to get the kid off the hook.'

Medel gave him a look. But Carter knew that if there had been a shooting during the exercise, he would have been held accountable. The ambassador would have hauled him in, dragged his feet over the coals. Demanded answers.

It would have been my neck on the line.

Not the kid's.

Medel grimaced. 'Just try to be diplomatic. He could make life difficult, you know.' He raised his hands and went on. 'You speak your mind, I can see that. But that mouth of yours will get you in trouble one of these days.'

'It already has, mate,' Carter muttered.

'What do you mean?' Medel asked, creasing his brow.

'Forget it. Just a figure of speech.'

'Look, I'm just trying to help.' The captain paused before adding, 'Trust me, OK? You really don't want to make enemies of the Vargas family.'

Enemies, thought Carter.

Too bloody right.

I've made enough of those to last me a lifetime.

Two

The Vargas family lived in a palatial mansion set in the foothills outside Santiago, fifteen kilometres from Carter's drab rented apartment. He'd returned to his lodgings straight from the training base, scrubbed and changed into his civvies, ditched his uniform in a pile in the corner of his room, next to the bag of paperback thrillers and military histories he'd brought with him from back home. Then he'd hopped into the Toyota Land Cruiser provided to him by the embassy and tooled north-east out of the city.

Twenty minutes later, he rolled up at the wrought-iron gate at the front of the Vargas property.

Carter gave his details to the bovine-faced security guard and arrowed the wagon down a stretch of tarmac flanked by aprons of manicured lawn dotted with exotic trees and shrubbery. At the far end the drive led to a wide carriage circle with a tiered water fountain in the middle. Beyond the circle stood a white-stuccoed house two storeys high, with a pair of ornamental balconies on the first floor and a porticoed entrance with columns as thick as ballistic missiles.

He steered clockwise round the carriage circle, pulled up at the twelve o'clock position and got out. A grinning valet bowed slightly and took the keys to the Land Cruiser. A maid greeted him in front of the entrance and ushered Carter through a lavish hall adorned with local artwork, with corridors peeling off on either side. They carried on down a long corridor, past a guest bathroom and a kitchen with a central island so big you could land a plane on it.

Carter crossed the living room, stepped through the French doors at the rear and emerged onto a broad flagstoned patio fronted by an infinity pool, facing out across a vista of gentle rolling hills and vineyards. Fire pits warmed the cool night air.

To one side of the pool, a powerfully built grill master with a bushy moustache tended to cuts of meat smoking on a stainless-steel grill. The mouth-watering aroma of fire-cooked lamb, chicken and sausage wafted across the garden.

A bunch of people were milling about or chatting in small groups, sipping bottles of beer or glasses of wine. Carter recognised a handful of the lads from the training group at the range. In among them, a few smooth-faced civilians dressed in casual shirts and jeans, pretty women in summer dresses with plunging necklines. Wives and girlfriends of the soldiers, he guessed.

'Carter. There you are,' a smooth voice called out cheerfully at his back.

Carter looked round and saw a slender guy in a dark grey suit strolling towards him.

Simon Langton, the British ambassador.

Langton had the bland appearance of a career diplomat. Carter had met his kind before, in embassies around the world. After a while, you started to recognise the type. The hair was side-parted and as grey as the suit he was wearing. The lips were tightly puckered, the eyes faded but alert, the jaw cleanly shaven, the brow slightly creased in restless calculation. Langton had that familiar mix of arrogance, insecurity and suspicion peculiar to those who worked in the backwater embassies. He gave the impression of a man who had spent his youth trying to claw his way to something more meaningful, had fallen short, and was now condemned to see out his career in a mood of perpetual frustration and disappointment.

'Good of you to make it,' Langton went on in his public schoolboy accent. 'Let's get you a drink. What's your poison?'

'Beer,' Carter said. 'Lager, if they have it.'

An eyebrow arched so far up Langton's face it threatened to disappear into his hairline. 'You're a Geordie, aren't you? Shouldn't you be drinking a hearty brown ale or something?'

Carter laughed drily and said, 'Just because I've got the accent, doesn't mean we're all the same.'

'There's a red on the go, if you'd prefer that. From the general's own vineyards, no less.' Langton indicated his glass. 'It's actually rather pleasant.'

'Beer's fine, thanks.'

Langton snapped his fingers and gestured to one of his flunkies, a round-faced redhead with heart-shaped lips. One of the embassy junior staffers. She disappeared through the kitchen door and came back a few moments later clutching a bottle of Heineken. Carter nodded his thanks, took a pull, and savoured the feeling as the ice-cold lager slipped down his throat.

Christ, that was good.

After the day I've had I needed that.

'Heard you had a spot of bother at the camp today,' Langton said. 'Something involving the general's son.'

Carter frowned. 'Who told you that?'

'The captain mentioned it. Confidentially, of course.'

Langton indicated a group of figures beside the infinity pool. Medel was among them, drinking *cervezas* with his fellow officers. Fabian Vargas sat a few metres away at a table with Garrido and Zamorano, sharing a bottle of Chivas Regal. As Carter looked on, Garrido leaned over to the kid, whispered something into his ear. Vargas nodded, and then the two of them rose slowly from their chairs and slipped into the mansion through the French doors. Zamorano remained at the table, smoking a cigar.

'Well, Carter?' Langton asked. 'What happened?'

'Nothing,' Carter replied bluntly. 'Just some differences of opinion. It's been straightened out.'

He didn't want to discuss the Tyre Village incident with Langton. If the ambassador knew that Carter had given the kid a bollocking in front of the unit, he'd never hear the end of it.

Langton exhaled and said, 'I sincerely hope that's the case. The last thing we need is any bad blood between you and Vargas junior to muddy the waters. Bad for business, you know.'

'I said it's fine.'

Langton glanced at his watch and said, 'Right, we'd better introduce you to the general. He's very keen to meet a genuine SAS legend, apparently. Come on. And for God's sake, make sure you keep the general and his son onside.'

Carter bit back his irritation as he followed Langton across the garden. He hated this part of the gig. Being wheeled out to meet the big boss, like some performing seal doing tricks for the crowd.

As if this job wasn't bad enough already, I've got to kowtow to a foreign Rupert.

They approached the grill master. The big guy with the moustache.

Langton coughed to clear his throat and said, 'General Vargas, may I have the pleasure of introducing Warrant Officer Jamie Carter, of the Special Air Service Regiment.'

The general was a heavyset guy in his early sixties. At first sight he looked more like a Mexican drug lord than a senior military man. He stood at around five ten, with a brush moustache, jowly cheeks and eyes carved like surgical incisions into the fleshy folds of his face. His thinning hair was shot through with streaks of grey.

General Vargas smiled thinly. 'So you're the man in charge of training the Pumas,' he said in thickly accented English.

'That's right, sir.'

'Good, very good.' The general tended to the grill, flipping burgers and sausages. Smoke drifted up from the sizzling meat. 'I like the SAS. Fine warriors. Yes, very fine. I was an elite soldier myself, once, you know.'

'Is that so, sir?'

'Oh, yes,' he said proudly. 'We were feared by everyone. We were the real deal. Killers. Our enemies trembled at the mention of our name.' He gave an ugly laugh. 'As a matter of fact, I think I would have made an excellent soldier in your unit.'

'I expect so, sir,' Carter replied tersely.

'I imagine you have been on many dangerous missions?'

'One or two, sir.'

'I have been on many myself, in my time.' Vargas smiled, revealing a set of stained yellow teeth. 'Perhaps one day, we shall sit down and enjoy a bottle of brandy, and I will tell you about my years purging my country of Communist scum.'

'Yes, sir. I look forward to it.'

I could be back at Hereford right now, Carter thought. *Preparing to go out and fight, or working on an anti-terrorist op.*

Instead I'm having to indulge this twat.

'And my son?' the general asked. 'You're teaching him well, I hope? No problems I need to know about?'

In the corner of his eye, Carter spied Vargas and Garrido strolling back to their table. Giggling and rubbing their noses. Vargas reached for the half-empty bottle of Chivas, poured himself a slug and knocked it back. Garrido exchanged a conspiratorial glance with Zamorano and passed him something hidden in his hand. Zamorano promptly got up from the table and strolled inside.

'None, sir,' Carter lied. 'No problems.'

Vargas nodded and said, 'I believe Fabian will make a fine commander one day. Who knows? Perhaps in time he will become a great general, like myself.'

'Yes, sir. I'm sure he will.'

The general smiled again. Carter tensed his jaw and felt the blood boiling in his veins. *I don't know who's the bigger prick*, he thought. *Fabian Vargas, or his father.*

Another guest bounded over requesting a word with the general in private. Vargas excused himself, much to Carter's relief.

He left Langton in conversation with one of the junior staffers and found a quiet spot near the balcony. Figured he'd stick it out for another hour before calling it a night. He'd make his excuses, leave the party and make the short drive to his apartment. Grab one of his books and head over to the local cantina. Carter was a regular at the joint. He spent a few hours most evenings at a table in the corner, reading and sipping black coffee.

The owner, a fanatical Blackburn Rovers supporter, jokingly referred to the Englishman as the Quiet Gringo.

In the SAS, Carter rarely socialised with the other guys, preferring to spend his downtime reading books or at the gym while they bonded over pints in the Hereford boozers. His fellow Blades regarded him as something of an unknown quantity. An outsider. Not really a team player, some of them whispered behind his back.

That was bullshit. He knew how to work in a team as well as the next guy. He just wasn't interested in going out on the piss once the job was done.

In the close-knit world of 22 SAS, Carter had soon discovered that his lack of allies had worked against him.

His actions at the siege in Mali should have been the crowning glory of his Regimental career. But the knives had been out for Carter almost as soon as he'd returned from his medal presentation in DC. He was a warrant officer class 2, one of the most senior non-commissioned men in the SAS, but he suddenly found himself being given the shittiest jobs at Hereford.

It didn't take him long to figure out that someone had been stitching him up behind the scenes. Trying to sabotage his career. He knew who was responsible. Brathwaite, the British ambassador to Mali. The bastard had vowed to destroy Carter's career. Now he was making good on his threat.

Eventually, Pete Boulding, his squadron sergeant major, had taken Carter to one side and given him the heads-up.

'You've dropped a bollock here,' Boulding had said. 'Word is, they're out to get you. Just keep your head down, ride the wave, and you'll be in the clear before long.'

Holding his tongue didn't come easily to Carter. He had a reputation among his fellow Blades as a straight shooter. Never a corporate player, Carter had no time for the bullshit of Regiment politics. He didn't butter up the top brass, never towed the party line and always told it exactly how he saw it.

That attitude had pissed off a lot of people. Particularly the higher-ups. The head shed did not take kindly to soldiers who questioned the wisdom of their orders. They wanted conformists. Guys who could be lions in the field, but sheep when they were back at the camp. It didn't matter if you were right – if you spoke out and dared to criticise, you were automatically the enemy.

In the wake of the Bamako attack, no one had taken his side. Carter had no close friends at Hereford; none of the lads had been willing to put their heads above the parapet. The only person who might have realistically defended him had left the unit years ago.

Which is why he now found himself working in Chile on a dead-end training job.

Maybe if I'd been willing to play the office politics game, Carter reflected, *things might have turned out differently.*

The bosses at Hereford would have been looking out for me, rather than trying to stab me in the back.

They might have given me a slap on the wrist, maybe, but they sure as fuck wouldn't have tried to ruin my career.

He helped himself to another swig of lager.

Every so often, he caught sight of Fabian Vargas sneaking inside the house. Each time, he followed the same routine. The kid crossed the lounge and headed down the hallway, in the direction of the ground-floor bathroom Carter had passed on the way in. A few minutes later he returned to the patio, buzzing with nervous energy.

Vargas and his two muckers had some kind of a system going on. Vargas went first. Garrido and Zamorano stayed outside, laughing and necking double measures of Chivas Regal. Then Vargas would swagger back over to the table, and the two other guys would make the same trip to the bathroom. They repeated the routine every fifteen or twenty minutes.

It didn't take a genius to figure out what they were doing.

Carter drained his beer, stepped through the French doors and made a beeline for the kitchen. He grabbed another bottle from the rack of drinks on the island countertop, prised off the cap.

He was about to head back to the lounge when he saw Vargas junior standing in the kitchen doorway.

The kid stood there for a long beat. Watching Carter. His pupils were the size of poker chips. His hands were restless, Carter noticed. The guy couldn't stand still. He kept shifting his weight from one foot to the other. Sweat ran down his puffy face.

All the telltale signs of a coke fiend.

The kid laughed and said, 'What do you think, gringo?' He indicated the surroundings. 'Nice place, eh?'

'Yeah,' Carter said tonelessly. 'Great. Very impressive.'

The kid drained the rest of his Chivas, set the glass down and held out his right forearm, showing off the rose-gold watch strapped to his fat wrist. 'Look, man. See this? Fucking Rolex. Genuine. Forty thousand American dollars.'

'Good for you,' Carter said.

'Got one for each day of the month. All kinds of fucking watches, man. Rolex, Blancpain, Patek Philippe. Whatever. I like to mix it up, you know.' Fabian Vargas tapped the face of his watch and grinned slyly. 'Maybe once I have passed the training course, I make you a little gift. Make you happy. What do you say?'

Carter forced a smile, the ambassador's words ringing in his ears.

Make sure you keep the general and his son onside.

Vargas said, 'Listen, I got something to show you. Something fucking cool.'

'Not interested,' Carter said. 'Ask one of your mates. I'll be leaving soon enough anyway.'

Fabian Vargas shook his head and pointed a limp finger at Carter. 'No. I want *you* to see it. I insist.'

He spoke as if he was giving an order to one of his servants.

Carter visualised his balled fist connecting with the kid's face.

'Trust me,' Vargas continued. 'You're going to want to see this.'

Carter sighed, considered the prospect of sitting alone in the lounge for the next hour watching shite TV, and figured whatever the kid was desperate to show him, it couldn't be much worse than that.

'Fuck it, then,' he said, setting down his bottle. 'Make it quick.'

Vargas rubbed his hands together. His dilated pupils flashed with cocaine-fuelled excitement. 'Come. This way.'

He led Carter out of the kitchen, past the lounge, and beat a path down the corridor towards the front of the house. They hung a right at the marble-floored entrance hall, continued down a smaller passage lined with family portraits and artworks, and then stopped in front of a door on the left.

Fabian Vargas wrenched the door open, flicked a light switch and gestured for Carter to enter ahead of him. A smile curled out of the corner of the kid's mouth.

'This is going to blow your mind,' he said.

Carter stepped inside a dimly lit study. A large mahogany desk dominated the middle of the room, with a throne-like chair behind it and a Chilean flag draped from a brass pole. A fitted bookcase ran down the length of one wall, the shelves crammed with leather-bound volumes. On the other side of the space, Carter noticed an AK-47 assault rifle fitted to a wall-mounted plaque. He saw a bunch of other stuff. Glass-front display cabinets containing memorabilia. Black-and-white photographs. Shadow boxes filled with medals and badges and ranks. More antiquated firearms.

Not a study, Carter realised.

A museum.

To the left of the AK-47 a large portrait of Augusto Pinochet hung from the wall, dressed in an army jacket and jodhpurs.

'My father's office,' Vargas said, a note of pride in his voice. 'We call this the war room.'

He gave Carter the guided tour, pointing out various items stored in the cabinets and elsewhere in the room. There was a presidential sash once worn by Pinochet, a semi-automatic pistol, a pair of dark glasses, two pairs of polished jackboots, plus a bunch of other stuff: a military cape, pens, watches, medals and awards, handwritten letters. Carter saw a ceremonial sword gifted to Pinochet by a foreign leader. Vargas even pointed out a comb rumoured to have been carried by the man himself, with strands of hair snagged on the metal teeth.

A wave of revulsion surged up into Carter's throat. *This isn't a museum*, he corrected himself. *This is a fucking shrine.*

Vargas said, 'My grandfather once served under our great president. They were in the army together. He was one of the general's most loyal officers. This was many years ago.'

'Fascinating,' Carter lied.

'Some people hate the president. Communists and traitors, who seek to sully his good name. Those of us who are true patriots, like my family, we honour the general's achievements. He made our country strong again. He was a great man.'

Carter said nothing.

Vargas waved an arm at the AK-47 on the wall and said, 'You see this?'

Carter nodded. The kid went on, 'My grandfather carried this weapon when he took part in the coup against the hated Marxists. Later, he served in the secret police.'

Carter stared at the kid, anger clamping like a fist around his throat. He considered telling Vargas junior what he really thought about his father's room of horror, then checked himself.

In another corner, Vargas indicated a framed poster of a glass soda bottle.

'Do you know why that is up there?' he asked Carter.

Carter didn't reply.

Vargas said, 'They used the same bottles. My grandfather and his colleagues. To torture the Marxists. They were inserted in places on the human body that would cause the prisoner intense suffering.'

Carter felt sick.

'My grandfather made sure the prisoners were shown the bottle first,' Vargas added. 'Before the interrogation began. That way, every time the prisoner saw a commercial on the TV or the radio after their release, they would remember what had happened to them.'

Carter had seen enough. He tore his gaze away from the poster and turned to leave. Vargas quickly shifted across, blocking the doorway with his corpulent frame. Carter could smell the whisky on the Chilean's breath, mixing with the aroma of stale cigar smoke.

'You don't like what you see?' he challenged.

Carter clenched his hands into tight fists. 'Get out of my fucking way.'

Vargas grinned and stood his ground. The kid was wired. Sweat leached out of his skin, beading his forehead.

'This is my family,' he said. 'This is who we are. You don't fuck with us. We're not the kind of people you want to mess with. You understand what I'm saying, bro?'

'I understand that you're a useless cokehead.'

Vargas wagged a fat finger. 'You should show me some more respect, gringo. I'm going to be in charge of the Pumas one day. I could be a useful friend.'

Carter snorted. 'You're a drug addict and a time-waster. You're not fit to run a brothel, let alone a Special Forces unit.'

Vargas's expression darkened. He took a step towards Carter and jabbed a fat finger at his chest.

'Listen real good, OK? My father is close friends with the President. One word to him, and you're on the next plane back to your piece-of-shit country.' His lips stretched into a vile grin. 'Who knows? Maybe we'll bring in some Americans next time instead. They know how to treat people like us.'

Something inside Carter snapped. All the pent-up frustration and rage of the past four weeks, the petty humiliations, the dull routine of life at the range and the knowledge that he was teaching some deeply unpleasant people how to kill, suddenly exploded in his chest. He grabbed hold of Vargas's index finger and bent it sharply backwards in a single clean move, snapping bone.

Vargas screamed in pain.

In the next instant Carter dipped his head down, tensing his muscles as he pushed himself off his feet, momentum driving him forward as he aimed for his opponent's face.

There was a dull crunch as Carter's forehead smashed into the soft flesh of the coke fiend's nose.

Fabian Vargas stumbled backwards, blood gushing out of his collapsed sinuses. Carter launched himself at the kid, stamped on his foot and followed up with a flurry of quick jabs to the ribs and chest. Vargas tried to counter with a wild right hook. The coke he'd shoved up his nose had boosted his confidence, but it had done nothing for his fighting ability. Carter read the move easily. He parried the kid's ragged punch and struck him again with a sharp blow to the chin, knocking Vargas off his feet. He fell away with a groan, arms pinwheeling, then landed on his back a few inches from the doorway.

Carter stood over his floored opponent, shoulder muscles heaving up and down.

He'd done a serious number on Vargas. The kid was writhing on the carpet, pawing at his face and calling out for help. Blood streamed out of his crushed nose. He wasn't going to be snorting any nose candy for a while.

Carter heard voices in the hallway. The urgent pounding of footsteps. Medel burst into the room. He took one look at Vargas, spared Carter a quick glance, and then dropped down beside the kid to inspect his injuries.

A few seconds later Langton, General Vargas and a handful of other guests came rushing inside. One of the maids gasped in shock. Medel shouted at someone to fetch towels and water. The kid groaned nasally.

The general's eyes narrowed to the width of coin slots. His face trembled with barely concealed rage.

'What the fuck is going on here?' the general demanded.

'He assaulted me,' Vargas moaned. Tears were streaming down his cheeks. 'Shit, my nose . . . it hurts so bad.'

'Jesus,' Langton hissed. 'Jesus Christ.'

The general shot Carter an evil look. 'Explain yourself.'

You don't fuck with us, the kid had said.

We're not the kind of people you want to mess with.

Carter said, 'It's his fault. This cunt started it. He's been on the cocaine all night, making threats and acting like the class idiot. He had it coming.'

The general looked towards his son. Medel handed him a white towel and the kid pressed it to his nose, staunching the flow of blood. 'Is this true, Fabian?'

The kid shook his head groggily. 'I was just showing him your collection. That's all, I swear. Next thing I know, he hits me. Shit . . .' He clamped his eyes shut against the pain.

'Good God, man.' Langton looked apoplectic. 'What in the hell were you thinking? Have you gone completely mad?'

Carter shook his head furiously. 'This twat's lying. He's a cokehead, for fuck's sake.'

General Vargas was glowering at him. 'You dare to strike my son, and then accuse him of being a liar? A decorated young officer, first in his class? This is an outrage!'

Carter ground his teeth. He knew it was pointless to argue his case. There was no way the general was going to take the word of a British soldier over his own flesh and blood.

The urgent buzz of a ringing phone broke the silence. Langton fished out his handset from his trouser pocket. Frowned at the number. He looked up at Carter and flared his nostrils.

'Get out,' he hissed. 'For Chrissakes, man, get out.'

Carter stood his ground for a long beat and stared daggers at the ambassador. He wasn't surprised that Langton had taken sides with the general.

The lucrative contract.

Hundreds of millions of dollars at stake for Whitehall, potentially. Langton wouldn't hesitate to throw Carter under the bus to salvage the deal.

A few paces away Garrido and Medel were helping Fabian Vargas to his feet. The kid winced in pain, weeping softly as Medel examined his broken finger.

'Leave, you bloody fool,' Langton repeated. 'Go home. We will talk later.'

His phone was still buzzing.

Langton muttered a curse under his breath. Then he gave his back to Carter and walked into the corridor to take the call. Carter brushed past him and quick-walked down the hallway towards the front door. Behind him, Langton was talking in a muted voice to whoever was on the other end of the line.

Sod them.

Sod them all.

The valet was already waiting at the entrance with his car keys. Even as he fired up the Land Cruiser and pulled away from the front drive, Carter knew that his career in the Regiment was over.

Langton would get straight on the blower to Hereford. Nutting a general's son in his own house was bound to cause a diplomatic uproar back home. They'd stick Carter on the next flight to London. The training package would be cancelled. Probably the big arms contract too. They might even charge him with assault.

Either way, he would be thrown out of the Regiment.

Carter had served nine years as a Blade. Nine years of hard fighting in some of the most hostile places in the world. Getting the job done.

Now my career is finished, he thought bitterly.

So much for keeping my head down.

Three

Carter stayed angry for the short drive back to his rental apartment in north-eastern Santiago. Home. For the next few hours, at least. His pad was on the fifth floor of a whitewashed block, a fifteen-minute stroll from the British embassy. One of the older buildings in an area of aggressive development. The district was chock-full of gleaming skyscrapers, chain hotels and sushi restaurants. The grand nineteenth-century homes, run-down bars and high-rises were disappearing, slowly submerged beneath the steel-and-glass tide of progress. The same story the world over. The old giving way to the new.

I know the feeling, Carter thought.

Ten o'clock at night on a Thursday in early April. The streets were quiet. At this hour, the temperature was somewhere in the low single digits, and the few pedestrians were wrapped up in more layers than a wedding cake. Carter steered the Land Cruiser down the blacktopped ramp at the side of the residential block, dumped the wagon in the underground car park and climbed the stairs to the fifth floor.

Carter had nothing to do but wait for the call from the embassy. Ten o'clock in Santiago was one in the morning in the UK. Langton would stay at the barbecue for a while, trying to patch things up with General Vargas before making the call to the Hereford duty officer. There would be a brief discussion with the head shed. Concerns would be aired. Conduct called into question. Following which he would be summoned to the embassy. There would be a brief formal conversation with the military attaché. Someone would hand Carter a ticket for the next available flight back home. He doubted anyone would miss him.

At least I won't have to spend another day working with Fabian Vargas, Carter consoled himself.

He couldn't sleep, so he fetched a bottle of ice-cold Escudo from the fridge, cracked it open and dropped into the black leather armchair in front of the TV. State of the art, twenty years ago. He snatched up the remote and channel-hopped, sipped his beer.

He was pissed off at Langton, at the Regiment. At the general.

But most of all, Carter was angry with himself.

He'd fucked up. A useless kid with a drug addiction and an attitude problem had needled him. Big deal. Any sensible soldier would have kept his mouth shut, but Carter had lost his cool.

Again.

His career was already in trouble.

Now it's in the bloody gutter.

He flicked through the channels until he found one of the news networks. Carter didn't speak Spanish, but he picked up the basic thrust of the report from the footage. There had been a meeting at the White House between POTUS and the British and Australian prime ministers. The three men were shown standing on a stage, grinning in front of the cameras and looking pleased with themselves. Some sort of major summit.

Carter recalled skim-reading an article about it on his newsfeed a few days ago. A new military alliance. To counter Chinese aggression in the region, it was said. Although none of the partners had mentioned China specifically, their intentions were obvious.

Good luck with that. It'll take more than a few nuclear-powered subs to rattle Beijing.

The report cut to a clip of the US president standing behind a lectern as he fielded questions from the media. A pair of advisers stood either side of their frail-looking commander-in-chief. A stern-faced man in a dark suit and a patterned silk necktie, and a slim red-headed woman wearing a bright blue jacket and a pair of matching trousers.

Carter had never seen the woman before, but he recognised the serious-looking guy in the necktie instantly. He was tall and slim and thin-lipped, with side-parted silvery hair and hard blue eyes so cold they were practically cryogenic. The man looked to be fifty or thereabouts, but he had the honed physique of someone twenty years younger, and the stiff bearing of a one-time military man.

That's him, thought Carter. *That's the bloke I met.*

Bill Ramsey, the former director of the CIA.

One of the president's closest confidants.

The same man who had hung the Medal of Honor around Carter's neck.

Carter cast his mind back to that day. Four months after the siege in Mali. The small ceremony in a side room in the Capitol. No photographers, no press. Just Carter, Ramsey and a few other US dignitaries. Ramsey had shaken his hand, looked him in the eye and in his slow Southern drawl he'd said that the American people owed him a great debt of gratitude for his actions.

'The President won't forget what you did, son,' Ramsey had told him. 'You can be damn sure of that. You've got yourself a friend for life right there. Count on it.'

Carter had been a man on the up. Or so it seemed. But then Brathwaite had done his best to destroy his career. Things had gone downhill for him ever since.

On the TV, the news had moved on to the other major international stories. A migrant caravan was slowly making its way north to the US border. There was a short segment on the famine in Afghanistan. Loggers were aggressively deforesting the Amazon. Inflation had hit a new twenty-year high. Carter drank his ice-cold beer and watched the world going up in flames.

He finished his drink. Grabbed another and tore it open, numbing the anger.

Ninety minutes later, his phone buzzed.

Carter dug out his Regiment-issue handset and glanced at the caller's name glowing on the screen.

Peter Treadwell. The embassy's military attaché.

Treadwell acted as the liaison for the Chilean SF training contract. Once a week Carter attended a meeting with the guy at his office at the British embassy to brief him on the training programme. Treadwell had even popped down to the camp on a couple of occasions to watch Carter putting the recruits through their paces.

As soon as he saw Treadwell's name flash up, Carter knew it was bad news.

Twelve minutes past midnight. Less than three hours since he'd stormed out of the mansion. *Christ*, he thought. *Langton has moved fast. He must have reached out to Hereford as soon as I'd driven away. The guy must really want me off the job.*

He skated a finger across the screen. Clamped the phone to his ear and said, 'Yes?'

'Jamie, this is Peter,' the attaché said, pointlessly. He spoke in a rich plummy accent, but not as posh as Langton. One of the lesser public schools. A grade or two below him in the social order. 'Listen, I'll get straight to it. We need you to come in.'

Even over the phone, Carter could sense the cold anger in Treadwell's voice.

Here it comes. The end of my life in the Regiment.

Terminated by a coked-up idiot with a crap haircut and a general with a fetish for Pinochet souvenirs.

He said, 'When?'

Treadwell said, curtly, 'Right now.'

'Send a car. I'll be ready.'

A contemptuous snort came down the line. 'I'm not sending you anything, you thick bastard. Not after the stunt you pulled earlier tonight. You've got legs, haven't you? Bloody well use them.'

Treadwell liked to think he was funny. Carter just thought he was a cunt.

He was about to kill the call when Treadwell said, 'One more thing.'

'Aye?'

'Bring your bags and documents with you. Packed and ready to go. Understood?'

Carter was about to ask why, but he already knew the answer.

I'm on the way home.

One-way ticket.

'I'll be there in twenty,' he said.

'Fine. Don't keep us waiting.'

Treadwell clicked off. Carter listened to the dead air for a beat. *Us*, Treadwell had said. Therefore not just the attaché. He wondered who else would be sitting in on the meeting. The ambassador, presumably. He'd want to gloat over the wreckage of Carter's SAS career. Maybe the communicator from MI6, ready to hand him his boarding pass.

He was out of the Regiment. No question. The head shed frowned on Blades who caused diplomatic shitstorms, and they didn't get much worse than battering the son of a general in the middle of a Whitehall charm offensive. He was gone.

Carter had no family waiting for him back home. He'd married young. Too young, in hindsight. Alex had caught his eye on a night out in Hereford not long after he'd passed Selection. Six months later, they had married. But things had quickly gone south. Afghanistan had done things to Carter's head. It put shit in there he simply couldn't get out again. When he came back home, he was a closed book. All the bad stuff had been buried in the blackest recesses of his mind. In the darkest moments, he turned to drink. Alex had told him to seek help, but he wasn't interested.

'You're like a different person, these days,' she had said, and she was right. They had limped along for a while before finally separating. Divorce had followed soon after. Now he could barely afford the monthly alimony payments.

Carter lived by himself, in a modest house a couple of kilometres outside Credenhill. In the mornings, when he wasn't at the camp, he went on long walks. In the evenings, he read.

'You must get lonely,' one ex-girlfriend had said. Carter didn't feel that way. Outside of training, he was comfortable in his own company. He had few friends. Nothing to keep him tied to Hereford. No reason to stick around. That had advantages.

Perhaps he'd try his luck in America after he'd left the SAS. He had contacts at Langley, in Delta and the SEALs. He had a Medal of Honor and a thumbs-up from the president himself. There would be opportunities over there, he figured.

Anything's got to be better than this shite.

He spent several minutes packing his very few possessions into his waxed canvas holdall: toiletries, civilian clothing, his stack of military history titles. Carter always took a few books with him whenever he went on ops. He was currently reading works on Stalingrad, D-Day, the Napoleonic Wars.

Years ago, while on a training exercise, he'd seen a veteran Blade engrossed in a history of Ancient Greek warfare. Carter had been puzzled. He'd asked the guy, a gruff Brummie, why he was reading that stuff.

'I'm a soldier,' the Brummie had replied matter-of-factly. 'Killing is my profession. Why wouldn't I take an interest in it?'

Which had seemed like a good answer. Ever since, Carter had made an effort to bone up on his history whenever he had some downtime.

I'll have plenty of that from now on.

Three minutes later, he checked out of his apartment for the last time.

Four

Carter stepped out into the lamplit gloom of the street and headed north. A chill wind was whipping through the city, slashing at every inch of exposed skin and tugging at his leather jacket. He walked for several minutes down a broad leafy avenue lined with swanky new-build condominiums, financial investment firms and boutique shops, until he hit a busy main junction. Then he hooked a right and carried north on a three-lane main road.

Few at Hereford would mourn his departure, Carter knew.

The other Blades respected him for his fighting skills, but there was an element of jealousy mixed in with it. And hatred. Carter had poked a lot of colleagues in the eye over the years.

There were two sides to life in the Regiment. Soldiering was only half the job. There was a political side to the SAS as well. Some of the lads thrived not because of their achievements on the battlefield, but because they kept their heads down. They dodged the big missions, got their postgraduate qualifications, and steadily worked their way up the ladder.

Carter had been brilliant at fighting, but he'd never come to grips with the wider system in place at Hereford. For a born warrior, negotiating the politics of the unit had been like wading through mud. He'd lambasted operators who were more concerned with their next appointment than doing the job properly. Carter had been right, but his outspoken attitude had landed him in trouble on several occasions.

Despite everything, he still loved being part of the Regiment. The thought that it was going to be snatched away from him made his blood boil.

The SAS had saved Carter. He had misspent his youth in a bleak town in Northumberland, a place the rest of the country had left behind, and every poor fucker who lived there knew it. In that environment, you had to learn to look out for yourself from an early age.

Carter had never known his father. He'd been raised in a squalid council flat with his mother and stepfather, a violent drunk who spent most of his time pissing away what little cash they had at the nearby bookies. At school, he fought and flunked his exams. He was an angry kid, lost and full of inchoate rage.

He had always wanted to be part of a team, but he'd never given the army much consideration. Until one day he found himself waiting for a bus opposite the local army recruiting office. For reasons he couldn't quite understand, he felt something drawing him to the place. Calling to him. The recruiter had given Carter the hard sell about life in the army. He'd talked about career opportunities, learning new skills and visiting far-flung countries.

But most of all, he had talked about the army as a family.

About being part of a team.

Soon after, Carter had joined the Parachute Regiment. He'd spent a couple of years in 2 Para before passing Pathfinder Selection, a common career progression for guys who were interested in one day applying for SAS Selection.

Now that chapter of his life was about to come to an end, he reflected bitterly.

Carter carried on for five hundred metres until he reached the British embassy.

From the outside, the place didn't look much like a diplomatic station. It was a drab brick building, with tinted glass windows and a plain facade, situated on the corner of a busy intersection. The only hint of its true purpose was the Union Jack hanging limply from the flagpole mounted above the entrance.

The embassy operated a skeleton staff outside of regular business hours. There was one guy on duty at the front desk. A bored-looking Chilean with a pot belly, his chubby face lit up by the bluish glow of a TV screen. Carter was beginning to think there was something in the national diet. The guard buzzed him in through the main entrance and motioned for Carter to pass through the metal detector fronting the lobby. He made a quick call to someone, then returned to his TV show.

Carter waited.

Sixty seconds later, the lift doors sucked open. A grey-haired figure stepped out, swiped through the optical turnstile and marched purposefully over to Carter.

Peter Treadwell greeted Carter with a firm nod.

'Jamie. Thanks for coming in,' he said.

The tone was civil, but the look in his eyes was filthy.

Treadwell had the build of an ex-rugby player gone to seed. He was round-faced and puffy-eyed and carrying enough timber around the midriff to open a lumber yard. Too many hours sat behind a desk, presumably. Too much time guzzling champagne and grazing on canapés at official functions. But the narrowed green eyes were cold and hinted at a latent ruthlessness. Carter guessed you didn't make military attaché unless you knew how to play the game.

Despite the late hour, Treadwell was smartly dressed in a crisp white shirt, plain grey trousers and tan leather brogues.

'Before we go upstairs, I'd like to tell you something. You're an absolute disgrace.'

Carter had nothing to say, so he stayed quiet. He didn't want to get drawn into an argument with a guy whose day job involved nothing riskier than the odd paper cut.

'You're an embarrassment to this embassy, and to your own unit,' Treadwell continued. 'Personally, I'm disgusted by your behaviour. You should be ashamed of yourself. The sooner you're out of here, the better.'

Carter still didn't reply.

Treadwell shot him another sharp look, his features twisted with contempt. 'Right. Come on. The others are waiting upstairs.'

He gave his back to Carter, walked briskly over to the turnstile and hovered his security pass against the reader. The gate swung open, and Carter followed him towards the lift. They rode the cab to the third floor, passed through a self-locking door and marched down a dull corridor, passing rows of darkened offices and glass-walled meeting rooms. At the far end they stopped in front of a solid unmarked door. Treadwell rapped his knuckles twice on the hardwood, waited a beat. Then he wrenched it open and gestured to Carter.

'Inside,' he said.

Carter swept into a grey-carpeted room, long and narrow and low-ceilinged, like a submarine, with ornate wall lights and wood panelling. A massive walnut conference table dominated the central area, enclosed by a dozen executive swivel chairs. There was a speaker phone in the middle of the table, a laptop. Plus a stainless-steel French press, ceramic coffee cups, bottles of water, a plate of stale croissants. An antique side table with a vase of fresh flowers. A flat-screen TV had been rigged up to the far wall. The walls were decorated with canvas artworks and photographs.

Carter had been in places like this before, on other jobs in other countries. This was a secure room, frequently swept for bugs. Somewhere embassy staff could hold extremely sensitive discussions without fear of anyone else listening in.

Four figures sat around the table. Two on the left, two on the right. All of them stared at Carter as he entered the room.

Langton was sitting on the nearest chair to the left, a look of silent fury drawn on his face.

Next to him was a guy Carter hadn't seen before. A pale-faced man, balding, with a long, slender nose and slanted eyebrows that gave a look of faint disapproval. He was fifty, Carter guessed, or in that ballpark, and dressed in a plain dark suit so sharp you could have used it to slice open a watermelon.

Carter slid his gaze towards the two guys sitting on the right.

And froze.

The nearest man was lean and sinewy. His thick beard was peppered with grey, and his lips were stretched in a wide grin. He wore a grey T-shirt and a pair of dark jeans. A frayed baseball cap crowned his grizzled head. He had a tattoo of a bone frog clutching a trident on his right arm, the kind of thing SEALs wore to honour fallen comrades.

'What's up, chief?' the guy said in a slow Kentucky accent. 'Been a while.'

'Mike.' Carter jolted in surprise. 'Fuck me, what are you doing here?'

Mike Mullins was with SEAL Team Six. Otherwise known as DEVGRU, for Development Group, or Task Force Blue, depending on who you were asking and when they had joined. American SF teams tended to have more names than an identity thief.

Carter and Mullins had worked together in the last years of the war in Afghanistan, as part of a joint task force comprising US and UK SF. The door-kicking team. They had been given the job of going out on raids, detaining terrorist suspects and gathering intelligence at lightning speed. Then getting back into the chopper and heading straight to the next target.

Counter-insurgency tactics on steroids.

The operations had helped to forge a close bond between the guys in the SAS and their counterparts in Delta Force and SEAL Team Six. The Tier One brotherhood. Carter had befriended a bunch of lads from those units. Including Mike Mullins.

Carter had got along well with the Kentuckian. They had both experienced difficult childhoods, had both had to overcome all the shit life can throw at a person. Mullins had told him his story one night over a few beers. He'd been raised by his grandparents in a bumfuck town outside of Louisville. His father had been in and out of jail, and his mother and aunts had become addicted to prescription painkillers. Industrial-strength meds. The whole town had been high at one time or another.

Mullins had been a hell-raiser in his youth, working in a tile factory and spending his downtime drinking, getting into bar fights and dabbling in drugs. Hanging out with the wrong crowd. Then one night, sitting in the county jail, he decided to turn his life around. He kicked the drugs, joined the navy. Mullins had spent a few years there before he'd passed SEAL Selection, then joined DEVGRU.

On the surface, Mullins came across as a laid-back whisky-guzzling country boy. But in truth he was a brilliant warfighter and a deep thinker, with a postgraduate degree in war studies. One of the best soldiers Carter had ever worked with.

'Long time,' Mullins was saying. 'What has it been, chief? Three years?'

'Something like that,' Carter said.

Mullins waved a hand at the guy beside him. 'You remember Bryan, right? From Afghan?'

'Hey, bud,' Ortega said.

Carter nodded a greeting at the second guy. Bryan Ortega was ex-Delta Force, he recalled. Otherwise known as CAG, for Combat Applications Group, or 'The Unit', or Task Force Green. Clearly there was some serious competition to be the most titled team in the US Special Forces community. Maybe there was a prize.

A hard-as-nails bloke from Phoenix, Arizona, Ortega was in his late thirties. He looked like the typical Delta operator, barrel-chested and muscular. The veins on his forearms were as thick as gas pipes. He was decked out in an olive-green shirt that barely stretched around his immense biceps, a pair of creased khaki trousers. His forearms were sleeved with gang tattoos. A large silver crucifix hung around his neck.

Carter didn't know him very well, but he'd heard second-hand rumours about Ortega from Mullins and a few of the other American operators. His parents, it was said, had fled Colombia during the years of the narco wars. There had been stories that Bryan had been involved with a local gang in his youth. People with connections to the Mexican cartels. Ortega had narrowly escaped the life, but some of his relatives hadn't been so fortunate. He was a serious, brooding guy, deeply religious. He never swore, said little, and mostly kept to himself on ops.

'Look like you messed up your hand, bud,' Ortega said. He grinned. 'What, you think you're Floyd Mayweather now?'

Carter looked down at his bruised right hand. The skin on his knuckles was torn and bloody. Collateral damage, from banging the general's son in the face. He hadn't even noticed at the time.

Treadwell stepped forward, indicating the balding guy in the sharp suit.

'This is Tobias Proudlock,' he said. 'He's from Vauxhall. Six's man in DC these days. Quite new to the role, so you won't have crossed paths before.'

Carter blinked and snapped out of his stupor. 'What the fuck is this about?'

Treadwell said, 'These three gentlemen would like a word with you.'

'About what?'

'That is something we would very much prefer to discuss in private,' Proudlock, the balding guy in the suit, said in a cut-glass accent. 'You know how it is.'

He smiled politely and turned towards Langton.

'We'll take it from here, Simon. Thanks.'

Langton took the hint, levered himself out of his chair with as much dignity as he could muster. 'Yes. Well. I'll leave you to it, then. Anything you need, let me know.'

'We'll be fine,' Proudlock said.

Langton turned to Treadwell and nodded. The latter started for the door. Langton followed, then stopped in front of Carter and gave him the stink-eye. Carter could smell the wine on his breath.

'Just so you know,' he slurred, 'I had already made the decision to get rid of you. On account of your outrageous conduct this evening.

Whatever business you have here with these fellows, don't think you're off the hook. I'll be filing a complaint with your superiors as soon as possible. I shall make my displeasure clear in the strongest possible terms.'

Carter shrugged. 'Fill out your forms if it makes you happy.'

'You don't have anything to say for yourself?' Langton snapped. 'Not even an apology, for Chrissakes?'

'No,' Carter replied. 'Because I'm not bloody sorry. I'll be glad to be gone.'

'That makes two of us.'

Langton snorted contemptuously before he marched out of the room. Treadwell followed them out and pulled the door discreetly shut behind him. Then Mullins smiled and said, 'You seem to have pissed him off pretty good, chief.'

Carter said, 'That's nothing. You should see him when the embassy canteen runs out of foie gras.'

Mullins's massive shoulders pumped like pistons as he started to laugh. Ortega soon joined in. Proudlock gave Carter a disapproving look and waved a hand at the chair Langton had just vacated.

'Have a seat,' he said. 'Get you something? Coffee? Water?'

Carter shook his head. His head was still spinning.

Mullins, the thickset Kentuckian, grinned and said, 'Chief, I'll tell you something. You have an impeccable sense of timing. You're one lucky motherfucker.'

'That's not how it looks from here, mate.'

Mullins laughed, took off his cap and scraped a hand through his mussed hair. Carter dropped into the empty chair opposite the Americans, his guts twisting into a knot.

'You figured this was something to do with that jerk you beat up earlier. Right?' Mullins asked, replacing his cap.

Carter shrugged. 'It crossed my mind.'

Mullins laughed again. 'Can't say I blame you. Would have done the same thing myself. Honestly, it sounds like the dipshit deserved it. Beating the shit out of the kid in the general's office, though. That takes some serious cojones.' He shook his head and smiled. 'I'll say this. You Brits certainly do it in style.'

Carter said, 'What are you lads doing here?'

Mullins uncrossed his legs and said, 'Full disclosure. Since we're all friends here. Bryan and I work for the Company these days. But then I guess you figured that out already.'

Carter stiffened.

The Company.

The CIA.

Which meant that Mullins and Ortega were ops officers with the Special Operations Group, the CIA's elite paramilitary unit. SOG was a close-knit team of veteran ex-SEAL Team Six and Delta guys tasked with carrying out black ops on foreign soil. Doing the Company's dirty work. The agency had hired a bunch of lads from the US SF community in recent years, either directly or as third-party contractors to create an extra layer of deniability.

Which prompted another question.

'What's going on?' he asked, searching the faces of the two Americans facing him. 'Why the fuck am I here?'

Mullins tipped his head at Proudlock. Giving the floor to the MI6 officer. Proudlock leaned forward and laced his hands in front of him. His silver cufflinks glinted sharply in the glow of the wall lights.

'We've been sent down from Washington to brief you,' he said. He shifted his weight and grimaced, like he had a serious case of piles. 'Luckily for you, I might add. If we had got here a few hours later, you would have been on a flight back to London by now.'

'That, ah, situation with the kid has been taken care of, by the way,' Mullins said. The Kentucky native poured himself a cup of black coffee and proceeded to tip the contents of four sugar sachets into it. 'The general won't be pressing any charges. You're in the clear, regardless of what your ambassador may think.'

Carter nodded slowly. He should have been elated. Two minutes ago, he had been facing the sack. The end of his life as a Blade. Now he was in the clear. But any sense of relief he felt was immediately tempered by the knowledge that the Company wouldn't have lifted a finger to help him without wanting something in return.

Whatever they wanted, Carter figured it had to be better than the alternative.

Better than running a crap training package and taking shit from the Vargas family.

'I'm listening,' he said. 'What's the craic?'

There was a pause of silence while Proudlock produced a manila folder from a leather satchel beside his chair. Ortega sat with his thick arms folded across his chest, stared at a point on the table like he had a problem with it. Mullins tore open a fifth sachet of sugar and tipped it into his mug. Carter was beginning to think the guy had a problem.

Proudlock placed the folder down in front of him, flipped it open and looked up. Then he said, 'What can you tell me about a chap called David Vann?'

'Dave?' Carter sat upright. 'He's ex-Regiment.'

'You knew him personally, I understand. Chum of yours.'

'Yes.' Carter sighed between gritted teeth. 'I knew Dave all right. He was one of the legends of the Regiment when I joined. He was my instructor on Selection.'

'You served under him directly, correct?'

Carter nodded. 'That's right. When he came off Training Wing, he took over as my troop sergeant.'

'Would you say you were close?'

Carter shrugged and said, 'We were both Para Reg.' He saw the blank look on Proudlock's smooth face and added, 'We both came from the Parachute Regiment before joining the SAS. We were both ex-Pathfinders.'

Proudlock furrowed his brow. 'What has that got to do with anything?'

'A lot of the guys who pass Selection come from Para Reg. They tend to form their own cliques at Hereford. Look at everyone else as a crap hat or a wanker.'

'Did you?'

'At first. There's a mindset when you're in the Paras.' Carter tried to find the words to explain it to a civilian. 'You can be a bit of an arsehole, but if you're ex-Para, you'll get away with it. The other Para lads will give you a break. Because of the loyalty to their old unit.'

'So Vann looked out for you? He was a mentor, you might say?'

'Yes.'

But there was more to it than that, Carter knew.

Vann had already been in the Regiment for several years when Carter had first joined D Squadron. Every lad at Hereford knew about Vann. He'd fought in Bosnia in the 1990s, Sierra Leone. Then Iraq, taking the fight to al-Qaeda and the insurgents lopping off the heads of Western hostages.

Vann had a reputation as a brilliant, occasionally reckless, soldier. One of the true hardcore operators. He was feared and respected by the other lads in equal measure.

Carter had looked up to Vann. Admired him.

And he'd saved Carter's career.

Some of the guys in the SAS were guilty of slacking off once they made it through the rigours of Selection. Once you got that beige beret on your head, it was easy to fall into the trap of thinking you had reached the pinnacle of your army career. For a while, Carter had made the same mistake. Instead of knuckling down and learning how to fight, he had started to act as if he was the greatest fucking soldier in the history of the world.

For the first year he'd regularly gone out on the piss with the other lads who came from Para Reg, getting into scraps with the locals. He was on a path to destruction.

Then Vann had pulled him to one side after training one day. 'Calm down, son,' he'd told Carter in his Belfast brogue. 'You're in the SAS now. Know what that means?'

Carter had just looked at him.

'You think you've hit the big time, right? But that's a load of bollocks,' Vann had continued. 'All you've done is join another unit with better kit. That's it. Now you're gonna have to prove yourself every day, all over again. If you don't, you'll get fucking RTU'd.'

If anyone else had spoken to Carter that way, he wouldn't have listened. But he respected Vann enough to realise that he was telling the truth. If Carter wanted a long-term career in the Regiment, he had to start looking after himself.

Learn how to live like a professional, Vann had said.

Take yourself seriously.

From that moment on, Carter had dedicated himself fully to life as an elite operator. But he never forgot Vann's advice. Without his intervention, Carter would never have survived in the Regiment. He'd be back in Para Reg now, wondering what might have been.

He said, 'What's your interest in Dave?'

Mullins and Ortega looked knowingly at one another. Proudlock sat back and glanced at the Company men, waiting for them to take over. Mullins frowned at his palms for a long beat, as if he was trying to read his own fortune.

He lifted his gaze to Carter. 'What we're about to tell you goes no further than these four walls. It's important you understand that. Soldier to soldier. OK?'

'OK,' Carter said warily.

Mullins sipped his sugar-plus-coffee and said, 'For the past five months, Vann has been running an operation for us. Strictly off the books.'

'What kind of operation?'

'A training job,' Ortega said. 'In Afghanistan.'

'Vann has been working with what's left of the anti-Taliban forces,' Proudlock explained. 'The resistance movement.'

'I'm surprised there's anyone left. I thought the Taliban crushed most of them lot during the takeover.'

'There's a small group of holdouts,' Mullins said. 'Veteran mujahideen fighters, soldiers, plus a few disillusioned Taliban. They're currently operating in the north-eastern pocket of the country, between the Panjshir Valley and the border with Tajikistan.'

'Your old stomping ground, I believe,' Proudlock interjected.

Carter gave a slight nod. 'I was an embed in them parts for a while.'

'This was . . .' Proudlock consulted the file. 'Between 2018 and 2019, I understand.'

'That's right.'

Afghanistan.

Carter had been embedded for eighteen long months with a Special Forces unit in the north of the country. The Regiment 'embeds' had been tasked with leading groups of elite Afghan soldiers on missions to gather intel and carry out attacks on Taliban positions. Acting independently of the coalition, they had sabotaged static targets, ambushed insurgent forces and neutralised heroin dealers. Taking out those enemies beyond the reach of conventional forces.

For a while, the operations had been devastatingly successful. But the stress of living in total isolation from his colleagues, dealing with the blood feuds and tribal rivalries, while waging a dirty war against the enemy, had eventually exacted a heavy toll on Carter.

He had returned from his rotation a changed man. As if he'd undergone a personality transplant. Something had broken during that long period of disconnect from the Regiment and the rigid structure of army life. He suddenly found he had no tolerance for the political bullshit at Hereford. For a man with no filter, that was a serious problem.

Eventually, the head shed had grown tired of Carter's outspoken attitude. His CO had accused him of not being a team player and packed him off to Mali on a training posting.

Then he'd intervened in the terrorist attack in Bamako. Made himself an enemy for life with the British ambassador.

He snapped back to the present as Mullins continued the briefing. 'The rebel fighters call themselves the National Alliance. They claim to be the legitimate government of Afghanistan and have vowed to fight the Taliban to the death. They're led by a guy called Jabar Hakimi.'

'Never heard of him.'

'You wouldn't. He's from the younger generation of Afghans. His older brother, Rashid, fought against the Taliban for several years before he was killed in a gun battle last year near Aybak. The Alliance elders promptly declared Jabar as the new leader. Before that he had served as one of the junior field commanders.'

Proudlock said, 'Hakimi is something of an unknown quantity. But his brother was a brilliant leader, which buys him a certain amount of support. Rashid was politically astute, charismatic, moderate. A humble ascetic who inspired fervent devotion among his followers. Did his thesis at Durham. Wrote about the tactics of the Viet Cong. A rather interesting read, actually.'

'You think his younger brother is up to the job?' asked Carter.

'He has the credentials,' Proudlock replied confidently. 'His brother's name carries a lot of weight among the tribes. Jabar has some military experience, and he knows his men. He's the horse we're backing in this race. We've invested considerable resources in him.'

Something clicked inside Carter's head. He suddenly understood why Six had agreed to run a deniable operation inside Afghanistan with the Company. Because Whitehall had staked its chips on Hakimi one day becoming an influential power broker in Afghanistan's political landscape. A risky strategy, with no certainty of a favourable outcome. But worth a shot, given the potential upside.

Ortega said, 'The rest of the rebel leadership fled the country after the latest Taliban offensive. They're out of the picture. Which means Hakimi is basically the last man standing.'

Mullins swigged his coffee and said, 'Shortly after the evacuations, we began supplying arms and equipment to the National Alliance. Small arms, mostly. A long-term project. As part of the arrangement, we agreed to send in a guy to teach the rebels how to use them. An outsider. Six recommended your buddy.'

Carter canted his head to one side. 'Why send in Dave? Why not one of your own lads?'

'We wanted a buffer. Orders from the very top, you understand. We were given the authorisation to equip the National Alliance, but on condition that nothing could be traced back to us. The commander-in-chief wanted clean hands on this one, in case of a clusterfuck. Which is why we brought you guys onto the team,' he added, gesturing towards Proudlock.

'I should point out that our involvement in this operation is strictly in an advisory capacity,' the latter said. 'We've facilitated the arrangement with Vann, but the financial muscle and logistics come from our cousins across the pond.'

Carter frowned and rubbed his stubbled jaw. 'I don't understand. What has any of this got to do with me?'

Mullins said, 'Vann was in regular contact with us, using an encrypted satphone linked to a secure line at Langley. Bryan has been acting as his handler,' he added, nodding at Ortega. 'The deal was, Vann would file a sitrep once a week, or whenever he needed supplies. Or to report an engagement with the enemy.'

'I know the drill,' Carter replied irritably. 'What's the problem?'

Ortega said, 'Six weeks ago, Vann went silent.'

Carter crinkled his brow. 'Dave hasn't sent back any more reports?'

'Negatory, bud. We haven't heard so much as a mouse fart from the guy. He's off the grid.'

Mullins said, 'We've been working with your people to try and find out what's going on out there. But we're short on reliable assets right now. Most of the local networks went underground after the Taliban takeover. Dismantled. We've got some contacts, but they're low-level guys. They don't have the right skill sets for a search operation. There was one potential candidate, but he was killed in a firefight a few days before the Taliban completed their takeover. So you see our problem, chief.'

Ortega said, 'We've got a lone British operator somewhere in the north of the country, in the middle of a war zone, and no one has any clue what he's doing or why.'

Carter said, 'What do you want me to do about it?'

Mullins paused and looked him hard in the eye. 'We want you to go into Afghanistan and locate Vann,' he said. 'Find out what has happened to him. Before the Taliban, or anyone else, gets to him first.'

Five

A tense silence hung over the room. Carter sat there, a bunch of questions cycling through his mind. Like symbols on a slot machine reel. He settled on the most obvious one. 'Why me?'

'Three reasons.' Mullins counted them off on his fingers. 'One, as I said, we don't have the contacts on the ground for this kind of operation. Most of our key assets flaked out once they realised the Taliban were going to overrun Kabul.'

'You must have a few guys left behind,' Carter said. 'Afghan Special Forces veterans and the like. You're the CIA, for fuck's sake.'

Ortega sucked the air between his teeth. 'It's not as easy as that, my friend,' he cut in. 'The remaining assets have gone cold on us. We think there are trust issues.'

Carter gave a mirthless laugh. 'That's hardly a big fucking surprise, is it? Your president made the poor bastards a load of big promises, then decided to cut his losses and run the moment it got a bit hairy. What did you expect them to do?'

'Yeah, well, it is as it is. But it means we're basically operating blind in Afghanistan right now.'

'What's the second reason?' asked Carter.

Ortega said, 'Deniability. We can't get officially involved in an operation we're not supposed to be running in the first place. If we start sending in American citizens to hunt for Vann, pretty soon someone will connect the dots and realise we're bankrolling the rebels.'

'There would be congressional hearings,' Mullins said. 'People would be asking questions. It could get uncomfortable. You see what I'm saying, chief?'

Proudlock shifted and said, 'I think the point our American friends are making, Jamie, is that their hands are tied. Politically speaking. Ours aren't.'

'Exactly,' Ortega said.

Mullins counted off another finger. 'Plus, you've got deep operational expertise. You were an embed. That means you know the terrain, the tribes.'

Carter nodded thoughtfully. Although Delta and DEVGRU had in many ways overtaken 22 SAS in terms of equipment and training in recent years, the Regiment still had an edge over the US SF community when it came to winning hearts and minds. If you wanted a door smashed in, the Americans were the best guys for the job. But if you needed someone to broker a relationship with a tribal headman, the Regiment had a better track record.

Carter didn't know why. A question of arrogance, perhaps. If you believed you came from the greatest country in the world, everyone else looked inferior.

He said, 'You don't need me to go in and find Vann. You say he's been using a satphone to file his sitreps with Langley?'

Mullins nodded. 'That's right.'

'So why not just trace the signal? You could pinpoint his location, stick a drone over the area and get eyes on his position, or get him out on a chopper. Problem solved.'

Mullins hesitated. He glanced quickly at Ortega. The two warriors exchanged a look Carter didn't like.

'The satphone is a dead end,' Ortega said after a pause. 'Vann deactivated it six weeks ago.'

'Why would he do that?'

'We don't know.'

'Are you sure he deliberately switched it off? The satphone might have been damaged in a contact. Or the circuitry could have malfunctioned. It's the oldest rule in the book. Murphy's Law. I've lost count of the number of ops I've gone on where the kit has broken down for one reason or another.'

Mullins said, 'We considered that possibility. But that doesn't appear to be the case here.'

'Why not?'

'Two weeks ago, we picked up another signal. From Vann's satphone.'

Carter felt a stab of unease in his guts. 'Hang on. Dave *reactivated* the phone?'

Ortega nodded. 'We tracked the signal to Kabul and sent in one of our last assets to investigate.'

'And?'

'He found a nineteen-year-old kid wandering around a flea market in the city, trying to hawk a military-grade satphone.'

The cold feeling slithered down Carter's spine.

'How the fuck did he get hold of Dave's phone?' he asked.

'The kid said he was from a village north of Panjshir. A speck-on-a-map kind of place. He claimed that a few days earlier a big white guy approached him, gave him the satphone and a fistful of gold coins and told him to drive to Kabul and switch the unit on.'

'Did you send someone to the village?'

'Of course. We're not amateurs.'

'And?'

'And, zilch. Nothing. Nada. The place is home to a handful of farmers. Nothing more. No one knew anything about Vann, and if they did, they weren't prepared to say anything.'

Carter asked the obvious question. 'Why would Dave pawn off his satphone to some random kid?'

'If we knew that, bud, we wouldn't be sitting here now.'

'You must have some idea, surely?'

Proudlock crossed his legs and said, anxiously, 'We're keeping an open mind. Perhaps Vann feared that he had been compromised and decided to throw his pursuers off the scent.'

'You think he's on the run?'

'It's the most likely explanation,' said Mullins. 'The Taliban have been pushing hard to crush the last pockets of rebel resistance in the country. Full-court press. Sustained pressure, day and fucking night. The guys in the National Alliance have been getting their asses kicked and the military commanders are too busy squabbling among themselves to get their shit together. Hence why we sent in your guy Vann.'

'Hakimi has got a lot of qualities,' Ortega said. 'But he's got his hands full dealing with infighting among the Alliance commanders, and he has no experience of coordinating a prolonged guerrilla war. That's why we turned to Vann. We were looking for a way to even things up.'

'A force multiplier,' Carter said.

Mullins nodded in agreement and said, 'This isn't 2001 anymore. We're not up against a rabble of bearded mullahs with rusty AK-47s. The Taliban are better equipped now. We're talking about Black Hawk helicopters, plus drones from China, and external support from Russia and Pakistan.'

Carter's eyes almost popped out. 'The Taliban have got Black Hawks?'

'A whole fleet of them, chief. Spoils of war. Piloted by Pakistani air force crews on secondment to the Taliban.'

The evacuation from Kabul, thought Carter. He'd seen the reports on TV. In the frantic dash to escape the chaos around the airport the Americans had left behind a staggering amount of equipment. Weapons, night-vision goggles, vehicles. Some of it had been destroyed, they claimed, but a lot more must have been left intact. Against those odds, the lads in the National Alliance wouldn't stand a chance. Not unless they had some outside help.

Carter bristled with anger. He thought about the burning frustration of wasted effort and lives. Twenty years of conflict. Thousands of dead. Brother warriors maimed for life.

All the shit we had to wade through, and when the last Hercules C-17 took to the skies, the country found itself right back where it started.

Mullins said, 'The point is, if the rebels have been attacked, Vann would likely have gone to ground. It would be the logical option. He'd have the Taliban hunting for him, and maybe ISIS-K. He'd want to keep his head down until things went quiet.'

'What about the rebels?' Carter asked. 'You must have a line of communication to Hakimi. Can't you reach out to him instead?'

'Vann was our primary point of contact,' Proudlock said. 'Everything went through him. Requests for extra supplies or funds, information, the lot.'

'Your mob has always got a back channel. Can't you use that?'

'We've tried already,' Proudlock said in exasperation. 'As far as we can tell, Jabar Hakimi and his closest advisers have also gone silent.'

'But you don't have a clue where they might be hiding?'

'No.'

Mullins said, 'Jabar's forces are constantly on the move from one camp to another. Standard procedure. Just because they're out of contact doesn't mean a thing. But equally it could also be that they've taken a beating and have scattered to the wind.'

Carter shook his head and said, 'How the fuck do you expect me to find Vann, though? He could be anywhere. For all you lot know, he might be en route to the embassy in Pakistan.'

'Possible,' Mullins said. 'But unlikely. Our people have been looking for him. He would have been picked up by now.'

'Just in case, we've alerted the embassies in every neighbouring country,' Proudlock said. 'In the event Vann does show up, they'll let us know immediately. But I have to say I agree with Mike. If Vann had left Afghanistan, we would almost certainly have heard from him by now. All the evidence suggests he's holed up somewhere in the mountains.'

'How do you know the Taliban haven't captured him? Or ISIS-K, for that matter?' asked Carter.

'If they had,' said Proudlock, 'chances are we'd know about it by now. The Taliban's social media team would be blowing up. We believe Vann is still at large.'

'Even if that's true, it'll be fucking hard to locate him,' Carter said. 'I can't just stroll around the place, knocking on doors and asking the local goatherds if they've seen a big white bloke lately.'

'There's a plan,' Mullins replied tersely.

'There'd better be. Dave's a good mate, but if you send me in there flying solo, I'll last about five minutes. Christ, how can you be sure he's even still alive?'

'We're confident that's the case.'

'Maybe you need to reconsider,' Carter said. 'Your int on the kid with the satphone is two weeks old. The picture might have changed by now. I might be going on a wild goose chase.'

'You won't, chief. Trust me.' Mullins grinned.

Carter looked at him questioningly.

'Vann is alive,' Mullins added.

'How do you know?'

'Because someone saw him.'

Six

Carter waited for the Americans to go on. Mullins dug out his smartphone and gave the screen his war-face, unlocking it. The Kentuckian tapped and swiped at the screen for a few beats. Then he slid the handset across the polished table.

Carter scooped it up and eyeballed the screen. He found himself staring at a picture of a burly Afghan male with a neatly stubbled beard, short dark hair and a scalp so flat you could play billiards on it. He was dressed in a shabby camouflage jacket, with a *shemagh* tied around his neck.

'Recognise the face, chief?' Mullins asked.

Carter nodded slightly. 'Omar Sharza. He was an interpreter for the Afghan Special Forces. I worked with him a few times on my embed posting. One of the good guys.' He lifted his eyes from the screen, squished his eyebrows together. 'What's he doing in Afghanistan now? You were supposed to get all them lads out.'

'Sharza elected to stay behind after the Taliban takeover,' Proudlock explained. 'Voluntarily, I hasten to add. He's been helping to organise rat runs from Afghanistan. Getting people out of the country before the Taliban can put them to death.'

Carter lifted his gaze. 'This guy reckons he spotted Dave?'

'Not exactly,' Proudlock said. He exchanged a nervous glance with Mullins.

'What's that supposed to mean?'

'Four days ago, Sharza was moving through a small place called Khordokan. He was helping to smuggle out an anti-Taliban official.'

Mullins said, 'Sharza got talking with one of his contacts in the village. This contact told Sharza that he'd seen a man matching Vann's description the day before. He'd stopped at the village to barter gold for a couple of mules.'

'Are we sure it was Dave?'

'As sure as we can be.'

'Sharza put the word out to his network after the satphone was reactivated,' Ortega said. 'Asking them to look out for a guy who didn't look or sound like a local but dressed like one.'

'Vann has been on the ground for five months,' Mullins explained. 'Which means he'll have a beard, and he'll be dressed in local clothing. The disguise would fool a passer-by, but if anyone saw him up close or heard him talk, they'd quickly realise he wasn't from the area.'

'Khordokan?' Carter screwed up his face. 'That's not far from the Tajikistan border.'

'Yes,' Proudlock snapped. 'What of it?'

'What's Dave doing all the way up there?'

'We don't know. It's possible that the location of the rebels' base of operations was compromised and they had to move further north at short notice.'

Mullins said, 'Khordokan is considered safe territory. Or as safe as can be in Afghanistan right now. The people there are fiercely opposed to the Taliban, so it makes sense as a safe haven. But that's obviously pure speculation. Could be any number of reasons why Vann is in the area.'

'Assuming he's still there,' Carter said. 'He might have moved on by now. The trail might have gone cold.'

'Even if that's the case, Vann can't have gone very far,' Ortega said. 'Not with the rest of the country crawling with Taliban and ISIS-K fighters, and rival militia groups.'

Carter shook his head forcefully and said, 'I know that area. It's sparsely populated. Scattered villages and farms, lots of narrow mountain passes and caves. Dave could be hiding anywhere.'

'Sharza is in the area as we speak,' Mullins said. 'He's making discreet enquiries, collating local intelligence. That should help narrow down the search area to something more manageable.'

Carter puffed his cheeks and exhaled. 'Even so, it's going to be bloody difficult. Like searching for a grain of sand on a beach.'

'This is our best chance of locating him, chief.'

Carter stared at him. Mullins sounded like a guy desperately trying to convince himself against all logic that his plan would work.

'It's more than that, mate,' Carter said. 'This second-hand sighting is your only lead. It's shit or bust.'

Mullins made a gesture with his huge hands. 'It is what it is. You know the deal. If the situation wasn't a fucking mess, guys like us wouldn't be called in to clean it up.'

'Obviously we can't trust Sharza to conduct the search for Vann by himself,' Ortega added. 'He's a good guy, as far as we know, but he's not trained in search-and-rescue operations. He doesn't have the skill set for this kind of job.'

Proudlock said, 'Your orders are to fly to Uzbekistan, cross into Afghanistan and rendezvous with Sharza. Once you've successfully located Vann, you'll notify Langley directly. We will then jointly assess the situation and decide on next steps. If it looks like we need to pull Vann out, we'll let you know.' He indicated the two Company men with his delicate hand. 'Mike and Bryan will brief you on the particulars. Any questions?'

'Why me?' Carter asked. 'I'm hardly flavour of the month at Hereford these days, in case you hadn't noticed.'

A smile teased out of the corner of Proudlock's mouth. 'Yes, I read about that unpleasant business after Mali. You seem to have a habit of pissing off ambassadors in every country you work in.'

Carter clenched his jaw tightly, burning at the memory of his encounter with Brathwaite in the aftermath of the Mali siege.

'I won't forget this,' Brathwaite had told him, his voice incandescent with rage. 'Disobeying orders. I'll bloody ruin you, man. D'you hear?'

Carter had dismissed the threat as a bluff, but the bastard had been as good as his word. Brathwaite had been ultimately responsible for his posting to Chile.

In a way, I'm only sitting here now because of that fucker.

'To answer your question,' Proudlock said, 'you know Vann, which means you'll know how he thinks. What he'll do in a particular situation. That may prove useful in locating him. Secondly, you've had experience of operating alone in Afghanistan.'

Carter considered for a beat. Proudlock saw the hesitant expression on his face and frowned.

'I must say, I thought you'd be champing at the bit to get involved.'

Carter glared at him. 'Why would you think that?'

He stabbed a finger at the folder in front of him. 'It's all there in the file, old boy. You hate authority and dislike taking orders from other people. This is an independent mission. Just the sort of thing for a chap like you.'

'It's Afghanistan,' Carter said pithily. 'If this goes south, I'll end up with my head on a bloody stake.'

'It won't,' Ortega insisted.

'You're the right guy for the mission, brother,' Mullins said. 'If anyone can find Vann, it's a goddamn war hero and a Medal of Honor recipient.'

'It's just a gong, mate. I didn't even want the thing. All it's done is make half the lads back home jealous. I would have been better off without it.'

'Screw them. Am I right? Me and Bryan, we worked with you before. We know your qualities. Fact is, we wouldn't send you out there if we didn't think you were up to it.'

'It, er, goes without saying that this operation is completely deniable,' Proudlock added hastily. 'If you're compromised or killed, we'll deny all knowledge of your activities.'

A deep groove formed above Carter's brow. He had his doubts. He'd seen the news reports about Afghanistan. The whole country was falling apart at the seams. Warlords were at each other's throats, terrorist groups were setting up training camps in the mountains, drug traffickers were slaughtering one another to gain control of the main smuggling routes. Famine, death and economic collapse.

I'll be going into the country, he thought, *when everyone else is trying to get the fuck out.*

But he owed Vann. The Ulsterman had taken Carter under his wing years before. Vann had guided him, put him on the straight and narrow. *I would have been kicked out of the Regiment a long time ago if it hadn't been for Dave*, he reminded himself.

Besides, Carter figured there might be an upside to working with the Company. Do this job, he reasoned, and there was the possibility that the CIA might take him on as a contractor. The Circuit was shrinking. Money and opportunities were drying up. Working for Uncle Sam didn't sound like the worst idea in the world.

At least I'm not toxic over there. Not yet.

He said, 'When do I leave?'

'Today,' Proudlock said. He frowned at his watch. 'Five o'clock this morning. A little over four hours from now. Our friends here have taken care of the logistics. We'll explain everything, then you'll be straight onto a private jet.'

Carter looked at him closely. Something had been gnawing away at him for the past several minutes.

'Why do you care?' he asked.

Proudlock stared at him blankly. 'Pardon?'

'About Vann. You're going to a fucking lot of effort to find a missing guy who's not even with the Regiment anymore. You could deny any knowledge of his operations, sit tight and wait to hear from him.'

There was a beat of silence. Proudlock shifted uncomfortably. Mullins and Ortega swapped anxious glances.

Mullins said, 'It's a delicate situation. We don't want Vann to end up as a guest of the Taliban, or ISIS-K. Or anyone else. That could make things complicated.'

'Dave wouldn't spill his guts. He's a committed operator.'

'We're not worried about that, bud,' Ortega said.

'Then why the sudden concern for his welfare?'

'Outside this room, only five other people know about this operation. Including POTUS himself. Everyone else is in the dark.'

'So?'

Mullins said, 'Vann is off-reservation in the most lawless place in the world. If he's taken prisoner, his captors won't need to get him to confess to anything. They'll just splash his face over social media and claim that he was doing all kinds of evil shit on our dime. If he's unlucky enough to get kidnapped by ISIS-K they could hold a gun to our heads. Use him as a bargaining chip. Hand over some of our friends from the prison camps in Syria, or your man dies. That sort of thing.'

'The president staked his political career on getting out of Afghanistan,' Ortega said. 'It was messy, sure, but whatever we felt about it personally, he wanted out because it played well in the polls. If word gets out that we're still involved, a lot of people will look like assholes. You get the picture?'

Carter said, 'I see it, all right. Your commander-in-chief doesn't want to get caught with his dick in his hands.'

'If that's how you want to put it, yeah.'

'There's another issue, of course,' said Proudlock. He shifted awkwardly. 'Your chum Vann left the Regiment under something of a cloud. An unsanctioned airstrike during his time as an embed, as I understand it.'

Carter stared at him. He remembered the story. Vann had been embedded with a team of Afghan SF in the south-east of the country, along the porous border with Pakistan. Towards the end of his rotation, he'd called in aircraft ordnance on a target near the Tora

Bora cave complex as part of an operation to flush out a group of hardened ISIS fighters. Four civilians had been killed in the attack. A subsequent investigation had discovered that the target had not been officially sanctioned by coalition commanders. Vann had attempted to cover up the mistake by subsequently inventing a legitimate reason for the strike, an act which had ultimately led to his dismissal from the Regiment.

'It wasn't Dave's fault,' Carter argued. 'He called in air support on what he believed was a legitimate target. He had no idea there were civilians in that area at the time.'

'Nonetheless, he appears to have a track record of going rogue. Disobeying orders. Perhaps history has repeated itself here.'

'Meaning what?'

'Perhaps he has taken the law into his own hands again. Maybe he's out there right now with the National Alliance fighters, settling scores with rival tribes. That could be problematic for us, for obvious reasons.'

Carter saw a flicker of anxiety in the spook's eyes. Despite his arrogant tone, it was obvious that Proudlock was under pressure. Carter could guess at the reason. The Company had approached Six asking for help. Someone – Proudlock or his superior – had recommended Vann to the Americans as a safe pair of hands for the job. Now the guy had gone AWOL.

Proudlock would be desperate to clean up the mess before heads rolled. Starting with his own.

Proudlock leaned across the table and dropped his voice.

'Just find Vann,' he said. 'Whatever it takes. If you fail, it'll be bad for all of us. Understood?'

'Is that a threat?'

'It's whatever you want it to be,' Proudlock said. 'But I promise you this. Let us down, and your career will go up in flames. I'll make damn sure of that.'

Seven

Proudlock stood up and left the room to make some calls. Then Mullins dug out a laptop and a tablet from a rucksack on the chair next to him. He flipped open the laptop, tapped a bunch of keys, and Carter saw a window expand on the screen displaying a satellite map of north-eastern Afghanistan. The rebel pocket. A wedge of land on Tajikistan's southern border, bounded by a range of snow-capped mountain ranges to the east. To the west, a wide river demarcated the border with Uzbekistan. Kabul was three hundred kilometres further south. Barren desert, mixed in with steep valleys, narrow rivers and grazing lands. A lot of territory. A lot of empty space.

Sparsely populated.

Scattered villages and farms.

Mullins pointed to a spot in southern Uzbekistan, five kilometres north of the border with Afghanistan. He said, 'You'll land here, in Termez. Our guide will RV with you at the airport and escort you across the border checkpoint east of the city.'

Carter said, 'Who's the guide?'

'An Afghan national. Former district police officer. One of the guys who got out of the country in time. One of the lucky ones.'

'Why not get Sharza to meet me in Uzbekistan instead?'

'Out of the question. Sharza is a wanted man, on account of the rat runs he's been organising. The Taliban have been searching everywhere for him. If he crosses the border, there's a chance he might be recognised.'

'Is this guide reliable?'

'He's legit,' said Ortega. 'He knows the borderlands as well as anyone. Don't sweat it.'

'Easy for you to say,' Carter growled. 'You're not the one risking your balls in the Taliban's backyard.'

'You don't trust us?'

'I don't trust anyone, mate. Force of habit.'

Ortega gave him a flinty look. 'If you have a problem, bud, why don't you just come out and say it?'

'I'm not looking for an argument,' Carter replied, meeting his gaze. 'I just want to make sure I'm not going in half-cocked.'

Mullins raised his hands in a placatory gesture. 'The guide is clean,' he said. 'He checks out. You've got nothing to worry about. I give you my word on that, chief. One warrior to another.'

'That's all I wanted to know.'

'Let's move on.' Mullins pointed to the screen, indicating the border between Uzbekistan and Afghanistan. 'Once you've RV'd with the guide, you'll head straight down to the border and cross the friendship bridge into Afghanistan.'

'What's my cover story?'

'You're an administrator working for an international NGO in the medical assistance sector. There are several such organisations operating inside Afghanistan at this minute, running various programmes. You're going in to oversee one of the projects, to make sure the money is being spent appropriately.'

'Will the guards buy it?'

'No reason they wouldn't,' Ortega said.

Mullins said, 'The Taliban are desperate for outside help right now. They're facing a humanitarian catastrophe. Massive food shortages, an energy crisis, skyrocketing inflation.'

'Sounds just like Britain, mate.'

Mullins half smiled. 'Point is, the Taliban can't afford to turn away the NGOs. Not if they want to avoid mass civil unrest. We've run this set-up multiple times for guys on reconnaissance patrols. We know how to get you inside.'

'What about documentation?'

'The guide will supply everything you need. He'll be driving a vehicle with the NGO branding. In addition, we've updated the relevant website so that your name is listed on the staff page.'

Ortega said, 'You'll be travelling into Afghanistan under your real name, of course. Simpler that way.'

Mullins said, 'Apart from ourselves and our two other American friends, no one else is aware of your connection to the Mali incident. Certainly no one outside of the SAS. There's a Whitehall blackout on any photographs or mentions of your name online, as I'm sure you are aware. So we don't see any problem with you entering the country under your own name. The chances of anyone recognising you are non-existent.'

Ortega looked Carter up and down and said, 'You'll need fresh threads. Something more appropriate for the job. You'll find bags of clothes on the jet.'

'What about survival kit?' Carter asked.

'All of that stuff is on the plane. Take whatever you need.'

Mullins worked the touchpad, sliding the map view to the east. Then he un-pinched his finger and thumb and zoomed in on the northernmost part of Afghanistan. Carter waited for the map to catch up and refresh, adding definition to the surrounding terrain. He saw a series of narrow defiles, mountains and dried-out riverbeds scored into a parched landscape pocked with slivers of greenery.

Mullins pointed to a location fifty kilometres due south of the Tajikistani border.

'This is Khordokan,' he said. 'It's three hundred and fifty kilometres from the Uzbek border. A four-hour drive from Termez. Maybe longer. Depends on the state of the roads. You'll meet with Sharza at a designated road junction across the border from Uzbekistan and continue your journey to a safe house. Once you've linked up, the guide will head back to Uzbekistan.'

Carter rubbed his brow and considered. 'I'll need supplies in-country. Weaponry, for starters. I'm not tooling around them parts without some proper hardware.'

'Sharza will source firepower from his contacts in the area. Whatever he can get his hands on. Which could mean pretty much anything these days – M4s, grenades, Russian pistols, RPGs. You'll have to make do.'

'I don't give a toss where the stuff comes from,' Carter said. 'As long as it shoots in a straight line.'

He studied the map with his professional soldier's eye. His brain was working overtime, looking at the bigger picture. Assessing potential obstacles, rehearsing scenarios. A few hours from now, he would be on his way to Uzbekistan, and there would be no turning back. He didn't want to leave anything to chance.

'We'll need money,' he said. 'Emergency cash. To buy supplies, or extra fuel, or horses if we need them. Some of them villages in that province are inaccessible by road.'

Ortega said, 'The guide in Uzbekistan will issue you with gold coins. Enough to pay for any situation you might find yourself in.'

'I'll try to keep the receipts.'

Mullins threw back his head and laughed. Even Ortega broke into a slight smile. A once-in-a-millennium event. Like a rare alignment of the planets in the solar system.

A few minutes later Proudlock walked back into the room. He parked himself on the edge of the table while Carter turned his attention to the satellite map.

He looked at the insertion point on the border between Uzbekistan and Afghanistan, and the major roads leading east towards Khordokan.

He said, 'That route will take us right through Taliban-controlled land. What's the plan for getting through?'

Ortega said, 'Your interpreter will know how to avoid the major checkpoints in the cities. If you stick to the back roads and keep a low profile, you should be OK.'

Mullins said, 'The Taliban have got their hands full right now. They're facing civil unrest, famine, the growing threat from

ISIS-K, fighting with rival warlords, defections to the rebels and the resurgence of al-Qaeda. They've got Islamic militants trying to sneak into the country to carry out attacks. They won't be overly worried about an aid worker and his interpreter tooling across the country.'

'Plus,' said Ortega, 'there's the PR angle.'

'Meaning what?'

'There are nine billion dollars in frozen assets belonging to Afghanistan. The Taliban want it unlocked. Best way to achieve that, they figure, is to go on a charm offensive. That means no terrorist training camps, no hostage-taking, no videos circulating of Western workers getting a neck shave with a machete.'

Carter laughed cynically. 'I can't imagine anyone falling for that shite. Only an idiot would think the Taliban are all nice and cuddly now.'

'Agreed,' said Mullins. 'Needless to say, that policy has resulted in a major fracturing within the Taliban's ranks. Some of them have started taking hostages for ransom. Others are opposed to the practice. Depends on who you run into, and where.'

'What if we hit trouble?'

'Then your best bet is to stay quiet, keep your head down and let Sharza do the talking. This is his home turf. Anyone starts asking questions, he'll deal with them.'

'If all else fails, you'll have to bribe them,' Proudlock put in. 'Buy them off with gold.' He smiled cynically. 'The Taliban like to pretend that they're above corruption, of course, but that's purely for public consumption. They're as corrupt and venal as anyone else in that godforsaken place.'

'I'll need backup,' Carter said. 'If this shit goes noisy, I'm going to be hanging out of my arse out there.'

Mullins didn't reply immediately. Instead, he reached into his rucksack again and retrieved a bulky satphone with a backlit display above a twelve-button keypad, housed in a rugged casing. An extendable black aerial as thick as a cigar tube jutted out of the top-left corner.

'Military-grade satphone,' Mullins explained. 'Encrypted on voice, which means you can talk plainly without having to worry about anyone trying to hack into it. There's a number stored in the memory. Call it and you'll be patched through to the ops team at Langley. If you find yourself in a situation where you need firepower or immediate extraction, reach out to us. We can get a hellfire on target or a helicopter dispatched to your location asap.'

He handed over the satphone and looked steadily at Carter.

'Whatever happens, do not lose this phone,' he continued soberly. 'That clear, chief? Your life may depend on it.'

'Did you give Vann the same speech?' Carter replied drily. 'Because if you did, it looks like he wasn't paying attention.'

Mullins's expression hardened. 'I'm deadly serious. This phone is your only link to the outside world. If you get into trouble out there, and you can't contact us, we've got no way of pulling you from the fire.'

Carter set down the phone and said, 'What happens once I find Vann? Assuming this all goes to plan?'

'Call us on that number on the satphone. We'll want to speak to him. Find out what's been going on. Then we'll figure out what to do.'

'Are you going to extract him?'

'Depends,' said Ortega.

'On what?'

'Whether your buddy has got anything to hide.'

Carter shook his head. 'You've got it wrong, mate. Dave wouldn't have gone underground without a good reason. Whatever happened, he'll have an explanation.'

Ortega smirked. 'We'll see.'

* * *

They spent another hour poring over the details of the plan. Times, locations, distances. Emergency extraction points. Routes in and out of the country. They showed Carter a photo of the Afghan guide, the ex-police officer, so he'd know who to look for when he touched down in Uzbekistan. When they had finished, Mullins and Ortega walked him through it all a second time. Committing the plan to memory, so that Carter understood every nook and cranny of it.

The less glamorous side of warfare, maybe. But just as important as the ability to drop a target or kick down a door.

Proudlock paced restlessly up and down the room, fielding calls and occasionally frowning at his watch. At around three o'clock, he stepped out of the room again.

Carter gulped down a second mug of bitter coffee, rubbed his tired eyes and refocused on the maps. Roadheads, rivers, villages. He wasn't trying to commit it all to memory, but he wanted to build up a solid picture of the environment. Three years had passed since he'd last set foot on Afghan soil. He was a little fuzzy on some of the details.

Some time later, Proudlock marched back in.

'There's a car on the way,' he said, glancing at his watch. 'Should be here in twenty minutes. The driver is one of our UKNs. He'll ferry you directly to the airport across town. Police escort to help clear the route. There's a private jet waiting for you on the runway, courtesy of our friends at Langley. Wheels in the air at five o'clock sharp.'

'What's the itinerary?'

'You'll hop up to Charleston and refuel. Then a second leg to London. From there you'll fly direct to Termez in southern Uzbekistan. Total journey time of around twenty-one hours. Arrival time in Uzbekistan is approximately ten thirty in the morning, local time. Tomorrow.'

'You might want to get some ice on that once you're airborne.' Mullins smirked and nodded at Carter's puffy right hand. 'That is one nasty bruise, chief.'

'You should see the other bloke.'

That drew a withering look from Proudlock. 'I wouldn't brag about that if I were you, chum. Your career is hanging by a thread here.'

'Story of the last year of my life, mate.'

Mullins said, 'Before I forget. There's a Company laptop on the jet. Rigged up to the on-board Wi-Fi. Give you a chance to study the search area in more detail before you land.'

They spent the last ten minutes talking through the plan one more time, making sure there were no grey areas. Then Proudlock left the room to draft a secure message to Vauxhall Bridge with the embassy communicator, updating them on the situation.

At 4.15, the same round-faced redhead Carter had seen at the Vargas family barbecue several hours ago knocked on the door and announced that his ride had arrived.

There was no big farewell. Mullins shook his hand and told him they'd grab a beer once he was back on friendly soil. He reminded Carter again not to lose sight of his satphone. Ortega nodded tersely.

Then Carter grabbed his holdall and followed the redhead out of the conference room.

He didn't see Langton or Treadwell on his way out of the building. Too busy sorting out his replacement for the training package, probably. They would be in contact with Hereford, urging them to send out a new body to run the course. Putting in grovelling calls to General Vargas, telling him how much they valued his friendship.

Well, fuck them. The Vargas kid is someone else's problem now.

I've rotted here for long enough.

He had been given that rarest of gifts in life.

A second chance.

Redemption.

After months of putting up with crap postings and Hereford bullshit, Carter had an opportunity to get back in the game. Back to doing what he did best. Proper soldiering.

Carter was a killer. He'd been good at it, had dedicated himself to his profession with a single-minded intensity that few could match. After the Bamako siege, the Regiment had tried to take away the only thing Carter had going for him.

For a while, he'd lost his purpose. Now he had a chance to salvage his career. And he was determined not to lose.

* * *

It was still dark when he stepped outside. Four fifteen in the morning. Rubbish tumbleweeded across the main road. The only signs of life were the lights blazing in the windows of distant apartment blocks.

A trio of vehicles waited for him in front of the building. At the rear was a BMW X7 in pistol grey, with heavily tinted side windows and a front grille the size of an electric gate. Two green-and-white liveried Dodge Chargers were parked up in front of the wagon. Engines purring, headlamps burning, roof lights flashing in alternating red and blue bursts. The police escort. The road-clearance team. At this hour Carter doubted they would get snarled in traffic. But you never knew. He'd been gridlocked in some pretty strange places.

As soon as he exited the building, the BMW driver hopped out and circled round to the rear of the vehicle. He was a European-looking guy. Pale and dull-eyed, with a long papery face surmounted by a widow's peak of grey hair. Probably an expat. Someone with a background in law enforcement or intelligence who had settled down in Chile and now saw out their retirement running errands for Six. Out of loyalty, presumably, or some misguided sense of patriotic duty. They certainly weren't doing it for the take-home pay.

Carter stowed his holdall in the boot, then hooked round to the passenger-side door and climbed into the back seat. The driver with the widow's peak slid behind the wheel and gunned the engine. Ahead of them, the lead Dodge Charger pulled away from the embassy into the empty road. The second Dodge followed a couple of metres behind, the BMW bringing up the rear.

The journey to the airport took just under thirty minutes. They drove in silence. Carter stared out of the window watching the city flicker past in a stream of garish light and shadow. Trying to ignore the apprehension tightening like an invisible band around him.

At a quarter to five, the convoy took a slip road off the motorway and carried on for another kilometre towards the airport hub. Whereupon the vehicles made a series of quick turns away from the main terminals until they stopped at a security checkpoint. A guy in uniform stepped out of the guardhouse and spoke with one of the officers in the front police car. Then the barrier arm raised up, like a span on a bridge, and the convoy rolled on down the access road as it curved round towards the concrete apron.

They carried on for two hundred metres, past a low glass-fronted terminal and a row of private aircraft and refuellers and fire trucks, before the tail lights on the Dodge Chargers suddenly flared, and the driver eased the BMW to a gentle stop behind them, next to a stationary executive jet. An ultra-long-range model, the kind frequently used by the CIA for rendition circuits. Operated by a shell company, to give the impression that it was an independent aviation transport firm, rather than a mobile interrogation cell.

Carter debussed, hauled his luggage out of the boot and made his way up the lowered airstairs. The cabin interior had been stripped of its luxury furnishings. Restraining points had been mounted to the floor. The kind of thing used to shackle prisoners by their legs. Carter saw blood stains on the carpet. Heavy-duty cargo nets hung from the cabin ceiling. There was a doss area in the rear compartment, and several large olive-green sacks stuffed with items of clothing and boots.

Two guys in green army kit were seated in the front section. One of them had a comb-over haircut and a forehead so big you could project a film onto it. The other guy was a greasy-looking fucker with slicked-back hair. The replacement crew. Working in eight-hour shifts, probably. The pilots had a long flight ahead of them.

The backup crew nodded a greeting at him, then resumed their conversation. A strong statement. *We're not here to talk.* Carter breezed past them and dropped into a seat in the middle compartment. He buckled in.

A few moments later, the guy with the comb-over got up, grabbed the lever on the airstair handrail and manually closed the cabin door. The pilots completed their pre-flight checks. Then the aircraft taxied towards the edge of the runway. The engines screamed, building to a deafening crescendo.

Three minutes later, they were climbing into the sky above Chile.

Carter looked out of the cabin window at the light-pricked city below. Three years after his last embed posting, he was going back to Afghanistan.

Back to where it all began.

He considered his chances of getting out of there alive at around fifty-fifty. Not odds that most people would accept. But Carter wasn't most people. He was a Blade.

The guys in the Regiment were by definition high-stakes gamblers. Which is what set them apart from everybody else. They were ready to crash through a door and neutralise a terrorist threat, even if there was a good risk of getting killed, because that was how you became a hero. A Blade would always take the shot at saving lives and killing enemies over playing it safe.

That mindset had been ingrained in Carter from a young age. He'd spent his whole life fighting the world in one form or another. He had a talent for it. Didn't know any other way to live.

But he also felt something else.

An obligation to an old friend. A sense of loyalty.

David Vann was in trouble, and there was only one person in the world who could help him now.

I've got a shot at saving my old mentor. From the Taliban, or ISIS-K, or whoever else is hunting him.

Dave's counting on me.

I won't let him down.

No fucking way.

Eight

Half an hour into the flight, the guy with the slicked-back hair got up from his seat and approached Carter.

'Heads up. We're about to dim the lights,' he announced in a flat, nasal Midwestern accent. He jerked a thumb at the guy with the comb-over. 'Me and my partner are gonna pop a couple of sleeping tablets and catch some shut-eye before we're on shift.'

Carter nodded and said, 'How long until we reach Charleston?'

'Eight hours. We'll land at around eleven thirty in the morning, local time. It'll be a quick turnaround before we're back in the air.'

'Roger that.'

The Midwesterner pointed with his eyes towards the rear of the cabin. 'You're welcome to sleep in the back. There's a sack of clothes back there. Shirts, cargoes, boots, whatever. Help yourself.'

'Where's the laptop?'

'Back of the cabin. With the rest of the equipment. It's already connected to the Wi-Fi network. You got any problems with it, let me or Kurt know.'

'That'll be fine.' Carter paused. 'Listen, can you spare us a pill? I'm too wired to kip.'

The guy hesitated for a beat. Then he dipped a hand into his trouser pocket and pulled out a white prescription pill vial. He unscrewed the cap, tipped an oblong-shaped tablet into the palm of Carter's hand.

'Thanks,' Carter said.

The Midwesterner shrugged. 'Knock yourself out, friend.'

'I will, mate. Literally.'

'Excuse me?'

'Nothing.'

The overhead and sideways lights blinked off, smothering the cabin in darkness. Carter snatched a bottle of water from the fridge in the kitchen area, chucked the sleeping pill into his mouth and chased it down with a glug of chilled liquid. Then he made his way to the rear compartment, lay down on one of the doss bags on the cabin floor and closed his weary eyes.

Sleep came on slowly despite the meds. Questions kept pricking at the base of his skull. The same ones Carter had been asking himself ever since he'd left the British embassy.

Why had Vann gone missing?

What the fuck was he doing in Khordokan?

And why had he decided to get rid of his satphone?

He decided that the most likely explanation was the simplest: Vann and his colleagues in the National Alliance had been compromised in a contact with the enemy. The Taliban, or ISIS-K, or some other group. The guy had somehow managed to escape the firefight and gone to ground to wait for help to arrive. Safer than trying to risk crossing the border, maybe.

But the satphone was harder to explain. Deliberately getting rid of it went against all the SOPs they had been taught at Hereford. Proudlock had suggested that Vann might have ditched the satphone to deceive his pursuers, but Carter wasn't so sure. The Taliban lacked the technology to track a signal, and he doubted they would be capable of reading Vann's messages either. The phones used the latest encryption, Mullins had said. Almost impossible to hack.

So walk through the alternatives. Perhaps the kid had been lying about his story. Maybe he'd got hold of it by some other means. Maybe his relatives belonged to the group holding Vann hostage. Possible, but unlikely. If Vann had been taken prisoner, his captors would have been bragging about their achievement. Or broadcasting a video showing his execution. The lack of noise suggested Vann was still at large.

So why else would Vann ditch his lifeline?

Carter didn't know. But he felt sure of one thing. David Vann was one of the finest warriors ever to don the beige beret of 22 SAS. A legendary operator, totally committed to the job. He wouldn't have abandoned his mission, not unless he felt he had no choice.

We're flying blind here, Mullins had told him.

Too bloody right, thought Carter.

I don't know why Vann went off the grid. But I know he's in trouble.

One way or another, I'm going to find him.

A sudden wave of tiredness came over him, settling like fog behind his eyes. The exhaustion of the last twenty-four hours, catching up with him. The fog thickened, his eyelids became heavy, and he fell into a troubled sleep.

* * *

He awoke six hours later. Two hours before they were due to refuel at Charleston. Carter got up from his doss bag and rooted around the sacks of clothes at the far end of the cabin. In a short while he'd found a pair of civilian cargo trousers, a T-shirt and shirt, all in his size and in muted shades of khaki and beige. Plus a pair of thick grey socks, salmon-coloured hiking boots and a North Face jacket. The jacket had a Velcro patch stitched to the front, with the logo of the aid organisation stuck to it. He took an extra T-shirt, an extra pair of trousers and socks, because you never knew what conditions you were going to face. He didn't want to have to wear muddy or wet clothing for days on end.

Carter found a waterproof rucksack stuffed with survival equipment. Specifically a one-size doss bag, a portable gas stove with four butane canisters, a set of three cooking pans, four twenty-four-hour civilian ration packs with boil-in-the-bag ready meals, snack bars, desserts and electrolyte drinks. Plus water purification tablets, a blanket, a foam mat, scarf, thick gloves, hat, compass, canteen, torch, solid-fuel hexamine block, emergency first aid kit, penknife and a notebook and pen, both with the NGO's logo.

Everything that he might legitimately need in the field as an aid worker. All of it was civilian-sourced, US-manufactured. The kind of stuff you could buy in any medium-sized outdoor shop.

Carter checked everything, repacked the rucksack and added two spare bottles of water from the cabin kitchen. He changed into his new civvies and dumped his old clothes in his canvas holdall, along with his Six-issued smartphone. His holdall would remain on the jet, pending his safe return from Afghanistan.

Assuming I make it out of there alive, Carter thought grimly.

He fired up the laptop and brought up the satellite images of north-eastern Afghanistan. He traced the potential routes Vann could have taken, paying particular attention to the locations of nearby villages along the way. Trying to identify areas where Vann might have decided to hide.

Almost immediately Carter realised that he had a problem. The search area was enormous. More than eighteen thousand kilometres squared of terrain. But he was confident he could shrink the area down to something more manageable. Much of the region was still contested territory. Some of the villages would have loyalties to the Taliban or ISIS-K, or a warlord who tried to gain favour with the Taliban by joining forces with them. Probably half the area in question was out of bounds.

But there was another issue. Even if Carter narrowed down the search radius, there were still hundreds of potential hiding spots. Vann could be bottled up in any number of locations. And while Carter was busy looking for him, the Taliban would be out in force in the surrounding area.

It'll be a bloody miracle if I find him before one of us gets bumped, he thought.

* * *

Two hours later, they landed at Charleston. There was a second brief stopover outside London at RAF Northolt. Carter drank more coffee and browsed news websites. He scrolled through the usual stories: illegal migrants crossing the Channel on dinghies, slum landlords raking in fortunes, people getting scammed out of their life savings.

One article midway down the newsfeed caught his attention. A report on the growing tensions between China and Taiwan. PLA aircraft were breaching Taiwanese air space, the story claimed. There was a lot of reported activity around the naval bases at Xiamen and Wenzhou. Flotillas were being mobilised. Infantry units and artillery were being assembled in staging areas along the southern and eastern coasts of the mainland. There were the usual bland quotes from defence analysts who couldn't agree whether the moves were a prelude to a full-blown invasion of the island or a strategic bluff. But something towards the end of the piece pricked Carter's interest.

A photograph of Bill Ramsey, the ex-CIA director and presidential adviser, with his trademark silvery hair, lantern jaw and silk necktie. The caption described him as the most influential unelected man in America.

Ramsey had been quoted in the article. He was clearly a China hawk. Not a friend of Beijing. He didn't explicitly mention Taiwan, but the implication was clear enough.

The Chinese Communist Party represents a grave threat to global peace and prosperity, Ramsey said in his characteristically blunt style.

For the Chinese Premier, I have a message: America is no longer prepared to look the other way while the rights of freedom-loving peoples are trampled under the boot of Beijing's totalitarianism. Anyone who threatens the interests of our allies would be making a terrible mistake. And I promise you this. The days of Chinese tyranny are numbered.

Carter shut down the laptop and slept some more.

Five hours later, Midwestern walked over and announced that they were about to make their final approach to Termez. Carter adjusted the time on his G-Shock and gazed out of the port-side window at the city below. He saw wide gridded streets, Soviet-era housing blocks and gold-domed mosques bordered on one side by a river. Three thousand years of history laid out in front of him.

Carter looked down at the scene and felt a quiver of unease in his guts.

In a few hours, I'll be crossing the border.

Heading into Afghanistan.

There's no going back now.

Nine

They landed shortly before eleven o'clock in the morning local time. Almost twenty-two hours since they had departed Santiago. A smell of hot concrete and jet fuel wafted across the air as Carter grabbed his rucksack and descended the lowered airstair. Termez in early spring, and the sun was already pulsing in the bright blue dome of the sky. An airport guard greeted Carter on the apron. He took one look at the SAS man and pointed him in the direction of the main terminal building.

Carter followed the signs for border control and joined a long line of passengers. Oil and gas workers, mostly. Rugged middle-aged guys dressed in heavy-duty kit, with hard faces and calloused hands. Therefore not tourists. Not here to admire the ornate mosques or the mausoleums of ancient kings. Carter flashed his passport and visa at the border guard. The guy scrutinised his documents closely, took in his NGO-branded clothing and the lanyard around his neck displaying his ID card. Then he stamped Carter's passport and waved him through.

Carter bypassed the luggage carousel and customs and emerged to a high-ceilinged arrivals hall. Posters advertised taxi firms and local restaurants, mixed in with companies promoting various pumps and tank vessels and heat exchanges. All kinds of complicated refinery equipment. Aimed at the site managers and oil execs passing through, he guessed.

He walked past the duty-free shops, found a garishly lit café that reeked of disinfectant and ordered a Coke Zero from the humourless guy behind the counter. He tapped his bank card against the handheld reader, took a seat and waited for the guide to show up.

Two minutes later, a broad-shouldered guy walked over to his table. Carter identified him straightaway from the photo he'd seen back at the briefing in Santiago. The ex-Afghan police officer. He was a few inches shorter than Carter and running to fat; a long moustache drooped down either side of his down-turned mouth, and his prominent paunch threatened to burst out of his shirt. His eyes were heavily lidded, as if he'd just roused himself from a deep slumber. They peered at Carter suspiciously from beneath a pair of wild eyebrows.

'You are Carter?' he asked in a gravelly smoker's voice. 'Jamie Carter, yes?'

Carter stood up and said, 'That's me.'

The guide offered a sweaty hand. His khaki shirt carried the same logo as Carter's shirt and cargo trousers. An odour of cheap tobacco permeated from every pore of his body.

'Najim Kabiri. I'll be accompanying you across the border.'

Carter pumped the Afghan's hand. Najim Kabiri had a fierce grip and the mean-looking face to go with it. He had spent years in the Afghan police, Mullins had told him. Which was a perilous job, with a high casualty rate and the constant threat of Taliban infiltrators putting one in the back of your head. You needed nerves of steel to survive in that role for any length of time.

Kabiri dropped his eyes to the rucksack at Carter's feet. 'Is that all your baggage?'

'That's it,' Carter replied. 'Nothing else.'

Kabiri nodded. 'I'm parked outside,' he said. 'We'll head straight down to the border crossing, OK? We meet with Omar there. I must be back here before nightfall.'

'Lead the way.'

He followed Kabiri across the hall and through the main entrance, past a throng of passengers and drivers milling about at the taxi ranks, then crossed the road and made for a short-stay parking lot. In which time Kabiri had managed to holler greetings at a couple of taxi drivers, fielded a call on his ancient-looking phone and puffed his way through another tab from his pack of Russian-branded cancer sticks.

They hastened across the lot until they stopped in front of a white Toyota Land Cruiser. One of the older models, with the logo of the NGO stickered down the side. A beaded pendant hung from the rear-view mirror. Kabiri dashed his butt on the ground, crushed it under his heel and gestured for Carter to get in. Carter dumped his rucksack in the back seat and hopped into the front passenger side while Kabiri squeezed his bulky frame behind the steering wheel.

'Got some gifts for you, my friend,' Kabiri said as he started the engine. Some sort of traditional folk music blared out of the car speakers. 'In the glovebox.'

Carter popped open the compartment. Inside, he found a series of laminated maps of north-east Afghanistan, plus a bag of five-gram gold bullion bars. Each one was about the size of a standard SIM card and worth somewhere north of £250. A year's salary in Afghanistan. There was also a separate double-sided sheet of letterheaded paper, written in both English and Uzbek, stating that the bearer of the document worked for the medical assistance programme and had the right to cross into Afghanistan. Project oversight. The signature at the bottom belonged to the company CEO. The document was bullshit, but the guards wouldn't know that. They'd just see the NGO's logo and signature and assume it was official.

Morally wrong, perhaps. There was always a risk of blowback when soldiers passed themselves off as aid workers or peacekeepers. Innocent people could become targets. But Carter couldn't worry about that now.

As long as it gets us across the border.

He stuffed the bag of gold tablets into his belt pouch, put the folded maps in his rucksack. Kabiri sparked up another foul-smelling cigarette and pointed the Land Cruiser east and then south through the outskirts of Termez. Carter saw crumbling houses and ramshackle teahouses and crowded bazaars. Decorative minarets loomed over weeded gardens. Mangy dogs roamed the streets, sniffing mounds of rubbish. An endless ocean of desert stretched out beyond the city.

Kabiri took another pull on his cigarette, glanced at the phone mounted on top of the dash and said, 'We'll get to the bridge in fifteen minutes. You let me do the talking, OK? I know these guys. They trust me.'

Carter looked at him and said, 'Have you done this before?'

'Many times,' Kabiri said. 'I usually work for the aid programmes, you know. Taking people to the projects across the border. Sometimes, the Americans ask me to do them a favour. Get somebody across, no questions asked.'

'Why would you risk your balls running blokes like me into Afghanistan if you've got a steady job?' asked Carter.

Kabiri said, 'I have relatives. In Kabul. I send them money. Whatever I can spare, to pay for rent and food. The Americans, they pay good dollar, you know?'

'Can't you get them out?'

'I have tried. Many times. It is not easy with the Taliban. They don't want people to leave. For now, I do what I can. Later, maybe the Americans help to get them out.' Kabiri paused. Smoke fumed out of his nostrils. He said, 'Omar is waiting for us on the other side of the bridge. Fifteen kilometres away. We meet him, then we're good. I go back. You understand? I don't stay there for a moment longer than necessary.'

'Roger that, mate.'

He glanced sidelong at Kabiri. The guy was sweating like a drug mule at an airport. Carter didn't blame him. He was going into Afghanistan with a white guy for a passenger. A risky proposition. *If they rumble us,* Carter thought, *they might take me hostage. Use me to secure a fat ransom. But they'll torture Kabiri and put him to death. Burned alive, maybe. Or thrown from the roof of a ten-storey building.*

Kabiri said, 'You know Omar Sharza?'

Carter nodded. 'We worked together. A few years ago.'

'Omar is a good friend of mine,' Kabiri said.

'Is that so,' Carter replied.

'Yes,' Kabiri said. 'He is Tajik, same as me. Since the Taliban came back to power, we do many jobs together. I think we will be doing this for a long time. Many people wish to leave Afghanistan.'

Kabiri buzzed down the window and flicked his cigarette into the road. On the radio station, the folk tracks had given way to a stream of noisy adverts in the local lingo.

'People are starving,' Kabiri went on. 'Nobody has money to buy food, and the drought has been bad again this year. Now they say Daesh-K is getting stronger. More fighters are crossing into Afghanistan every day. Not only Daesh-K, but al-Qaeda. Even the Taliban cannot control these people. It is a tragedy.'

Carter didn't reply. He wasn't interested in shooting the shit with this guy. He just wanted to get across the border so he could link up with Sharza and start looking for Vann.

The sooner we begin the search, the better our chances of finding him.

'None of my business, of course,' Kabiri said. 'But if you ask me, you have to be a crazy man to go back there now.'

'You're right,' Carter replied tonelessly. 'It is none of your fucking business.'

Kabiri fell silent and refocused on the road ahead. Carter watched the landscape roll past, mentally running through the next few hours in his head. He figured maybe half an hour to cross the border into Afghanistan. Then a thirty-minute ride south to the RV with Sharza. Then a two-hundred-mile journey east to the safe house near Khordokan. A four-hour drive, maybe longer. Assuming they steered clear of trouble along the way, they'd reach the safe house some time before nightfall. Carter could spend the evening assessing potential locations to recce with Sharza before they began their search at first light.

They motored east, away from the city, passing through a parched landscape interrupted with a few isolated settlements. Something caught Carter's eye at the side of the road. Hundreds of flimsy makeshift tents had been pitched in a field, he noticed. Some were little more than sheets of tarpaulin held together with sticks. In the gaps between the tents he glimpsed skinny children rooting through piles of festering rubbish. Dishevelled old men sat around in groups, baking under the oppressive desert sun. At the edge of the road, veiled women pleaded at passing motorists with outstretched hands, begging for scraps of food.

'Refugees,' Kabiri said, noticing Carter's expression. 'From across the border. The lucky ones.'

'Christ. There must be thousands living in there,' Carter said. He thought: *if these are the lucky ones, the country must have really gone downhill since I last saw the place.*

We're entering the gates of hell.

'At least they got out before it was too late,' Kabiri said. 'They have no money, no clothes. Life will be very hard for them here. But at least they will not starve to death.'

Carter ran his eyes over the endless rows of makeshift tents. Emaciated figures stared vacantly into the distance. Mothers tried to comfort wailing babies.

'Things will get better,' Kabiri said. 'When the world hears of the plight of our people, they will have to help. They cannot let us suffer like this.'

'Maybe,' Carter replied.

But he knew the hard truth. The rest of the world didn't give a toss about these poor souls, not really. Western celebs and worthies would post sympathetic messages on their social media accounts, declaring their support for Afghan women, or whatever happened to be the fashionable cause of the moment. Then they'd lose people's attention and move on to the next thing.

No wonder the rest of the world hates our guts.

Seven minutes later, they hit the border checkpoint. Which was a heavily policed zone roughly two kilometres from the river crossing. Carter saw lots of barbed wire. Lots of sandbags and concrete security barriers. Half a dozen border officials stood around a large guardhouse, armed with Russian-manufactured assault rifles, plate armour and holstered pistols. Above them, an Uzbekistani flag rippled like a tongue in the faint midday breeze.

In front of the guardhouse, a stream of vehicles waited to be let through. Aid convoys, mostly, representing NGOs and charities from several countries. Germany, France, Canada. Usually there would be a stream of traders crossing back and forth to sell their wares, Kabiri said, but no one bothered now.

'The traders say the people have no money to buy anything. Some barter their gold jewellery or sell whatever else they have in exchange. But most have nothing left.'

Kabiri hastily extinguished his cigarette, took the crumpled packet from the dash and stuffed it into his trouser pocket. A smart move. The Taliban took a dim view of smoking. They didn't want to piss off the border guards unnecessarily.

As Carter scanned the convoys he spotted a Land Rover belonging to a well-known British NGO at the rear of the queue.

'Shit,' he muttered.

Kabiri glanced anxiously at him. 'What? What is it?'

Carter indicated the Land Rover directly ahead. 'Stay away from that vehicle,' he said. 'Slow down and get behind them guys,' he added, pointing out a German convoy immediately behind the Land Cruiser.

'Why? Is there a problem?' Kabiri asked, panic rising in his voice.

'Just avoid that wagon,' Carter ordered. 'It belongs to a British aid organisation.'

'So?'

'They'll have security with them,' Carter said. 'Some of them might be ex-Regiment guys. They might recognise me.'

'Are you sure?'

'Just fucking do it.'

Kabiri eased the Land Cruiser down to a slow crawl and pulled over at the side of the road, letting the three German wagons pass before he tucked in behind them and joined the line of traffic. As they edged forward, Carter glanced out of the corner of his eye at Kabiri. The guy was sweating buckets, looking more jittery with each passing moment.

Fuck me, thought Carter. *His nerves are shot to pieces, and we haven't even reached the border yet.*

After what felt like a long time but was probably no more than five minutes, a stern-faced border guard motioned for them to move forward. Which turned out to be the easier part of the crossing. The local border forces didn't give a toss about people trying to get into Afghanistan. They only cared about who might be coming the other way. The guard had a brief exchange with Kabiri and took a cursory glance at Carter's paperwork before casually waving them through.

Kabiri steered the Land Cruiser along the road, sticking close to the three-car German aid convoy in front of them as they passed over a Soviet-era road-and-rail bridge extending across a murky stretch of river.

On the far bank, Carter saw a cluster of half-ruined buildings, rusted pickup trucks and sagging power lines.

Afghan soil.

They cleared the bridge, motored on for another two hundred metres, and then Kabiri slowed the Land Cruiser to a halt as they reached the bottleneck at the Afghan checkpoint.

The scene in front of them was chaotic. A long line of vehicles clogged the road, motors running, spewing out exhaust fumes while the driver of the British aid wagon leaned out of his side window, waving paperwork at a Taliban soldier.

More soldiers patrolled the checkpoint, glaring at the new arrivals. They were nothing like the poorly equipped fighters

Carter had encountered on his last rotation in Afghanistan. These lads had US weaponry and kit. Pilfered from the stores left behind by American forces, no doubt. Carter saw one guy armed with an FN Minimi light machine gun. His shoulders were garlanded with belts of 5.56 x 45 mm NATO link.

This isn't 2001 anymore, Mullins had said. *We're not up against a rabble of bearded mullahs.*

The Taliban are better equipped now.

Up ahead, the British NGO crew was finally waved through.

Kabiri edged the Land Cruiser forward, gripping the wheel so tightly Carter thought it might snap. Sweat patches the size of reservoirs stained the front of the guide's khaki shirt.

On the other side of the road, a fleet of large cargo trucks snaked towards the Taliban-manned checkpoint. As Carter looked on a trio of Taliban soldiers stepped out into the road, shouting and signalling for the driver of the lead truck to pull over.

Directly ahead, the wagon at the rear of the German convoy had passed through the checkpoint.

A pair of heavily armed soldiers next to the guardhouse yelled something incomprehensible at Kabiri, motioning for him to ease the Land Cruiser forward. Kabiri drew the vehicle level with the guardhouse, buzzed down the side window and killed the engine.

The two soldiers marched over. A tall guy and a much shorter guy. Like opposite ends of a matryoshka doll set. The shorter guy was squat and wide-necked and wore a pair of wraparound shades. The second soldier stood about six inches taller than his mate. He had a mean-looking face and a scar shaped like a crescent moon below his left eye.

Their gear and clothing might have changed. But the Taliban still looked like a bunch of evil bastards.

The scar-faced soldier stopped a couple of paces from the Land Cruiser. He gave Carter his best screw-face while the taller guy with the crescent scar approached the driver's side window. Kabiri gave him a nervous smile. His stained rotten teeth looked like a mouthful of stubbed-out cigarette butts.

The scar-faced soldier barked at Kabiri and extended his left hand. Carter understood the guy's demand easily enough. *Show me your papers.* Carter handed over his passport and the fake letter from the NGO, and Scar-Face creased his brow in concentration as he studied the documents.

Across the road, the driver of the lead transport truck climbed down from the front cab and raised his hands above his head. One of the soldiers started questioning him while his two mates inspected his vehicle, searching the cab and kicking the tyres.

Carter looked back at Scar-Face. He was still frowning at the letter. Shades came over to cast an eye over it. They had a quick consultation in front of the guardhouse. Then Scar-Face marched over to the Land Cruiser, pointing to the document as he shouted at Kabiri.

Kabiri held up his hands in mock surrender and made a series of apologetic gestures. As if to say: *What do you want me to do?* Scar-Face shook his head and snapped angrily as he shoved the letter back at him.

'What does he want?' Carter asked.

'He says that this letter is not sufficient,' Kabiri replied in a strained voice. 'He says he cannot let us through without the rest of the documents.'

'Tell him that's all we've fucking got,' Carter said angrily. 'If he's got a problem, tell him to check the NGO's website. He can find all my details on there.'

Kabiri hastily translated. Scar-Face uttered a quick-fire reply.

'He says he doesn't know about any website,' Kabiri said. 'He says if you don't have the paperwork, you have no right to be in Afghanistan.'

Carter leaned over, showing the soldier the identity card attached to his lanyard. 'Tell this fucking idiot we're working on a major project with the support of his government. If he doesn't let us through, he'll be in a world of shit with his bosses.'

Kabiri translated again. But Scar-Face didn't appear to be listening. He caught sight of Carter's right hand and narrowed his eyes in suspicion. The soldier pointed to it as he snapped at Kabiri.

'What is it?' Carter asked. 'What's he banging on about now?'

Kabiri swallowed nervously. 'He says he wants to know why an NGO worker has got a bloodied fist.'

Carter glanced at his purpled hand. He'd been so busy focusing on the mission during the flight from Chile that he'd forgotten to clean the dried blood from his knuckles. A stupid mistake.

Scar-Face waited impatiently.

'I fell down the stairs coming off the plane,' Carter said. 'On the connecting flight. Wasn't looking where I was going. Bloody typical.'

Kabiri relayed the explanation to Scar-Face. The Taliban guard snorted and grooved his brow. The guy wasn't buying it, Carter realised. The man shouted furiously at Kabiri, gesturing at him with the business end of his assault rifle. Kabiri gave a panicked response. The argument was getting heated. Carter realised the whole operation was about to turn to shit. If Scar-Face saw through the cover story, he was fucked.

Just then he heard a commotion from the direction of the cargo trucks. Screaming voices. Shouting. Carter looked across the road. Towards the lead truck, fifteen metres away.

So did Kabiri and Scar-Face.

The two soldiers beside the truck were dragging out a pair of shrieking kids from the underside of the chassis. They pulled out two more boys from beneath the truck and forced them at gunpoint to stand next to the first pair. None of the kids looked a day older than eleven or twelve.

Carter looked on through the dirt-flecked windscreen as the soldiers ripped the threadbare clothes from the four boys, revealing dozens of dark-coloured packs strapped with duct tape around their chests, arms and legs.

Heroin.

Black tar.

The two soldiers tore the heroin packs free and started thrashing the half-naked kids with their long wooden sticks. Almost immediately the other guards hurried over to join in, kicking and punching faces and torsos while their mates stood around and laughed.

Carter saw another trio of kids crawl out from beneath one of the rear transport trucks. They turned and began running back down the road in a desperate attempt to escape the same fate as their friends. One of the guards spotted them and shouted what sounded like an order at Shades and Scar-Face. Telling them to give chase, perhaps.

Scar-Face glanced back at Kabiri and drew his eyebrows together, as if making a quick decision. Then he said a few words to the guide before he started after the fleeing kids.

'He says we can go,' Kabiri said. 'We are free to continue our journey.'

'Thank fuck for that,' Carter muttered.

As they accelerated away, Carter glanced back at the checkpoint. Scar-Face and Shades had caught up with the kids. The soldiers yanked them to their feet while their mates marched the other boys at gunpoint towards a windowless concrete building at the side of the road.

'Smuggling,' Kabiri said. He lit a celebratory cigarette and sucked on it, exhaling with relief. 'Very big problem on the border now. Lots of gangs use the children to try and get through. Most make it. Some do not.'

Carter said, 'But the Taliban run most of the smuggling operations in these parts, don't they?'

'Yes.'

'So why the fuck would they arrest some kids for trafficking heroin? Surely they'd want the gear to get through.'

'Supply and demand,' Kabiri said. 'Today, there is too much opium on the global market. It is, as you say, saturated. Which makes it cheap. So now the Taliban cut the supply. Drive the price up. Make more money.'

Sharza rubbed his thumb and forefinger together to emphasise his point.

'What will happen to the kids?' Carter asked.

'They will be flogged and beaten. One or two may be used for *bacha bazi*.'

Carter wrinkled his nose in disgust. During his time in the country as an embed he'd heard plenty of stories about the rural custom of *bacha bazi*. Boy play. Adolescent boys who dressed up as females and danced in front of groups of adult men. Many were sold or kidnapped and sexually abused by powerful Afghans.

He said, 'I thought the Taliban had outlawed all them dancing boys.'

Kabiri said, 'This is true. But the Taliban also use them for honey-traps sometimes. To get close to the warlords and commanders who are opposed to the rule of the Taliban. They force the boys to win the trust of their enemies, then poison or shoot them.'

Carter shook his head in disbelief. 'The drug gangs never used to use kids. Not for this shite.'

'Times have changed,' Kabiri said.

'What does that mean?'

Kabiri shrugged and said, 'People are desperate. Families will do anything for a little food. Some sell their kidneys or other organs. Girls are sold into marriage with older men, sometimes when they are still just infants, so the father can receive a down payment on the dowry. Boys are forced into labour. Whatever work they can find. Some go to work for the smugglers. They pay money to the family if the children make it across the border.'

Carter stared at him in disgust. 'People are selling their kids now?'

Kabiri said, flatly, 'They have no choice. A bride can fetch two or three hundred dollars. Enough to put food on the table for a while. Many parents cannot afford to feed their children anyway. If they do not sell them to someone else, they will starve to death.'

'Jesus Christ.'

'Like I told you. Only a crazy person would come back here.'

Ten

They headed east from the checkpoint, passing through the strategic border town at Hairatan. Carter looked out of his side window as they drove past a tableau of poverty and despair. Long lines of people queued up for handouts outside a food relief distribution centre. Others sat begging on the sides of the road, their malnourished children lying on blankets at their feet. There was a palpable sense of desperation in the air. Carter could see it in their faces. A people forced to the brink.

Twenty years of war, and this is how we've left the country.

He recalled that Afghanistan was in a different time zone and changed his G-Shock to the local time, thirty minutes behind Uzbekistan. After several kilometres the road curved south and they pushed deeper into the country. Carter saw groves of apricot trees, neglected farmsteads and impoverished villages. Columns of people trudged along the roadsides, many of them barefoot, the men dressed in a variety of waistcoats, tunics and trousers. Some walked alongside underfed donkeys weighed down with the family's worldly possessions.

They continued east on the main road, heading in the direction of Kunduz. Twenty minutes later, they hit a road junction with an abandoned truck stop at the side. In the distance, the rusted metal carcass of an Afghan light-armoured vehicle baked beneath the sun. From his study of the maps, Carter swiftly recognised this place as the prearranged RV point.

Kabiri dropped the Land Cruiser to fifteen per and steered off the highway, then parked next to the derelict truck stop. Carter glanced round.

'Where's Omar?' he asked.

'We are too early,' Kabiri said. 'Omar will be here soon. Don't worry, my friend. Patience. He will come.'

They sat and waited. Kabiri chained his way through another rancid-smelling cigarette. Carter pulled out a plastic bottle of water from his rucksack and took a couple of sips.

Eight minutes later, he descried a cloud of dust on the road further west. A white Toyota Hilux scudded towards them. Carter watched it turn off the metalled road before it pulled up next to the Land Cruiser. The Hilux was one of the four-door models, with a shortened rear bed. It looked several years old, with worn tyres, and the paintwork was coated in a patina of sand and grime. The perfect vehicle for blending in with the local environment.

Kabiri tipped his head at the pickup and said, brusquely, 'There. That is Omar. Go. I'm done here.'

'Good luck, mate,' Carter told him. 'With your relatives.'

Kabiri smiled. 'I think, my friend, I do not need the luck as much as you.'

Too fucking right, thought Carter as he climbed out of the Land Cruiser.

He hooked round to the rear door, opened it and snatched up his rucksack from the back seat, pausing to tear off the NGO badges from his shirt, trousers and bag. He stowed the Velcro patches in his pockets: if they ran into any more Taliban checkpoints along the way, Carter would slap them back on and try to bluff his way through, sticking to the original story that he was here on official business.

He slammed the door shut. Kabiri quickly accelerated away in a swirl of hot dust and churned dirt as he steered the Land Cruiser back onto the highway. At the same time Carter jogged over to the pickup. Omar Sharza hopped out and greeted him with a fierce handshake.

'My brother,' he said in faintly accented English. He stood back and gave a weary smile tinged with sadness. 'I did not think I would see you here again.'

'That makes two of us, mate,' Carter replied.

Sharza looked exactly the same as Carter remembered him. He was big all over, a great bear of a man with meaty paws and a full beard. But his eyes were bloodshot, and there was a strained look on his face. The constant stress of running people out of the country from under the noses of the Taliban.

'You are ready?' asked Sharza. He had a soft voice that seemed completely at odds with his grizzly-bear physique. Carter nodded, and Sharza said, 'OK, then. Let's go.'

Carter bundled his rucksack into the back of the cab and jumped into the shotgun seat. Then Sharza punched the start-stop button on the dash, the Hilux engine fired up, and soon they were cannoning east on the highway.

Towards Khordokan, and the last known location of David Vann.

Every few minutes Sharza glanced in the rear-view mirror, as if he was worried that someone might be following him. But the road behind them remained clear of vehicles and after several kilometres the interpreter visibly relaxed.

'I am sorry I couldn't meet you in Uzbekistan,' he said at last. 'But you must understand. People are hunting for me. I could not take the risk.'

'None of that, mate,' Carter replied. 'You don't have to apologise.'

Sharza smiled sadly. 'It is a shame we must meet again.'

Carter shot him a questioning look and said, 'What are you still doing here, Omar? You should be out of the country by now, bedding down with your family in Kent, or wherever.'

Carter surprised himself with the feeling in his voice. But he liked Sharza. Respected him. He had spent eighteen months living with the bloke while he'd served as an embed with Afghan SF. The two of them had taken meals together, shared jokes and fought against the Taliban. In that environment, you quickly learned who you could trust, and who wasn't up for the job. Over time, Sharza had proven himself a man of dedication, loyalty and toughness.

The guy had risked his life to serve alongside Carter. If anyone warranted a shot at a new life, it was him. He certainly deserved better than staying put in Afghanistan.

'I couldn't leave,' Sharza explained quietly. 'The British government offered to help get me out, but I could not accept.'

'Why not?' asked Carter.

'There are people here . . . people who need my help. I could not abandon them.'

'You've got a wife and kids, Omar.'

'I know.'

'So why stick around here? You're putting your neck on the line every time you set foot outside your home.'

Sharza stared dead ahead for several beats. Then he swallowed and said, 'I have a nephew. My brother's son. Amredin. Nineteen years old. He is still here, in Bazarak. Hiding.' He glanced at Carter. 'If the Taliban find him, they will kill him. This I know.'

'What about your brother?'

'He's in Greece. In a refugee camp. With the rest of his family. Amredin was supposed to join them, but my brother received a warning from a friend that the Taliban planned to arrest him, so he had to flee in the middle of the night, without any notice. They did not even have time to pack their things.' Sharza paused. 'Amredin was staying with his grandparents at the time. My brother had to leave him behind.'

Carter was silent for a moment. Then he said, 'That's why you're still in-country? Because of your nephew?'

'Yes,' Sharza said. He scratched his beard. 'The Americans, they promised that they would get Amredin to safety if I agreed to help others escape.'

'Did they?'

'Not yet. They are waiting for the right moment, they say.'

'What about your family?'

'They are waiting for me in Britain,' Sharza said. 'At a place called Cardiff. You know it?'

Carter laughed heartily, breaking the sombre mood. 'Aye, I know it.'

'What's so funny?'

'You might speak English better than some of our lads, but you won't understand a word the locals are saying. They speak a whole different tongue in them parts.'

'Then I shall learn,' Sharza said, proudly. 'I am keen to educate myself, learn many things. My children too. I will get out of here soon, I hope. Once we find your friend.'

Carter said, seriously, 'How much have they told you about the mission?'

'Only that your friend is in danger.' Sharza hesitated. 'They said this friend of yours, Vann, he is close with Jabar Hakimi, the leader of the National Alliance. This is true?'

'As far as I know,' Carter said. 'Why?'

'I have contacts, in Kabul and elsewhere. They say the Taliban are planning to destroy the National Alliance while it is still weak. They have vowed to hunt down and kill anyone who is guilty of working with them.' Sharza paused. 'Including your friend.'

'Then we'll have to find him first,' Carter said.

Sharza nodded. He said, 'I have done as the Americans have asked. I have spoken with people I trust about your friend. To see if any of them have seen or heard of such a man.'

'Any news?'

'Nothing. No one has seen him since Khordokan.' He looked across at Carter. 'Your friend, he is like a ghost.'

Carter rubbed his jaw. 'We'll have to take a closer look at the maps later. Find out where he might have taken refuge. If Vann was in that area a few days ago he can't have gone very far.'

'No.'

'Where's the safe house?'

'I have found a place for us in a village, fifteen kilometres from Khordokan. We will stay there tonight.'

'Is it secure?'

'I know the people who live there. They are good people,' Sharza replied confidently. 'They do not like the Taliban. They will shelter us. I would trust them with my life.'

You already are, mate, Carter almost said.

Carter consulted his G-Shock. A little past one o'clock in the afternoon. A two-hundred-mile journey on Afghan roads equated to a journey time of around four hours. They were looking at an ETA of around five o'clock. Two hours before nightfall. Plenty of time to start casting an eye over the maps before beginning their search the next morning.

They continued east, through the major cities at Kunduz and Taloqan. Taliban-controlled territory, but Sharza had explained that there was no other way of reaching the safe house. But he knew the locations of the main police checkpoints, and the spots where Taliban were likely to be found in large numbers: guarding mosques, government buildings, food distribution centres.

Besides, most of the police officers were former Taliban soldiers, Sharza added. Many of them came from tiny villages. They had never set foot in a city before in their life and knew nothing of the backstreets and the side roads in a place like Kunduz. Sharza expertly navigated his way through chaotic back roads crowded with beggars and packs of feral dogs. Women rooted through bags of rubbish while homeless people wrapped themselves in tattered blankets.

East of Kunduz the situation looked even more desperate. They rolled past narrow strips of fertile land and meadows on either side of the river, hemmed in by forbidding mountain ranges. Small, dirt-poor villages clung to the riverside, many consisting of nothing more than a scattering of dismal hovels and poppy fields.

Carter said, 'Looks like this area hasn't changed much.'

Sharza smiled. 'You mean the opium?'

'That's still the big trade, I'm guessing.'

'For now,' Sharza replied. 'But not for much longer, maybe.' He waved a hand at the surrounding mountains. 'The people here are poor, but this land is very rich. Many minerals here. Coal too. The Chinese are opening mines now. All across this area. Many Chinese come here to work.'

'Got to be a dicey place to operate,' said Carter. 'They're at risk of getting caught up in the fighting.'

Sharza said, 'That is one of the reasons why the Taliban wish to crush the National Alliance as soon as possible. The Chinese want the government to guarantee the safety of their workers. Otherwise they have threatened to end their operations and leave. This the Taliban cannot afford.'

Same old bloody story, thought Carter. *One foreign power pulls out, and five minutes later another country moves in to take advantage of the situation. These people can't catch a break.*

Sharza continued, 'Things here are bad. But I fear they will get worse.'

'Worse than this?' Carter asked, arching an eyebrow.

Sharza nodded. 'The Taliban came to power because people believed they would not be as corrupt as the old regime, and they were willing to give them another chance. But if they cannot feed their own people then they will not stay in power for long. Already their enemies are gaining support.'

'You mean the National Alliance?'

'Some have joined their cause, yes. But others are siding with ISIS-K.' He sighed wearily. 'They are taking advantage of the misery of the people. They say that the Taliban is a puppet of the American government and cannot be trusted. Lots of disillusioned Taliban are joining them. Soldiers who thought victory over the Americans would bring peace. Every week, ISIS-K grows stronger.'

'Do you think they'll topple the Taliban?'

'One day, who knows? Perhaps they will eventually grow strong enough to defeat the Taliban. But I hope not. That would be very bad for us.'

Carter decided to change the subject. 'What happened to them other lads we worked with?' he asked. 'Hamidullah and the rest? Did they get out in time?'

Sharza shook his head and said, gravely, 'Hamidullah was killed in the fighting with the Taliban in Panjshir. Faysal was arrested in his village and strangled to death. The Taliban killed his sons, raped his daughter and forced his wife to marry a Taliban commander. Mustafa was tortured and buried alive.'

'Fuck me, did anyone get out?'

'Ahmad. He escaped across the border just before the Taliban took Kabul. He is in a camp in Iran now, I think. The others, I do not know.'

He stared at the road ahead, his expression devoid of emotion. Carter tried to think of something comforting to say. He came up empty. There was nothing you could say to a bloke who had lost most of his mates.

They carried on in silence for twenty minutes until they hit another Taliban checkpoint manned by a pair of slovenly soldiers. Carter could tell from their gait and the way they carried their AK-47s that these guys were the dregs. He slapped the Velcro badges back on his clothing and let Sharza do the talking. The interpreter waved the NGO letter at the two soldiers, but they showed no interest in it and Carter guessed they were both illiterate.

The guards looked at one another, sized up the car and Sharza's white passenger. Reached the obvious conclusion.

Then one of the fighters thrust an outstretched hand at the driver's side window. Making the universal gesture for a bribe.

Carter dug out a couple of gold tabs from his pouch and handed them over. Five hundred pounds' worth of bullion. The Taliban fighter stepped back from the road, motioning with his rifle for the Hilux to proceed.

'Good to know some things haven't changed around here,' Carter said as they drove on past the checkpoint. 'The place is as corrupt as ever.'

'Worse now than it ever has been.' Sharza laughed.

'Why's that?'

'Most of the Taliban's soldiers have not been paid for months now. The government has no money. The treasury is empty, and they cannot pay the salaries of their own men. Which means the men cannot afford their rent and bills, not even food for their families.'

Carter grinned. 'Lucky for us.'

Sharza shrugged his shoulders. 'Today it is good for us. But tomorrow, maybe not so good.'

'Meaning?'

'If the Taliban are not paid soon, they will ignore the orders from Kabul and start taking hostages. Then it will be very hard for people like you to operate here.'

Shortly before five o'clock they crossed a decaying bridge over the river and then Sharza hung a right, pointing the Hilux east along a single-lane track. Which they followed for three kilometres until they pulled up in front of a crude shack, with a front yard enclosed by a waist-high mud wall. A pair of scrawny mules grazed among the rocks and dirt.

Sharza cut the engine and said, 'We are here, brother.'

Carter debussed from the Hilux and snatched his rucksack from the back seat. Then he followed Sharza towards the weathered wooden door built into one side of the farmhouse. A dry wind gusted fiercely across the valley, blasting sand in Carter's face and gritting his teeth.

As they approached the door swung open and an older-looking guy wearing a light patterned turban emerged from the gloom. He had a cobwebbed beard and a face like shrivelled fruit. Sharza greeted the man warmly and the two of them talked for a short while, exchanging pleasantries, before the interpreter gestured towards Carter. The old man looked impassively at his guest. He didn't seem surprised to see a Brit on his doorstep. But then again, thought Carter, the bloke had probably seen it all in his lifetime. The Soviets, the Taliban, the War on Terror, and now the Taliban again.

'This is Khaibar,' Sharza translated, indicating the old man. 'My father fought alongside him in the Northern Alliance, when they battled the Taliban. He says he is honoured to welcome you to his home.'

They shook hands. Carter looked at the interpreter. 'How much does this bloke know about me?'

'I have said that you are a close friend of mine, from years ago. He does not need to know anything else.'

'Tell him I'm very grateful for his hospitality.'

He knew the risk the old man was running in sheltering a Western soldier under his roof. If the Taliban found out, he could expect nothing less than the death penalty.

Khaibar chatted to Sharza as he led them across the front yard. Carter paused to take off his shoes before he followed the Afghans into a modestly furnished abode. He peered into the rooms leading off the main hallway but saw no one else inside. Which struck him as odd. Usually a dwelling this size would house several families. But this place was emptier than a pub in lockdown.

'Where is everyone?' he asked Sharza. 'Where's the rest of the family?'

'Most of them have left. Those who did not die in the fighting. Some went to Kabul to look for work, others have fled the country. Now there is no one here except Khaibar and his grandson. It is the same in many other villages in this area.'

'How does this fella get by?'

'He finds a little work here and there in the other villages, doing odd jobs. But it does not pay very much, and he barely has enough to stave off hunger.' Sharza added despondently, 'You see, brother. This is what the Americans have left us.'

They followed Khaibar through to a spacious room with frayed rugs covering the floor and richly decorated cushions stacked against the walls. Tattered curtains were draped across the rear window. In the middle of the floor space was a scuffed metal tray with a teapot and a set of glasses. Carter saw bowls of rice, a few slabs of coarse bread, some fruit. The walls were bare except for several framed family portraits. An old stove provided the only source of heat.

A small boy in a dark brown tunic sat beside the stove, watching a video on his smartphone. Apart from the clothes, he could have been any other child in any other corner of the world.

'This is Zohib,' Sharza said. 'Khaibar's grandson.'

The kid glanced up at Carter. There was a numbed look in his eyes that Carter had seen before, on the faces of children in other war zones. He gave the boy a friendly smile. Zohib blinked and returned his attention to the phone screen.

Khaibar gestured eagerly for Carter to sit down. Carter sat cross-legged while the old man spoke through the interpreter.

'Khaibar apologises that he does not have more to share with you,' Sharza said. 'But food is scarce these days, he says, especially since the markets closed down.'

'Tell your man not to worry,' Carter said. 'This spread will do just fine. Tell him I appreciate it.'

He remembered how generous the Afghans had been during his time as an embed. How most of the families he'd stayed with didn't have a pot to piss in, but still insisted on sharing everything they had with you.

He sat and ate while the two men conversed. Carter didn't refuse the scran, even though he had his ration packs, because he didn't want to cause offence to the old-timer. He scoffed down his food with his right hand and feigned interest when the old man described the latest developments in the nearby villages. Basic stuff, but the kind of details most of the Americans he had served with in Afghanistan had failed to grasp.

After the meal, the boy got the stove going, filled the kettle with water and they went through the familiar ritual of drinking green tea. As Carter sipped his brew, he noticed the kid staring at him expectantly. Something about his expression moved Carter. He finished his drink, reached into his rucksack, dug out a chocolate bar from one of the ration packs and offered it to the boy. Sharza looked at him with an anxious expression.

'What are you doing?'

'Giving the lad some chocolate. No harm in that.'

'Don't,' Sharza hissed. 'Don't do that.'

'The kid's hungry.'

Sharza shook his head forcefully. 'You can't.' He dropped his voice so low it could have slithered across the floor. 'If these people get caught with Western food, it will be a death sentence for them. They'll be accused of collaborating with the enemy.'

'The Taliban would kill him because of a chocolate bar?'

'Anyone who works with the West is a traitor.' Sharza composed himself. 'I know you want to help, brother, but please. This is not the way to do it.'

Carter glanced at the kid. He was staring wide-eyed at the chocolate bar in Carter's hand. *Sod this*, he thought. He tore off the wrapper and handed the bar to the boy.

'Tell him to eat it now,' he said to Sharza. The latter began to protest, but Carter cut him off. 'Look, I'll keep hold of the wrapper, so there's no risk of the kid getting in any trouble.'

Sharza sighed and uttered a few words to the boy. Zohib tore off a chunk of the bar and chewed enthusiastically, his face glowing with innocent delight. A small gesture, maybe. But better than nothing.

After a while the old man got to his feet and gestured for Carter and Sharza to follow. He guided them down the hallway, into another bare-walled room carpeted with richly decorated rugs. Khaibar stood back, arms at his sides while Sharza dropped to his knees and rolled back one of the rugs, revealing a hole in the ground covered with a strip of wood. The sort of thing a family might use to hide their cash and valuables. Sharza dug his fingernails into the slender gap between the edge of the hole and the board and prised it off.

Inside, Carter spied the gleaming tip of a rifle.

'This is all I could find at short notice,' Sharza said. 'If you need anything else, maybe we can get from another village. But it will cost money.'

Carter reached down into the hole. He hauled out an M4 assault rifle swathed in blankets, with a bungee sling clipped to a mounting point on the underside of the receiver. He took out five thirty-round clips of 5.56 x 45 mm NATO ammunition, set the rifle and magazines down on the floor and thrust his arm in again and retrieved a semi-automatic pistol. An MP-443 Grach. A Russian nine-milli firearm, with a stainless-steel barrel and a sturdy polymer grip. Weapon of choice for Spetsnaz operators.

Carter pulled out four spare magazines, each one containing eighteen rounds of 9 x 19 mm Russian 7N21 ammunition. Plus a black leather pancake holster. At the bottom of the hole, he found a Soviet-built NRS-2. Which at first glance looked like a survival knife, but also functioned as a single-shot weapon, capable of firing a round of 7.62 with an effective range of up to twenty-five metres. As an added bonus, the knife also came equipped with a pair of bolt-cutters.

'Where did you get this lot from?' asked Carter.

'A friend,' said Sharza. 'Over in Fayzabad. He served in the army, before the Taliban returned to power. He has many weapons from an American cache they left behind at the firebase. He sells to anyone who is willing to pay. Smugglers. Warlords. Al-Qaeda.'

'Must be a lucrative side hustle.'

'Very lucrative, yes. But dangerous. If the Taliban find this out, they kill him and his entire family.'

Carter inspected the hardware, disassembling the M4 and the pistol. They both looked to be in good working order, no rusted parts or signs of wear and tear. He reassembled them, then transferred the extra mags into his rucksack. He tucked the gun knife into the pocket of his cargoes, slid a clip into the mag feed on the underside of the M4 and switched the fire selector to the safety setting. He kept the rifle by his side, within arm's reach, the way every Regiment man had been taught. Then he loaded the MP-443 Grach and sheathed it in the pancake holster threaded through his belt.

While the old man tended to the fire, chucking in rags and bits of rubbish as fuel, Carter unfolded the maps and spread them out on the floor in front of him. Sharza leaned in closer and by the flickering light of a kerosene lamp, he talked Carter through the area in close proximity to Khordokan.

Vann's last known location.

Carter was familiar with the layout of the area, the names of the villages and biggest towns. But a map only told half the story, he knew. To narrow down the search, he needed to understand the loyalties of the people living in each district. Their tribal, ethnic and cultural ties. He listened closely while Sharza described the area to the east of Khordokan.

'These elders in this place are in alliance with ISIS-K,' he explained, indicating a tight grouping of villages. 'ISIS-K recruits many fighters from this area.'

'Would Dave know that?'

Sharza scratched his jaw and thought for a moment. 'I think so, yes,' he replied. 'Everyone understands this is ISIS-K territory. If your friend is working with Hakimi and the National Alliance, they would have told him of such things. He would know to avoid the villages there.'

'What about this area?' Carter tapped a finger over the terrain to the south. 'Who lives here?'

'Few people,' said Sharza. 'Even less than here. Most of the villages in that valley have been abandoned. Many are home to only one or two families.' He bit his lip. 'But I do not think we will find your friend there.'

'Why not?'

'That district is under Taliban control now. They guard all the main entry and exit points along the mountain passes, they patrol the major settlements. Your friend would be captured as soon as he tried to leave.'

Carter mentally eliminated that area and concentrated instead on the terrain around Khordokan. Six days had passed since Vann had been spotted on the outskirts of the village. Assuming the information from Sharza's contact had been accurate. Carter ran his eyes over the nearby roadheads, rivers and footpaths. He visualised the route Vann would have taken from the rebel hideout to the south, then on to Khordokan. Tried to put himself in his mucker's position.

Vann would want to avoid the villages. Someone sympathetic to the enemy might catch sight of him and report his location. Therefore, Carter was looking for a remote location. Somewhere on raised ground, with an unobstructed view of the main approaches, a good backstop to cover the rear and an escape route if the position was compromised and things got ugly. He'd also need food, or a means of acquiring it, which meant he couldn't base himself too far from the villages. Plus access to fresh water. In a region suffering from historic drought.

'Is there a well in Khordokan?' he asked.

'Not now. It dried out last year. The drought . . . But there is one in the next village, I think,' Sharza replied uncertainly.

'What about him? Would he know?'

Carter inclined his head towards Khaibar. The old man prodded at the weak flames with a gnarled stick. It was dark outside now, and noticeably colder. Carter felt a chill draught whispering in through the cracks in the window.

Sharza put the question to his friend. Khaibar stabbed at the fire some more, as he made his reply. Then Sharza translated.

'He says there is a well in Zarangir, but it has almost run dry. Now there is only a little water.'

'What does everyone use, then? They have to get their water from somewhere.'

'There is a stream to the north. Three kilometres away.'

The interpreter indicated the place on the map. Carter frowned at it. *Zarangir.* Another tiny settlement. A speck on a map. The next village over from Khordokan, eight kilometres to the east. Fifty kilometres or so south of the Tajikistan border.

'The stream freezes in the winter,' Sharza went on. 'But now it is the only source of water in the area. Many people rely on it.'

'What else is there?' Carter said.

'Not much,' Sharza replied. 'The area used to be grazing land. This was many years ago, before the Russians came. Now there is hardly any vegetation left. Just dust and rocks,' he added sadly.

'What about Zarangir? What's in that place?'

Sharza stroked his beard thoughtfully. 'There are a few families there, as I recall. Thirty or so. But it is a poor village, very isolated. In the winter there is heavy snow and they are cut off for months from the rest of the country. Beyond it the land is mostly inaccessible.'

'Pro-Taliban?'

Sharza smiled and shook his head. 'Many of the people in Zarangir grow the red gold. The same is true of the other villages in this area. It is the only way they can earn a living.'

Red gold, thought Carter.

The poppy trade.

'Who do they sell to?'

'Local barons. Different people. They have no allegiance to the Taliban or anyone else. But they don't like outsiders. They are afraid of reprisals from the Taliban if they discover they are growing the poppy.'

Carter looked down at the map once more, an idea slowly taking shape in his mind. He noticed a road stretching up from Zarangir and traced the route with his index finger. The road ran in a northerly direction for fifteen kilometres, past the stream and the old hunting grounds, before it abruptly stopped near the base of a mountain range.

'This road,' Carter said. 'Where does it go?'

'Nowhere,' Sharza replied. 'It is, how do you say, a dead end.'

That puzzled Carter. 'Who would build a road that goes nowhere?'

'There used to be a village here, many years ago,' Sharza said, indicating the roadhead abutting the mountains. 'But it was abandoned during the war with the Taliban. Nothing left now.' The Afghan canted his head to one side. 'You think your friend might be there?'

'It would make a good base. He'd have a clear view of anyone trying to make an approach, and there's plenty of drinking water within easy access.' Carter looked up, the thought quickly gaining definition. 'Is there another escape route from there? Any other way out of them mountains?'

Sharza shook his head firmly. 'No escape. Why?'

Carter said, 'Wherever Vann is bottled up, he'll need a way out. He won't choose a location that doesn't have a secondary exit. Standard doctrine in the SAS. Never let yourself be cornered.'

Sharza gave a shrug and exhaled. 'Then your friend cannot be there.'

'You're sure it goes nowhere?'

'I know that area very well. Trust me, brother. The road ends there. It goes no further. Beyond it is only mountains.'

Carter clenched his jaw in frustration and dropped his gaze to the map. He focused on the dead end beyond the abandoned village fifteen kilometres north of Zarangir.

The perfect location. Almost. But Carter was certain that Vann wouldn't choose somewhere without giving himself an escape route.

He said, 'Let's take a closer look at Zarangir anyway. If that stream is the only water supply in the vicinity, then maybe Vann has been using it. One of the locals might have seen something.'

Sharza clicked his tongue. 'It will be a pointless journey. I'm telling you, there is nothing else in that area. No villages, nothing. Nowhere a person could survive, at least,' he added quietly.

'Maybe not. But it's worth a shot.' Carter sighed heavily. 'Look, we've got to start somewhere, mate. We've got to try.'

Sharza shook his head again. 'The people in Zarangir will not want to talk. Not even to me. They don't like outsiders.' He repeated the phrase like it was a religious mantra.

Carter said, 'You must know someone there, Omar. Come on.'

Sharza pursed his lips. His face was taut with unease. Then he gave a weary sigh and said, 'There might be someone. But I cannot make any promises. It will be dangerous for this man to talk to me. I am an outsider.'

'Just try, mate. That's all I'm asking.'

'OK. We can try to ask people in Zarangir. We do it your way,' Sharza replied guardedly. He paused. 'You will have to stay out of sight. If they see you, no one will talk.'

'Fine by me,' Carter replied. 'When do we leave?'

'Tomorrow morning,' said Sharza. 'First thing, I will take you to Zarangir. Then we will find out if anyone has seen your friend.'

Eleven

Carter awoke shortly after first light, in the cold grey gloom of the farmhouse. He crawled out of his sleeping bag, packed his kit in the Hilux and ate some cold rations while he waited for the others to finish their morning prayers. The old man insisted on serving more green tea, and then Sharza announced that it was time to go. Carter gave the boy another unwrapped chocolate bar as a leaving gift and got a beaming smile in return. He thanked the old man for his help, but the guy refused his offer of a gold bar for his troubles. They were good people, Carter thought, doing their best to eke out a living in a hard place. He hoped they would make it through the terrible years to come.

Three minutes later, they were heading east again, following the road as it curved round the edge of the mountains. Carter had studied the route from the safe house to Zarangir earlier that morning. The village was eight kilometres east of Khordokan, twenty-five kilometres from their present location, and accessible only via a series of narrow dirt roads. Sharza reckoned it would take them around thirty minutes to reach Zarangir. According to the old man they would have to watch out for Taliban in the area. Khaibar had said that the group had been increasingly active in the districts to the east, going out on frequent patrols in the villages as part of their drive to curb the poppy trade.

Carter had asked how the guy knew all this stuff. Sharza had merely laughed and said that word travelled fast in Afghanistan.

'Do you really think your friend is hiding in Zarangir?' he asked.

'The place ticks a lot of boxes,' Carter replied after a pause. 'It's remote, and there's access to food and drinking water. If he's not there, he can't be far away.'

'Perhaps.' A doubtful expression played out on the interpreter's face. 'But I am not sure, brother.'

'Why not?'

'The people in Zarangir have no allegiance to the resistance groups. They don't like—'

'Outsiders,' Carter interrupted. 'Aye, I know. What's your point?'

'No one would dare to shelter a British soldier. It is not worth the risk.'

Carter said, 'Maybe so. But even if Dave isn't hiding in Zarangir, someone might have seen something. He might be close by. Another village, perhaps, or a farmstead.'

Sharza made a pained face. 'I'm sorry, my friend. But there is nothing else beyond Zarangir. Nothing at all.'

Twenty minutes later, the road abruptly snaked away from the river and coursed north through a small valley devoid of vegetation. After another kilometre they neared the outskirts of a village set in the floor of a sandblown plain bordered by a series of steep mountains. Sharza kept the Hilux ticking along at twenty per until they were two hundred metres from the settlement. Then he pulled over at the side of the road and cut the engine.

He said, 'Wait here. I will go and speak with my contact. I won't be long.' He sprang the door handle, started to get out, then turned to Carter. 'I forget. I will need some gold.'

'What for?'

'My contact,' Sharza said. 'Sometimes the tongue needs to be loosened. Also, we need fuel.'

Carter did a quick mental calculation. Figured out that they had already covered well over three hundred kilometres in the Hilux. Equivalent to a third of the eighty-litre tank capacity. They had an unknown amount of ground to cover, plus whatever distance they might need to travel to extract Vann from the country. Carter grudgingly parted with two more gold bars from his belt stash.

Another five hundred quid from the survival fund. He was down to his last four tablets. The equivalent of a thousand quid in sterling.

Which would have to cover their fuel, food and other expenses for however long it might take to find Vann.

Assuming we find him at all.

He watched Sharza set off on foot towards the village and glanced at his watch. Eight o'clock in the morning. Less than three hours since dawn had broken. A long day ahead of them, possibly. Depending on the outcome of Sharza's enquiries.

Carter sat in the Hilux and waited. He rested his M4 rifle between his legs in the footwell, barrel pointing down. Ready to put down rounds if things got hairy. Every few minutes he flicked his gaze to the side and rear-view mirrors, keeping an eye out for approaching Taliban patrols or civilian vehicles. He felt dangerously exposed out in the open. Like a swinging dick in a room full of eunuchs. Any passers-by would surely take notice of the pale-faced bloke sitting in the pickup truck. News would quickly get back to the Taliban if they were in the area.

There's a Westerner in the village to the north.

Asking questions.

Time crawled past.

Carter concentrated on next steps. What would he do if the trail went cold in Zarangir. He had no other leads to follow, no other scraps of intelligence that hinted at Vann's whereabouts. He would have to speak to Langley after he'd exhausted his enquiries. Tell them that the search mission had failed.

Someone would then have to make a call. Someone above Mullins's pay grade, in all probability. *Do we continue the search, or pull our guy out?*

Pros and cons would be weighed up. Different scenarios played out. There would be political angles to consider. Risk assessments would be made.

Eventually, it would come down to a basic question: how much time and effort were they willing to throw into the hunt for a missing ex-Blade?

It didn't take a genius to guess the answer.

If Vann didn't show up soon, Vauxhall Bridge would conclude that he had been killed in a firefight, perhaps left behind by the resistance fighters in the mad dash to escape, which would explain the absence of a corpse. Maybe his headless torso would show up on a riverbed a few weeks from now. They wouldn't want to keep Carter in Afghanistan for longer than necessary. He reckoned he had another four or five days before they pulled him out.

An hour later, Sharza emerged from the muddle of buildings two hundred metres to the north. The interpreter was alone, his back slightly stooped as he carried a jerry can in either hand.

As he headed towards the Hilux, Sharza abruptly stopped in his tracks. He set down the petrol cans and wheeled round. Carter looked on as a second figure hurried over from the direction of the village. An older guy, a long beard as white as snow, with a dark shawl draped around his shoulders. The white-bearded man spoke with Sharza for a couple of minutes. He did most of the talking, pausing to glance back at the village, flapping a hand in the direction of the mountains.

After a couple of minutes they said their goodbyes, slapping each other on the back like old friends. The man headed back to the village. Sharza hefted up the jerry cans and lugged them over to the pickup. He loaded them into the back seat, then scooched behind the wheel.

Carter said, 'Who were you talking to?'

'My contact,' Sharza said. 'He says he was afraid to tell me anything in front of the elders. He did not want to be seen to be helping a friend of the British. This I understand.'

'What did he say?'

'He thinks he saw the man you are looking for.'

Carter felt his breath hitch in his throat. 'Is he sure?'

'Yes. Very.'

'Where?'

‘At the stream. Three kilometres from here.’ Sharza pointed in the same direction the man had indicated. The mountains looming to the north of Zarangir.

‘The man says he went there with his son to collect water,’ Sharza continued. ‘When they arrived, they saw a man at the edge of the stream, filling . . . I do not know the word in English. The American soldiers carry one and drink from it. A green bottle.’

‘A canteen?’

Sharza nodded. ‘Yes. That is it.’

‘What did he look like?’

‘The man was dressed like an Afghan, and his beard was long, but he did not respond when the father called out a greeting to him. Instead, he turned and left with his mule.’

‘When was this?’

‘Two days ago.’

‘Then he must still be in the area,’ Carter said, his mind racing.

‘Yes,’ Sharza replied. ‘I think so.’

‘Which direction did he go?’

‘North. My contact was very certain on that point. He says your friend took the road north of Zarangir.’

North, thought Carter.

The only other route out of the village. The road to nowhere. The single-lane track that ran from Zarangir to the dead end fifteen kilometres away.

A dead end, Sharza had told him. Not the kind of place Vann would select for a hiding spot.

No escape.

Sharza stared at him. ‘Do you really think your friend is there? In the abandoned village?’

‘Only one way to find out,’ Carter said.

* * *

They continued north on the road. After three kilometres they passed a bridge over a gently flowing stream edged with ribbons of grass and stunted trees. A loose throng of Afghans lined the water's edge, elders and children dressed in colourful clothing, filling up torpedo-sized plastic bottles with water. The menfolk all looked exhausted, worn down by a lifetime of war and grinding poverty.

They motored through an increasingly barren landscape, populated with a few clusters of flat-roofed buildings and animal pens fringing the foothills of the distant mountains. Goatherds shuffled along the roadside, driving on their scrawny livestock. As they cantered along Sharza pointed out how many people had once lived in a particular settlement, how many had fled after the Taliban's return to power. How many remained. Providing a running commentary of destruction and despair.

Carter turned his restless mind back to the problem of finding Vann's hideout. He imagined Vann taking this same route north from the stream. He wondered where the guy might have chosen to bed down. Somewhere safe. That would be his priority. Somewhere that wouldn't put him at risk of getting compromised by the enemy.

The road passed along a dried-out river, and then it degraded into a gravel track. Ten minutes later, they reached a narrow valley interspersed with clumps of drooping pine trees and dwarf shrubs. The abandoned village was at the far end of the valley. It looked even more decrepit than Carter had imagined: a handful of decaying buildings set near the base of a densely forested mountain. From a distance he saw no obvious signs of habitation.

Sharza downshifted and nosed the Hilux towards a patch of dirt at the side of the gravel road. The two men hopped out. Carter snatched up his M4 and threw the attached bungee sling over his head, allowing him to carry his weapon close to his chest, barrel-down, with his right hand clasped around the trigger guard. Ready to bring the rifle to bear on any threats that might be lurking around the area.

They spent the next hour methodically clearing the village, building by building. They started with the biggest homes and worked their way down, searching them room by room. Looking for any signs of recent habitation: a carelessly discarded wrapper from a ration pack, a piece of clothing, mouldy bits of food.

Carter saw a lot of rubbish. He saw frayed rugs caked in dust, plastic bags filled with old junk, an old TV that looked like it predated the invention of the printing press. Insects scuttled through the rooms. But he found nothing to suggest that Vann or anyone else had recently been in the area.

They looked under rugs and behind frayed curtains. They checked the homes for every conceivable hiding place and rooted through the smaller outbuildings.

The village was more deserted than Bigg Market on a Sunday morning.

Your friend is like a ghost.

Once Carter was satisfied that they had thoroughly searched the place, they circled back round to the Hilux.

'He is not here,' Sharza said in a resigned tone of voice. 'I'm sorry, brother. I did try to tell you.'

'I don't get it,' said Carter as he cast his eye over the valley. 'Dave must have travelled in this direction from the stream. He couldn't have gone anywhere else.'

'Maybe he sheltered in one of the other villages we passed,' Sharza suggested.

Carter considered, then shook his head. 'No. There are people in them places, even if it's only three or four families. Dave wouldn't do it. He'd be taking a big risk.'

'Perhaps he left the area, then. After my friend saw him at the stream.'

'That was two days ago,' Carter said, thinking aloud. 'Even if he had moved on, there would be signs of activity here. Footprints or something.'

'Then he cannot be here.'

'So where is he? He can't have vanished into thin air.'

Sharza gave a shrug. 'I don't know.'

Carter squinted as he scanned the ground beyond the village. He looked towards the mountain to the north. The gravel road ran on for a hundred metres past the edge of the village before it stopped at the foot of the thickly forested lower slopes. Higher up, the trees thinned out as the slope inclined sharply towards a forbidding rockface some distance below the peak.

Nowhere to go.

A dead end.

Carter dropped his eyes to the gravel road again. A short distance further along the road, something caught his eye. Fifty metres away from his position. A cluster of hard round lumps.

Animal droppings.

Carter stared at the mound of shit.

A thought pickaxed the back of his mind.

He set off down the road, moving at a quick walk as he beat a path towards the droppings. Sharza hurried after him, following a few metres behind.

'Where are you going?' he asked. 'There is nothing around here, brother. I am telling you.'

Carter didn't reply. He knelt down beside the pile of animal shit and picked up one of the stinking clods. Sniffed it, then broke it apart. The moist turd came apart easily in his grip. Sharza stood over him, his brow knitted in confusion.

'Goat droppings?' he asked.

Carter shook his head. 'Not goat's. This is mule shit, mate.'

'So what?' Sharza scratched his elbow and shifted. 'This could have been here for months. Maybe longer. Doesn't mean a thing.'

Carter shook his head. 'It was left a lot more recently than that.'

Sharza gave him a puzzled look. Carter indicated the soft lump in his hand and said, 'This came out of the arse of a mule between two and two and a half days ago.'

'How do you know that?'

'The inside of the turd is still moist,' Carter said. 'There are blades of grass in here that are still green, probably from the mule's last but one feed. If this shit was any older, it would have hardened by now, and the grass would have discoloured.'

The Afghan's frown deepened. 'But there are no mules around this place. No people. No nothing. Look for yourself.' He swept an arm across the abandoned valley to emphasise his point.

Carter nodded at the rest of the droppings. 'Some of this shit is a few days old. Some of it is about a week old. You've got month-old turds mixed in here as well. I bet if we inspected the roadside from here to the stream bed, we'd find loads more droppings along the way.'

'So?'

Carter said, 'Someone has been bringing a mule up and down this road on a regular basis. As recently as a few days ago.'

'You think that is your friend?'

'Your contact in Zarangir said Vann had a mule with him,' said Carter. 'When he spotted Vann at the stream the other day. He must have taken this route back from the village.'

'To here?' Sharza looked sceptical. 'But we have already searched the village. There is nowhere else to go. Nowhere else for your friend to hide. Dead end,' he added despondently.

Carter tossed the softened lump aside and wiped his hands on a tuft of grass. Then he turned his attention to the ground immediately downstream from the gravel road. North of the roadhead was the densely wooded area at the base of the mountain. He looked at the point higher up where the trees thinned out and the incline sharpened. He looked at the near-vertical rockface rising towards the summit high above.

The thought picked at his skull again.

Carter walked on past the edge of the gravel road. Towards the foot of the wooded slope, fifty metres away. Along the route he spotted two more mounds of mule shit. He stopped at the edge of the treeline and scanned the ground keenly. Sharza stood a couple of paces away, watching Carter with a curious expression.

'What are you looking for?'

'Sign,' Carter said.

'Of what?'

Carter didn't answer. He was looking at tangle of felled branches strewn across the ground between a pair of straight-trunked trees. Beyond the tangle he saw a scattering of dead leaves and loose grass, running on for half a dozen metres towards a patch of thick forest.

He marched over to the branches. Looked at them closely. Looked at the deadfall further up the gentle incline. Gears turning inside his head.

He thought about Vann. Thought about what he would do if he was in his mate's position. Alone, on the run from the Taliban, in a remote corner of Afghanistan.

A seeming dead end.

But maybe not.

'What is it?' Sharza asked.

Carter began clearing the ground. He worked quickly, chucking aside the cut branches and sticks. Then he moved further up, brushing away the leaves and grass until he had swept the area clear of deadfall. Beneath it, he found what he was looking for: a patch of densely compacted earth running between a narrow gap in the pine trees.

He turned to Sharza and said, 'This isn't a dead end. This is a trailhead. It'll lead up through them trees higher up the side of this mountain.' He pointed up the slope.

Sharza looked at him in surprise. 'But . . . how did you know?'

'This is ground cover.' Carter indicated the deadfall. 'Someone laid this here to disguise the entrance. That's what they taught us to do in the Regiment. It's basic fieldcraft when you're looking to hide your tracks.'

Sharza lifted his eyes to the mountain. 'You think your friend is up there?'

'Has to be. It's the only route Vann could have taken.' Carter stretched to his full height. 'I'll grab the kit. Let's get moving.'

He collected his rucksack from the Hilux. His professional eye told him that the climb from the valley floor to the plateau would take between one to one and a half hours. He wanted his kit with him in case the trail ran over the ridgeline and descended on the far side of the mountain. They could be trekking for hours, depending on how far away Vann had based himself. In which case they'd need food, clothing, blankets, water, maps, torches. All the basics.

He switched on his satphone, checked the battery. Four bars left. He made sure that he had the remaining gold bars in his belt pouch. Then he ordered Sharza to move the pickup out of sight, behind the grouping of derelict buildings in the village. He was sure they hadn't been followed by anyone since leaving Zarangir, but there was a small chance that a patrol of Taliban or ISIS-K soldiers might stumble upon the pickup truck. Better to err on the side of caution.

Two minutes later, as the sun reached its zenith in the cloudless sky, they started up the trail. Carter led the way, setting a brisk pace as the path zigzagged up the slope, meandering through clumps of pine trees and dense undergrowth. After two hundred metres the incline rapidly increased, and Carter dropped to a slow walk. Sharza followed a few metres behind Carter, moving effortlessly despite his bulk. The benefit of living in the wilds of Afghanistan. He had spent his whole life walking up and down mountain trails.

As they picked their way through the woods, Carter scanned the ground three paces in front of him, looking for telltale hints of recent movement along the track. In one place he noticed a snapped branch. In another he caught sight of a patch of dampened soil bearing the faintest imprint of a human boot. Further along, he saw more mule deposits, a few of them containing bits of recently digested grass and hay. Easily missed by a casual observer.

But to the trained eye of a Hereford man, they stood out like blood spatter at a crime scene.

At one point they seemed to lose the trail. It took Carter a few moments to establish that a section of it had been brushed over. Someone had made a poor attempt to cover their tracks. Carter pointed out the swept area to Sharza before they picked up the trail six metres further up the hill.

'How do you know all this stuff?' Sharza asked.

'You learn about it in the Regiment,' Carter replied. 'Every guy who goes through Selection spends a week doing tracking and anti-tracking.'

The Afghan angled his head. 'Will your friend know about this as well?'

Carter gave a dry laugh. 'Dave helped write the manual, mate.'

'Then why has he left all these tracks? Why not cover up everything?'

'He might not be alone,' Carter speculated. 'He might have some of the other guys from the National Alliance with him. Guys who aren't as well trained. They might have been sloppy on their way up the track.'

After half an hour they reached a narrow gap between the pine trees. Carter shaded his eyes against the sun as he looked up towards the sheer rock wall further up the slope. He saw no visible means of access to the ridgeline nearer to the peak. There didn't appear to be any footpaths cut into the rockface, either. He doubted Vann could have made his way up there. Not unless he had climbing equipment.

They pushed on again in the early afternoon heat. A hundred metres later, the track flattened as they neared a patch of level ground about the size of a tennis court. The track ran on for twenty metres before it wound its way past a mass of weathered rock and thorny shrub. He detected more signs in the surrounding vegetation and felt a prickle of excitement on his neck.

We're getting closer.

Not long to go now.

He glanced over his shoulder again. Sharza was three metres behind, moving easily as he followed Carter up the track. The guy had barely broken into a sweat.

Carter looked ahead again.

Stopped.

Something caught his attention to the left of the track, at eye level. A scrap of bright red fabric snagged on a bush.

Torn clothing.

Carter felt his pulse quicken. The fabric could only mean one thing, he knew. Someone else had recently taken this same footpath. He took a step towards the shred of material, intending to take a closer look at it.

Then he heard a metallic click.

Coming from directly beneath his right foot.

A sound Carter had heard before. He recognised it instantly, in a half-second of cold terror.

The triggering of a landmine.

Twelve

Carter waited to die.

A second ticked by.

Then another.

Nothing happened.

He stood very still. Wondered what the fuck was going on.

Anti-personnel mines were normally triggered by a pressure plate fixed to the surface of the mine. Once you stepped on the plate, the downward weight rammed the firing pin into the detonator, triggering the explosion. As soon as Carter had placed his right boot firmly on the mine, it should have kicked off. *Right now*, he thought, *I should be lying on the ground clawing at a bleeding stump.*

Which could mean one of three things.

Either I've stepped on a dud, or this is an old mine.

Or it's something else.

He heard footsteps at his six o'clock as Sharza approached him. 'Brother?' he asked. 'Are you OK? Why have we stopped?'

'Stay back,' Carter said urgently. 'Don't come any closer.'

He swallowed hard. Carter lowered his eyes to the ground and carefully scanned the patch of trampled soil around his right boot. Looking for any signs of recent disturbance. He couldn't see anything. Whatever he'd stepped on might have been in the ground for a long time. Years. Maybe longer. Planted by the Northern Alliance during their long war against the Taliban, perhaps.

But he was speculating. He couldn't know for sure. Not until he took his foot off the plate.

'What's going on?' Sharza asked, stepping closer.

Carter swallowed again and said, 'Move away from me, mate. Slowly. Do exactly as I say.'

'What for?'

'I've stepped on something.'

He looked over his shoulder. He saw Sharza standing four metres away, eyes as wide as frisbees.

Sharza said, 'You are . . . sure?'

'I heard a definite click. Something was armed, but it didn't go off for whatever reason. I'm guessing it's either a dud or an old model.'

Sharza edged back from Carter, blinking rapidly.

'Listen carefully,' Carter went on, trying to mask the tension in his voice. 'If this thing detonates, it'll take my leg clean off. I'm going to need your help. Understand?'

Sharza nodded quickly and licked his lips. 'What do you want me to do?'

'I'm going to take off my belt and throw it to you. You'll have to use it as a tourniquet. If the mine blows, get that belt around the stump of my leg and pull it tight to stop the flow of blood. There's no way you'll be able to help me back to the wagon from here, so you'll have to keep the leg elevated until help arrives.'

'But we are very far from the hospital.'

Carter said, 'I've got a satphone. I'll throw it to you. There's a number stored in the address book. Call it once you've secured the tourniquet and tell the person on the other end of the line what's happened. They'll send an emergency medevac to get me out. Got it?'

'Yes,' Sharza replied quickly. 'OK.'

Carter closed his eyes momentarily and steadied his breathing.

He had a decision to make.

He could assume the mine was defective, remove his foot and simply hope for the best. Or he could rake away the surrounding dirt to see what was underneath. Take a closer look at the landmine.

He went for the second option.

Carter de-slung his M4 rifle and placed it on the ground at the side of the trail. Then he wriggled out of his rucksack and dumped it next to his weapon, taking great care to keep his right foot pressed firmly down on the plate at all times. Applying pressure. Sharza offered to help, but Carter ordered him to stay well clear. He figured there was a reasonable chance the whole track might be littered with mines. Standard procedure when denying entry to ground troops. One guy steps on a plate and loses a foot. His mucker hurries over to help and sets off another explosion. A brutally efficient way of whittling down an enemy patrol.

Carter unbuckled his belt, yanked it free of the loops and chucked it over to Sharza. He threw over the satphone, reached into the side pocket on his cargo trousers and extracted the gun knife. Then, very slowly, Carter lowered himself to the ground, bending his right leg at the knee and dropping his left knee to the parched earth, giving himself a stable platform. He took another deep breath and started scraping away layers of dirt from the area either side of his boot.

He moved very carefully, trying to ignore the fear clenching his arsehole. The slightest mistake could accidentally trigger the device, he knew, tearing off a limb or mangling his eyes.

He brushed away more dirt with the edge of the blade, moving with surgical precision. Like an archaeologist excavating an ancient grave. After several agonising moments Carter uncovered something buried just below the surface of the ground.

Then his stomach dropped.

He was standing on a piece of plywood, the approximate shape and size of an A4 piece of paper.

Therefore, not a mine.

A booby trap.

Carter cast his mind back to the Regiment dems course. He was looking at a fairly primitive trap design. Wires sandwiched between two pieces of plywood. The kind of thing Blades had taught the fighters in the Northern Alliance to construct, back in the 1990s, when they were trading blows with the Taliban. Depressing the top plate drew the wires together in an arc, arming the trap and triggering the blast. For whatever reason, the explosive hadn't gone off. Carter didn't know why. Corrosion of the wires, perhaps. Or faulty design. Maybe both.

He slowly twisted at the waist, turning ninety degrees to his right until he was directly facing the side of the track. Sweat greased down his back, pasting his shirt to his skin as he scanned the handful of trees and bushes fringing the path. He conducted a brief visual inspection of the terrain, looking for any signs of disturbance. Something concealed in the undergrowth or attached to the trunks. Anything that looked unnatural.

Nothing.

He turned to the right and swept his eyes over the other side of the track. He saw nothing and frowned. Carter knew there had to be an explosive device planted somewhere in close proximity to his position. A basic trap worked by sending an electrical charge down a wire rigged up to the detonating device. Whoever had laid the mine had chosen a good spot. In the confined space of the trail the explosion would push outward from the surrounding treeline. Laws of physics. The kinetic energy from the blast would reflect back off the opposing side of the narrow path, showering Carter in a seething mass of debris, splintered wood and stones.

Worse than a landmine, from a medical point of view.

Much worse. Almost certain death.

Carter wore no plate armour. He had no ballistic helmet. Nothing that would help to shield him from the barrage of shrapnel. He would bleed out long before he'd receive medical attention.

I'm fucked.

He looked to the left again. Then to the right. He saw no trailing wires, no obvious areas where an explosive device might have been placed. He wondered if perhaps the wiring had been disconnected.

Why else wouldn't the blast have been triggered?

He tried to stay calm and think. Sweat was dripping down his face. His hands were trembling involuntarily.

He said, shakily, 'Get well back. Get that tourniquet ready. When I give the signal, I'm going to take my foot off this trap.'

'OK,' Sharza replied in a nervous tone.

The Afghan backed away, putting a distance of eight metres between himself and Carter. Staying well outside the kill zone. Carter tucked the gun knife into his side pocket, then reached for his daysack and hoisted it up by the straps, holding it close to his chest to protect his face from the potential blast. The sack wouldn't stop him from getting fragged, but it might save his eyesight or prevent his jaw from getting blown off.

One of two things would happen when Carter removed his foot from the plywood. Either the trap had malfunctioned, and he would be fine. Or the system would trigger, and he would be in a world of pain.

He drew in another deep breath, tensing his muscles as he braced himself for the next few seconds.

Maybe the last of his life.

'Raising my foot,' he called out to Sharza. 'Get ready.'

Carter clinched his eyes shut and held up the rucksack to his face, his jaw clenched tight as he started to lift his right boot.

His foot was halfway off the ground when a familiar voice at his twelve o'clock said, 'Jesus, fuck. Geordie. It's you.'

Carter froze.

The voice didn't belong to Sharza. It spoke in a rich Belfast accent, softened slightly around the edges.

He lowered the rucksack and looked up. A bearded man gripping an M4 rifle stood fifteen metres upstream from Carter, at a point where the footpath curved to the right and disappeared behind a screen of pine trees.

The guy had the build of a greyhound, slim and wiry. He wore a plain cloak over a collared tunic that came down just below the knees, and a pair of light-coloured trousers plaited around the ankles. He had a leathery sun-bleached face, light blue eyes and a jaw so square you could use it as an angle grinder. His eyebrows sloped down towards the bridge of his nose, giving him a stern-faced look.

David Vann.

Carter stared at his old mentor in slack-jawed silence. A second figure stood to one side of the ex-SAS man. A heftily built Afghan with a thick walrus moustache and bushy eyebrows, armed with an AK-47. He jabbered something at Sharza. The interpreter edged forward, glancing from Carter to Vann, his face stitched with anxiety.

Vann moved down from the trail bend and said, 'When you're done looking like a slapped arse, you can move that foot of yours.' He grinned. 'I know what you're thinking, but there's no explosive. The trap's a fake.'

Carter stared at him in bemusement.

'I'm serious,' Vann continued. 'You can move your foot, Geordie. Nothing will happen to you. Swear on me fucking life.'

Carter edged his foot away from the plate. Nothing exploded.

He eased out a breath of relief as Vann walked over and grinned. 'Doctor Livingstone, I presume?'

The two soldiers shared an easy laugh. Carter felt the tension of the last few minutes quickly draining from his body. Then Vann's face tautened as he looked steadily at the younger soldier.

'No, seriously,' he said. 'What the fuck are you doing here?'

'The Company sent me,' Carter replied. 'To get you out, mate.'

Vann smiled bitterly. 'I should have known,' he said in his rolling Ulster brogue. 'That's just their style.' He slapped Carter playfully on the back. 'Sweet Jesus, I can't believe it's you, Geordie.'

Carter wiped sweat from his brow and pointed to the plywood. 'What was that all about?'

'Early warning system,' Vann explained. 'The plate's rigged up to a light bulb. Up there.' He cocked his chin in the direction of the upper slope. 'Someone steps on it, the bulb flashes. Lets us know whenever anyone is trying to sneak up the trail.'

'Jesus Christ.'

'It's a necessary precaution,' Vann said. 'This whole area is crawling with Taliban right now. Patrols all over the fucking shop.'

Carter suddenly understood. *That's why I noticed so much sign further down the trail*, he realised. And why Vann had left the scrap of brightly coloured clothing on the bush. He'd deliberately planted a trail of sign to lure any pursuing forces or enemy patrols into the kill zone at the trail bend.

Carter looked at him and thought: *Vann might be out of the SAS now, but he's still got the mentality of an elite soldier.*

'Of course,' Vann went on, 'most idiots would have stepped on the plate without realising that they'd activated it. As soon as I saw the bulb glowing non-stop for several minutes, I knew it couldn't be local Taliban. I thought maybe the bastard was banjaxed. Never imagined you were here.' Vann grinned widely. 'Seems I trained you too well, Geordie.'

Carter smiled warmly at his mentor. David Vann looked almost unrecognisable from the legendary Blade he had once known in the Regiment. He seemed to have aged ten years in the past three. Prominent crow's feet protruded from the corners of his eyes. His brow was heavily lined, like old parchment, and his unkempt beard was tinged grey at the chin.

Whatever had happened to him since he'd been kicked out of Hereford, it had taken a heavy toll on the guy.

'What the fuck is going on here, mate?' he asked. 'Why haven't you been in contact with the Company?'

Vann's eyes shifted from left to right. 'I'll get to that shortly. Once we're off the trail. It's not safe out here, not with all them bastard Taliban combing the area.'

He nodded at the guy with the walrus moustache and said something in the local tongue. Then he turned to Carter.

'We'll head back up the trail. Mansur will bring up the rear. You and your mate will follow me.'

Carter frowned. 'Where are we going?'

'The compound.' Vann pointed to the ground above. 'The others are waiting up there. I'll explain everything then.'

Thirteen

Carter threaded his belt through his trouser loops, took the satphone from Sharza, shouldered his daysack and started after Vann as he scrabbled up the track. They passed the tight bend in the trail as it curled past the mass of rock twenty metres ahead. The kill zone. Then followed the path as it zagged sharply to the right. The ascent quickly became brutal. Their pace slowed to a plod. Vann led the way, moving along at the head of the column. Sharza trudged along a few paces behind, occasionally glancing back nervously at Carter, as if looking for reassurance. Mansur took up the position as the tail-end Charlie, to guard against any Taliban patrols who might have picked up their trail further down the slope.

As they trudged along the upslope Carter tried to make sense of the whole situation. He guessed they were being taken to the rebel hideout. A mountainside refuge. The Taliban offensive had probably forced Vann and his Afghan colleagues to relocate further to the north. Hence the move to a new camp, and the precautions they had taken with the signs along the trail.

This whole area is crawling with Taliban.

But there was a problem with that scenario, Carter reflected. If Vann and the rebel forces were in serious trouble, why hadn't he tried to reach out to his handler at Langley to call for support, or immediate extraction? Instead Vann had ditched his satphone. His only link to the outside world.

Another thing troubled him. The early warning system. Vann had told him that he'd rigged up the light bulb to alert him to any approaching hostiles. But a regular landmine or trap would have worked just as well. The sound of the blast would have been heard for several kilometres across the valley, with the added advantage of decimating the enemy patrol.

So why use a light bulb?

Carter didn't know. The whole thing made his fucking head hurt.

The track steepened again as it looped round a clump of cedar trees. After fifty metres they moved clear of the treeline and hit a plateau, snooker table-flat and roughly the size of a football pitch. A hundred metres away, on the far side of the plateau, a trio of mud-brick buildings had been erected in a natural cul-de-sac at the base of a broad escarpment leading up to another ridgeline.

Camouflage nets covered the flat-roofed structures. Presumably to conceal them from drones or aircraft passing overhead. There was a separate tented area to the side of the compound, Carter noted. Beneath the strung-out camo nets six mules were tethered to a wooden hitching post, weighed down with a variety of panniers, saddlebags and leather rifle scabbards.

'This way, Geordie,' Vann said. 'Come on, lad.'

He led Carter and Sharza towards the compound in the middle of the plateau, fifty metres away. They drew to a halt in front of the largest of the three structures. Then Vann turned to Carter and said, 'Wait here. I won't be long.'

'Where are you going?'

'I need to explain this situation to Hakimi.'

'Hakimi?' Carter repeated as he recalled the name of the National Alliance's new leader. 'He's here?'

Vann nodded and said, 'He'll want to speak with you, I imagine. But it's better if the fella hears it from me first.' He dropped his voice to a murmur. 'Between you and me, the guy is a wee bit paranoid. He doesn't like surprises. If he sees your mug, he'll shit a brick.' He grinned broadly. 'Although let's face it, most women would react the same way.'

'Piss off.' Carter smiled, then relaxed his face. 'Fine. We'll wait.'

'Good man.'

Vann disappeared through the entrance, closing the timber door behind him. Carter looked round, observing the compound. Fighters with shoulder-slung AK-47s were coming and going from the other buildings, loading heavy-duty sacks onto the mules.

'Looks like we got here just in time,' Sharza remarked. 'Your friends are preparing to leave.'

Carter nodded but didn't reply. He was gazing up at the cliff-face above.

Why would Vann set up shop in this place? Carter asked himself. *We're in a cul-de-sac. No way out.*

An enemy force, attacking in strength, could keep Vann and his rebel mates rammed into this area, with nowhere to go.

Further away, he noticed a low-ceilinged cave set into the base of the cliff-face, close to a copse of pine trees. There was a circle of blackened earth near the mouth of the cave. As if someone had recently lit a cooking fire. Forty-five-gallon drums lined the walls on both sides of the scarred earth. Amid the gloom Carter spotted a pair of shovels, several large wooden stirring paddles, bundles of firewood.

An industrial-sized cooking vat.

'Do you recognise any of this lot?' he asked Sharza, indicating the guys marching over to the mules.

'Sorry, brother,' Sharza said in a whisper. 'I've never seen these men before. I don't know where they are from.' He hesitated. 'But something is not right here. I can feel it.'

Eight minutes later, the door groaned open again. Vann strode back out and cleared his throat.

'Right. I've spoken to the big fella. He wants to have a word with you. Both of you,' he added, tipping his head at Sharza. 'Follow me. You can leave your stuff here, Geordie.'

Carter unshouldered his rucksack and dumped it beside the exterior wall. Then he followed Vann and Sharza through the doorway, into a squalid room measuring roughly eight metres by eight. A thick odour of sweat and cigarette smoke filled Carter's nostrils as he stepped inside. And something else, too. Something bitter and chemical.

Ammonia.

There was a hive of activity in the room. A pair of rebel fighters knelt on a beaten rug beside a pair of scales, processing tar-coloured bricks wrapped in cellophane. One guy weighed the bricks, while the other packed them into waterproof sacks, ready for two more guys to carry outside to the waiting mules. The floor was littered with plastic moulds filled with some sort of dark brown resin. Carter saw cut lengths of rubber tubing, white sacks of industrial chemicals, piles of dirty blankets. A whole factory of stuff.

A queasy feeling seeped like acid into his guts. Carter stopped in his tracks and looked at Vann in horror.

'Fuck me, Dave,' he said in an undertone. 'Don't tell me you're in the drug business now.'

Vann met his gaze steadily. 'It's not what it looks like.'

'Bollocks,' Carter growled. A hot wave of anger swept through his veins. 'I've busted plenty of sites like this before, mate. That's black tar,' he added, waving a hand at the plastic-wrapped bricks. 'You're processing heroin, for fuck's sake.'

Vann's expression tautened. 'Wind your neck in, Geordie. I can explain everything, I promise.'

Carter looked numbly at him. He felt as if someone had just punched him square in the face. A million questions bounced around inside his head.

'Have you lost your fucking mind? They'll arrest you for this back home. You're looking at twenty years behind bars.'

'Save it,' Vann hissed. 'Come on. Hakimi is waiting.'

He marched across the room, towards an opening at the far end. Carter followed him, his head spinning madly. Half a dozen belt-fed PKM Russian machine guns rested on their bipods on the floor near to the rear wall. The Russian equivalent of the GPMG. Chambered for 7.62 x 54 mm R. A cartridge first produced back when Russia still had a tsar. Each weapon had a green metal-cased ammo box fixed to the underside of the receiver. Twelve more boxes of ammo were stacked against the wall.

They're not taking any chances, Carter thought. Which made sense. Vann and his accomplices were running a heroin lab. Right under the noses of the Taliban. They wouldn't want to be caught cold if things went noisy.

Vann ushered them into a smaller room off to one side of the compound. A middle-aged guy with the build of a retired weight-lifter sat behind a large desk. The man had a dead-eyed look, flocked grey hair, pockmarked cheeks and a knot of scar tissue on his chin. He was dressed like a guerrilla fighter, with a wood-pattern camo jacket over an olive-green T-shirt.

There was a half-finished bottle of cheap vodka on the table in front of him, a pair of disposable cups, a set of walkie-talkies, a pack of cigarettes. An AK-47 leaned against the wall.

Carter had seen the man's face before. Back in Chile. At the British embassy.

The briefing. Nine million years ago.

Jabar Hakimi, the leader of the National Alliance, looked up as the three men swept into the room. His eyes narrowed into a calculating stare as he studied Carter and Sharza. Something about his features reminded Carter of a hawk.

'You are a friend of David, I understand,' he said, addressing Carter in a harshly accented voice.

Not a question, but a statement.

'That's right,' Carter responded tersely.

'And you, my friend?' Hakimi skated his gaze across to Sharza. 'Where are you from?'

'Shahr-e-Bozorg,' the interpreter said.

Hakimi proceeded to ask him a string of questions. He spoke in English, for the benefit of his British accomplice, Carter assumed. He grilled Sharza on his tribal affiliation, his leader. His kinfolk. The people he had worked for in the past. He seemed particularly interested in Sharza's years as an interpreter for the British army. Carter heard a note of strain in the guy's voice as he answered each question. Sharza was bricking it.

'Tell me,' Hakimi said as his flat eyes slid back to Carter. 'Who else knows that you are here? Answer me truthfully,' he added. 'I have a talent for smelling lies.'

Carter decided not to risk bluffing it. He knew Vann would instantly pick up on any bullshit. He said, 'There are two people at the CIA who know about the operation. Another person at MI6. Three in total. The ones I know about. Probably more.'

'You can't be sure?'

'I'm a soldier,' Carter said. 'The suits don't tell me any more than they need to. If there are other people involved, I wouldn't know about them. That's the way it is.'

'He's telling the truth,' Vann put in. 'I've been in the same boat plenty of times myself.'

'What orders did your people give you?' Hakimi asked.

'I was sent here to locate and extract Dave,' Carter said. 'That's all they told me.'

'They didn't say anything about heroin? Nothing about our smuggling operation?'

'No.'

'Were you followed here?'

'No.'

'You are certain? No Taliban?'

'Geordie is from the Regiment,' Vann interjected. 'He's a good operator. One of the best. If he had someone on his tail, he'd soon know about it.'

Hakimi looked at the Ulsterman with raised eyebrows. 'You seem very confident in your friend's abilities.'

'I trained him,' Vann said. 'I took this lad on Selection. Taught him almost everything he knows. You won't find a better soldier. Or a more loyal one,' he added.

Hakimi's expression shifted. The eyes narrowed again, the head angled in thought. His fingers steepled on the table.

Carter stood still and said nothing. He'd dealt with guys like this before while he'd been embedded with the local SF. Gangsters. Men who took advantage of the chaos of Afghanistan to enrich themselves. They had no loyalty except to money, and no scruples about killing anyone who defied them. In many ways they were just as ruthless as the Mexican cartels or the Russian mafia.

Six and the CIA had dropped a bollock putting their faith in this bloke, Carter thought. That was for bloody sure.

'You know what this place is, yes?' Hakimi asked.

'I'm not fucking blind,' Carter said.

Hakimi gave him a thin smile. 'It would be wise to treat me with more respect. It would be in your best interests.'

A cold silence fell over the room. Then Vann stepped forward and said hastily, 'Take no notice of him. Geordie is just wound up, that's all. He'll get over it.'

'Do you think we can trust him?'

Hakimi directed the question at Vann but stared at Carter with a tightened expression. Carter felt a sudden prick of anxiety in his guts. He didn't like where this conversation was going. Didn't like it at all.

Vann said, 'Geordie is on the level. He won't spill his guts. You've got my word on that. We're both ex-Para Reg. That still counts for something, where we come from.'

The rebel leader stared at him for a long beat. Carter remained quiet, his stomach doing somersaults. Then Hakimi shrugged and poured himself a slug of vodka.

'It's up to you to take the risk with your man,' he said to Vann. 'If you are prepared to vouch for him, that is good enough for me. But I don't want him to go anywhere . . . not until we have finished our business here.' He smiled. 'As a precaution, you understand.'

Carter felt his stomach unclench slightly.

‘What about him?’ he interrupted, nodding at Sharza.

‘Your friend is free to go,’ Hakimi said. ‘Him I have no use for.’

The warlord tipped the booze down his throat, stood up and glanced at Vann. A look passed fleetingly between the two men.

They filed out of the smaller room and crossed the main space. The drug-processing site. Hakimi led the interpreter outside, into the piercing glare of the afternoon sun. Carter followed them through the doorway and clamped a hand around the interpreter’s bicep before the latter turned to leave.

‘Go and find your nephew,’ he said. ‘The one in Bazarak. I’ll see you back at your friend’s place . . . the house we stayed at last night. Meet me there twenty-four hours from now. As soon as I’m done, we’ll head for the border with your nephew.’

Sharza nodded. ‘I will. Thank you, brother.’

‘Go, mate. Get moving.’

He smiled softly, then turned on his heel, giving his back to Carter.

As he started across the plateau Carter caught a blur of movement off to his side. He skimmed his gaze across to his left. Then he saw Hakimi reaching for something tucked into the waistband of his trousers. Something dark and bulky.

A pistol.

A cold tingling spread through Carter’s chest.

He opened his mouth to shout a warning.

Then Hakimi drew the pistol level with Sharza and shot him in the back of the head.

Fourteen

Sharza had no time to react. He was two metres away from Hakimi when the warlord squeezed the trigger. At that range, it was impossible to miss. A deafening boom echoed across the plateau and rolled down the valley as a round flamed out of the barrel. The interpreter spasmed as the bullet slapped into the back of his skull. Blood, bone and brain matter sprayed out of the exit wound, like water out of a sprinkler. Sharza was dead before he dropped to the ground.

Carter stared at the rebel leader in horror and disgust. He felt the blood pounding in his bloodstream. 'Jesus Christ.'

Hakimi laughed meanly. 'You are upset? Over the death of this worthless swine? This I do not believe.'

Carter shook his head angrily. 'It wasn't necessary. The guy was all right. He brought me here, that's all. He didn't know anything about the operation. There was no fucking need to drop him.'

'The man was a threat,' Hakimi explained casually. 'He came from another tribe. Different allegiance. He could not be trusted. He would have reported us to the local Taliban and collected the reward.'

'No, he wouldn't,' Carter insisted furiously. 'This guy was working against the Taliban, for fuck's sake. He wouldn't have shopped you.'

Hakimi shrugged his indifference. 'This is Afghanistan. Allegiances can change very quickly. It is safer this way.'

Vann stared at the dead interpreter, his brow puckered in deep thought.

He looked up at the warlord. The muscles on his neck were tightly bunched, his hands clenched into white-knuckled fists.

'Geordie's right. That was a fucking mistake,' he said.

'Is there a problem?' Hakimi challenged him.

'Aye, there is,' Vann raged. 'You've just signposted where we are, you idiot.'

Something like anger flashed in Hakimi's eyes. 'There was no choice. If we had let that man walk away, he would have gone straight to our enemies to collect a reward.'

'You've just saved them the bloody effort.' Vann thrust a hand towards the valley. 'That gunshot will have travelled for kilometres. Every Taliban patrol in the area will know where we are now. We've spent four weeks on silent, and you've just shafted it.'

Hakimi shrugged again. 'We are leaving this place soon anyway.'

'I don't give a toss. You don't go making noise when you're on silent. That's fucking basic.'

Hakimi glowered. 'Remember who you are talking to, my friend.'

Vann managed to bite back on his anger. 'Fuck it,' he said. 'There's no time for this. You'd better send a couple of your guys down the trail to that vantage point. Tell them to keep an eye on the roadhead. If they see anything coming this way, they can let us know.'

'As you wish.'

Hakimi shoved his pistol back into his waistband and called out an order to the men in the main building. A moment later, two fighters hurried outside. A grey-bearded guy wearing a black waistcoat and a patterned turban, and a stick-thin bloke with a pencil moustache and a mop of dark wavy hair. Both had AK-47 rifles slung across their backs.

Hakimi barked at them both. Issuing orders. The men promptly turned on their heels and hurried across the plateau, making their way back down the trail.

Once they were out of sight, Vann said, 'We'll have to accelerate the packing. Get the mules loaded and ready to go. We need to be ready to bug out of here at short notice.'

'I will tell my men,' Hakimi replied.

'We'll need to alert our man in Tajikistan as well. Let him know we're running ahead of schedule. His guys will have to meet us at the roadhead a few hours earlier than planned.'

'Leave the Tajik to me. I'll notify him.' The warlord gestured towards Carter. 'Keep an eye on your friend until we are ready to leave this place. You can wait in the office. After that, it is up to you to decide what you want to do with him.'

The warlord promptly swaggered off in the direction of the mules, shouting at two of the fighters and clapping his hands, gesturing for them to get a move on. While the fighters rushed to load the bricks onto the mules, Vann ushered Carter back inside the building, through the door at the opposite end of the main room. Back into the makeshift office space. He unscrewed the cap on the vodka bottle, poured generous measures into two disposable cups. Took one and offered the other to Carter.

'Drink?'

Carter looked at the cup and felt sick. 'No thanks.'

'Suit yourself.' Vann shrugged, raised the cup to his lips and necked the booze in one gulp. He poured himself another slug, filling the cup almost to the brim.

'He's a madman,' Vann said quietly. 'Hakimi. In case you haven't noticed. Totally unbalanced. Addicted to the killing. His brother had all the charisma and the tactical intelligence. Frankly I'm surprised he hasn't fucked things up before now.'

'What are you doing here?' Carter demanded. 'Trafficking drugs? Have you lost your mind?'

'I've got my reasons,' Vann muttered darkly.

'No, mate.' Carter gritted his teeth so hard he thought his jawbone might crack. 'There's no way you can justify this shit.'

Vann scowled at the younger man. 'You don't know my life, Geordie. Ain't got the first clue what I've been through these past few years. So button it, all right?'

Carter shook his head. 'I risked my balls coming here to find you. The Company thought you were in serious trouble. Jesus, a good bloke just got himself killed helping to track you down.'

'Don't look so scundered, you prick. You must have known I was up to something illegal. Fuck me, why else do you think I ditched the old satphone?'

The words slapped Carter in the face. So that's why Vann got rid of the phone, he realised.

A hollow feeling spread through his chest as he stared at Vann. A legend of the SAS.

The guy who took me through Selection and helped me to find my feet in the Regiment, Carter reminded himself. *The same guy who taught me how to soldier is now in cahoots with a psycho warlord.*

Processing heroin.

He couldn't believe that a man of Vann's calibre had sunk so low.

'How long has this been going on?' he asked.

'A couple of months,' said Vann. He grabbed the bottle and helped himself to another measure. His third drink. 'Give or take.'

Carter shook his head. 'You're supposed to be training up the rebels. Getting them ready for the insurgency. Not doing this shite.'

'Yeah, well. Things changed.'

'What the fuck is that supposed to mean?'

Vann snorted and said, 'Open your eyes, Geordie. There is no insurgency. I knew this was a waste of time as soon as I linked up with the rebels. The Taliban have got the Chinese, the Russians and the Pakistanis on their side. Serious firepower and assets on the ground. Any idiot with half a brain cell could see that Hakimi and his mates were going to get walloped by the enemy. Lambs to the fucking slaughter.'

'So you convinced him to go into the drug business instead?'

'Wrong way round.' Vann gave a rueful smile. 'It was Hakimi's idea, originally. He took me to one side after his older brother got whacked by the Taliban. He didn't want to end up the same way, and he was smart enough to know that we wouldn't get any serious support from the Yanks. Just enough to keep us on life support for a while, so some dickheads in Washington could give themselves a pat on the back and pretend that they hadn't abandoned their allies totally. Hakimi had contacts in the opium trade. People he knew who would pay top dollar for premium-quality smack. It was an easy decision. Stay here on a doomed op or make millions and live like a king. Anyone else would have done the same.'

Carter gave him an accusing stare. 'You're ruining lives. I can't believe you let yourself get dragged into this shite.'

'Fuck off.' Vann returned the hard look. 'I'm not interested in your moralising. You don't know what I went through when they kicked me out of Hereford. All because of a fucking mistake with that airstrike. Those bastards ruined my life, Geordie.'

Carter pursed his lips. He thought about the unsanctioned strike Vann had called in while serving as an embed. The four dead Afghan civilians. His clumsy attempt to cover up the attack by inventing a legitimate target, an act that had resulted in his dismissal from the Regiment.

'I screwed up on the job. I know that,' Vann confessed. 'But the Regiment shouldn't have put me in that position in the first place. They shouldn't have put that kind of stress on my shoulders.'

Carter shook his head, anger sweeping through his bloodstream. 'What happened to us embeds has got nothing to do with this.'

'You're wrong. That rotation messed with me up here, see?' Vann tapped a finger against his temple. 'Messed me right up. I lost my moral compass. Got drunk on fighting. I was teetering on the edge. Running them ops turned me into a war junkie.'

'Why didn't you reach out? You should have told someone.'

'I tried. I got in touch with the head shed, told them I needed some R&R. Decompression. A month or two out of the country to get my head straight.'

'What did they say?'

'What do you think?' Vann laughed bitterly. 'They didn't want to know. They never do. They just ordered me to carry on. Said I was doing a great job and told me I'd be in line for a gong at the end of it. All of the usual crap. That's when I started going feral.'

'Feral?' Carter repeated. He felt something shift inside his bowels.

Vann nodded. 'Me and the guys from the SF team, we were going out on sanctioned hits, right? Following orders and all the rest of it. But then some of the lads started getting clipped by fighters from one of the neighbouring tribes. I took that personally, see. These were my boys. Good warriors. I didn't like seeing them get chopped up. The lads wanted revenge. So I took them up to the next village and we slotted the other lot. Job done.'

Vann contemplated his vodka for a beat. Then he necked it and went on.

'After that, we started going out more often. Me and a few of the Afghans. The most capable soldiers. We were still doing the sanctioned stuff, but in between jobs we'd go out and do our own hits. Killing anyone we didn't like. Rival warlords, tribal militia, people who were trying to muscle in on our turf.'

'Jesus.'

'I stopped seeing clearly,' Vann said. 'All that time out there by myself, with no support or backup . . . it did something to my wiring, d'you see? I couldn't help getting mixed up in it.'

Carter felt a chill on the nape of his neck as he listened. He'd always known that Vann didn't like to play by the rules, but that was true of most of the guys at Hereford. The nature of the SAS tended to attract rogue soldiers. Guys who had no time for the yes-sir-no-sir bullshit of the parade ground. And there had been rumours that Vann's SF team in Afghanistan had been a little too gung-ho. Nothing concrete, just the occasional whisper in the camp cookhouse.

But Carter had never imagined that Vann had been secretly orchestrating a campaign of illegal murders.

He wondered how such a good operator had allowed himself to go over to the dark side. Where it had all gone wrong.

'That's when the business with the airstrike happened,' Vann continued. 'I'm responsible for calling it in, and I've got to live with the consequences of that decision. Got blood on my hands, haven't I? But the Regiment is guilty as well. They sent me in there, with no support, no nothing.' He gestured towards Carter. 'You were an embed. You know what I'm talking about.'

Carter nodded as he recalled his own time working alongside Afghan SF. Eighteen months spent in near-total isolation from the outside world. No downtime, no way of letting off steam. The constant stress of running deniable operations, knowing that if you suddenly found yourself in the shit, no one was coming to your rescue.

The commanders had cynically encouraged the use of embeds, because it gave them the ability to launch attacks against the enemy without the inconvenience of political accountability. Some guys had flourished in that environment. Others had struggled.

Guys like David Vann.

'The Regiment shafted me,' Vann continued. 'Left me all bitter and twisted. When I landed this job, I saw a way out. A chance to put all of the shit behind me and get on with my life. You might not agree with it, and that's fine. But I don't owe those idiots back home a fucking thing.'

Carter made a screw-face. 'Come off it, mate. Don't tell me you're so hard up that you needed to make a few quid on the smack track. You must have found good work on the Circuit.'

'I did, at first,' Vann said. 'One of the lads sorted me out with a contract in Kazakhstan. A security job with one of the big oil companies. Had me a nice penthouse in Almaty, fifteen hundred quid a day after expenses.'

'So what happened?'

Vann wrinkled his nose. 'The long arm of the Regiment, fella. They got me sacked. All of a sudden, I was out on my arse. Penniless.

What did you expect me to do? Reinvent myself as a social media influencer?'

'You didn't have to start dealing drugs,' Carter hit back. 'The Company must have been paying you good money for this job. Not millions, maybe. But enough to get by.'

'Aye, and what am I supposed to do once this gig is over? Tell me that. Most of the big companies won't touch me with a barge pole. Fuck me, I only got this gig because I had the embed experience and a couple of contacts at Langley. Everyone else has ghosted me. After this, I'm looking at ten years of crap security jobs, if I'm lucky.'

Vann pressed his lips together in suppressed anger and looked away for a beat. Carter let the silence play out between them. He didn't know what to say.

'I'm just doing what's right for me,' Vann said. 'Looking out for number one for a change. I'm not going to end up like some of them other lads, living in a council house in Hereford, scraping by on a piss-poor pension, wondering how I'm gonna pay the gas bill.'

Carter remained silent. Conflicting emotions swirled in his chest. On the one hand, he felt a pang of sympathy for Vann. No doubt about it, the guy had been treated shabbily by the Regiment. But no one had put a gun to his head and told him to go into the heroin trade.

'You'll never get away with this,' he said quietly. 'They'll catch up with you eventually.'

'No, mate. They won't.' Vann sounded confident. He flapped a hand at the main room and said, 'This is the last batch of gear. We're cashing in our chips. After today, that's it. Job done.'

Carter searched his face, looking for any sign of a lie. He saw none.

'We're going to smuggle this last package across the border,' Vann continued. 'There's a courier route to Tajikistan. We've used it before, it's safe enough. We'll sneak across it with the mule train and sell this stuff to our contact over there.'

'How much is in them bags?'

'Five hundred kilos of high-quality heroin,' Vann said. 'Heroin is more profitable than selling raw opium. You cut out the middleman. Increase your margins.'

Carter made a quick calculation. One kilo of heroin, he knew, was worth something like six thousand dollars on the wholesale market. Five hundred kilos of premium grade black tar would fetch around three million bucks. Or somewhere in that ballpark. Minus the expenses of the operation, paying for the guards and the raw materials. But still a lot of pocket shrapnel. And they had been doing this for months.

They must have raked in a fortune, Carter realised.

Vann said, 'This is me, lad. Once this is over, I'll retire to some isolated spot in the Maldives. See out my days sipping ice-cold beers and watching the rugby. No one will hear from me ever again. You've got my word on that. One Blade to another.'

Carter wondered why Vann was telling him all this stuff. The dream retirement plan. But then he saw the pleading look on the Ulsterman's face, and he understood: Vann was giving him the hard sell, leaning on their close bond in the hope that Carter would let him get away with it.

A last favour to an old friend.

A long pause of silence passed between the two men. Then Carter heard footsteps at his back, and a moment later Hakimi strode into the room, killing the call on his burner. He put the phone away and said to Vann, 'That was the Tajik.'

'And?'

'He's going to meet us at the roadhead on the other side of the border. Him, and the rest of his guys.' He stole a glance at Carter. 'At the same place we used on the last run.'

'When?'

'Tomorrow. First light. They will wait for us there.'

'What if we run into problems?'

'Won't happen.'

'You said that last time. I don't want any more scares with them border patrols. The last thing we need is things getting tasty.'

'The Tajik says we should send him a message confirming our position when we are close to the border. He'll check the area and let us know when we are clear to cross.'

'Good.'

Carter checked his G-Shock. One thirty in the afternoon. Ninety minutes since they had set off up the side of the mountain. Back when Sharza didn't have a hole in the back of his head.

'This isn't right,' he said with feeling. 'Think about what you're doing, Dave. There are lads at home getting hooked on the gear. You're helping to put people in early graves.'

'Save your breath,' said Vann. 'I couldn't give a shit about the morals. If I don't flog this stuff, someone else will. Same outcome.'

Carter tried again. 'Come back with me, mate. We can go home, sort this out with the Company. Tell them about the stresses you've been under, your financial troubles.'

Carter knew he couldn't make a hard arrest. Hakimi and his rebel fighters would plug him long before he could get away. His only hope was to persuade Vann to leave willingly. He could worry about what to tell Six and the Company later.

'I can't,' Vann said. 'Sorry, fella, but it's too late for that. Way too fucking late. If I go back now, they'll send me down. I'm looking at a long stretch behind bars.'

'It's got to be better than living as a fugitive, looking over your shoulder for the rest of your life. This is criminal.'

Hakimi glared coldly at him, trench lines carved into his brow.

'I don't care for your friend's opinions,' he said to Vann. His voice was laced with menace.

'Geordie will be fine,' Vann insisted. 'I gave you my word, didn't I? He's just a bit emotional.'

Hakimi sneered and said, 'I knew it was a mistake to remove that landmine. If you had left it there, this man would have been blown to bits, and we wouldn't have a problem.'

'I'll take care of it,' Vann replied firmly. 'It's under control.'

'It does not look like that to me. It does not look like that at all.' Hakimi tilted his head at Carter. His green eyes were trained like a couple of laser pens on Carter.

'No,' he said after a long pause. 'I don't think we can trust your friend. The risk is too great.'

Carter felt his heart jump with shock. The sides of his head pulsed viciously. Every muscle in his body tensed.

Fucking hell, he thought. *This bastard wants to kill me.*

Vann started to speak but Hakimi cut him off with a brisk wave of his hand. 'This man is like a brother to you, I know. You vouched for him, and that was understandable given your position. But we all have to make sacrifices.'

The colour drained from Vann's face. 'You can't. You fucking can't, fella. I'm not having it.'

'No one tells me what to do.'

Adrenaline shot through Carter's body. He started sweating heavily as he looked around the room, frantically searching for an escape route. A side-exit leading outside the compound, or a window he could breach. There was nothing. He'd have to shoot his way out, he realised. He had the shoulder-slung M4, the holstered Grach. He could drop Hakimi, and hope that Vann didn't retaliate, but he'd still have to deal with the warlord's loyal footsoldiers in the next room.

No way I'd be able to get through that lot.

I'm fucked.

'Geordie is a serving British soldier,' Vann said in a tense voice. 'Kill him, and you'll put a load of heat on us. We're in enough trouble as it is.'

'Like I said. I don't like loose ends.'

Hakimi glared coldly at the ex-Blade. Vann stood his ground. For a moment no one moved. The temperature in the room felt arctic. Carter couldn't breathe.

My life's hanging in the balance, and there's nothing I can do about it.

Nothing at all.

Then he heard the urgent thud of approaching footsteps. A moment later, a pair of fighters burst into the office. The grey-bearded guy in the patterned *shemagh*, and the thin guy with the pencil moustache. The two men Hakimi had sent down the trail to watch for any signs of the enemy.

Greybeard caught his breath while Pencil hurriedly made his report to the rebel leader. Hakimi listened with interest, stroking his disfigured chin. Then his body stiffened, and Carter saw a glimmer of fear in the man's eyes as he looked towards Vann.

'What did your man say?' Vann asked.

'There's a force approaching,' Hakimi said. The tone of his voice betrayed his alarm. 'Heading right for us.'

Fifteen

'How far away?' Vann asked urgently.

Hakimi said, 'My men saw them coming down the road from the south. One kilometre, he thinks.'

Vann drew in a sharp breath and said, 'It won't take them long to find the track. They'll start making their way up here any minute now.'

'How many vehicles?' asked Carter.

'My men saw two dust clouds,' Hakimi replied. 'Two vehicles. Could be anything up to nine or ten men.'

'Taliban?'

'Has to be,' Vann said. 'I'd bet my right bollock on it. No one else is active around here.'

Carter hurriedly thought back to the trail, calculating the time it had taken to climb the slope. The hard slog up the zigzagging footpath. He figured they had about forty minutes before the Taliban rocked up.

Vann turned to Hakimi and said, 'Tell your men to get into their positions. We'll set up the kill zone. Same place we've used for the training drills in the past. Geordie,' he added, nodding at Carter. 'With me.'

He swiped a pair of walkie-talkies from the desk and charged out of the room ahead of Carter. Hakimi and the two other Afghans hurried after them, the warlord bellowing orders at the other fighters in the main room. In an instant, everyone sprang into action. Like employees responding to an unscheduled fire alarm. Pencil, Greybeard, Mansur, Hakimi and the two fighters who had been weighing and packing the heroin bricks rushed over to the six Russian PKM machine guns resting on the floor at the back wall.

They grabbed one weapon each, clasping them by the wooden carry handles, then rushed out of the building.

As they emerged onto the plateau, Vann began shouting orders at the Afghan fighters, pointing towards a pair of large rocky outcrops two hundred metres further down the slope.

'Get them guns in place,' he thundered, gesturing towards the outcrops. 'Hurry.'

Hakimi hastily relayed the commands to his men. Greybeard, Pencil and a third guy with a brown pancake hat scrambled across the plateau, carrying their PKMs. Hakimi, Mansur and a long-haired fighter wearing a yellow scarf sprinted after them. All six guys started descending the footpath while Vann beckoned Carter to join him at the edge of the plateau.

'See them outcrops?' Vann asked.

He pointed to the two mounds of rock two hundred metres downstream from the plateau. They were set at a distance of a hundred metres from one another, Carter noted. One to the left of their position, the other to the right. Both outcrops had vantage points overlooking the bend in the trail further south. The tennis court-sized area of flat ground Carter had been approaching when he'd stepped on the early warning system.

He nodded. 'I see them.'

Vann said, 'This is what we're going to do. You take the fire team on the outcrop on the left flank. I'll lead the guys on the right. We'll wait for the enemy to come up onto the level ground. This is the only route up or down the mountain, so they'll definitely come that way. Once we've got line of sight on all the targets, you'll let rip on our side and our guys will open up from the other flank. We'll get a crossfire going, so there won't be any dead ground for the fuckers to hide in. Between us, we'll turn that area into a killing zone. Got it?'

Carter said, 'How many rounds have we got? For the PKMs?'

'Two spare belts per weapon, plus one box on each gun.'

A standard box for the PKM contained a hundred rounds of 7.62 x 54 mm R, Carter knew. Which gave them three hundred bullets per weapon. Two thousand rounds in total, when you factored in the AK-47s and the two M4s Carter and Vann were packing. Plenty of firepower. More than enough to deal with a group of half a dozen Taliban fighters.

'Here.' Vann thrust out a hand and gave him one of the walkie-talkies. Made by a company Carter had never heard of before. One of the cheaper brands, he assumed. 'They're both preset to the same frequency. As soon as you're ready to open fire, get on the radio and tell us, so we can coordinate the attack. We want to hit them at the same time.'

'Roger that,' Carter said.

Vann pointed to the flat ground below. 'Make sure you wait until they're all in sight. There's no cover down there, so they won't have anywhere to hide once the rounds start flying. Do this properly and we'll go through them like a dose of salts.' He grinned. 'It'll be just like the old times, boy.'

Almost, Carter thought to himself.

Except Vann wasn't transporting bricks of black tar back then.

'Start taking the boxes down,' Vann said. 'I'll join you in a minute.'

Carter hurried back over to the compound. He dropped to a knee beside his rucksack and hastily dug out the four spare magazines of 5.56 mm for the M4. He shoved the mags into his side and rear trouser pockets, clipped the walkie-talkie to his belt and ran back into the building. He scooped up two green-cased boxes of ammo for the PKMs from the stack on the far wall, grabbing them by the canvas handles, then ran back outside.

Twenty metres away, he spied Vann and Hakimi beside one of the smaller buildings. Deep in conversation. Vann appeared to be doing most of the talking. Carter wondered what they were discussing. The plan for the smuggling route, maybe. Logistics. They had been forced to ramp up their departure from the compound. All of a sudden, their carefully laid plans had gone to shit.

Carter set off down the dirt track at a quick trot. He'd considered reaching out to Langley for help, but instantly ruled it out. The Company wouldn't be able to come to their rescue. It would take hours for them to send a drone over from the base in Qatar. By which time the firefight would be long over. Besides, Carter reasoned, sticking a few Hellfires into the enemy would almost certainly blow the op. The Chinese were extremely active in Afghanistan now. So were the Pakistani security forces. Both of them would be monitoring activity around the country. A US drone strike in the remote mountains to the north-east would definitely get their attention.

We're going to have to tackle this the old-fashioned way, he thought.

With bullets and aggression.

After descending for two hundred metres, he reached the two large mounds of boulder-sized rocks situated to the east and west of the slope. Both outcrops overlooked the footpath two hundred metres below. Further downslope, he could see the thick woodland stretched across the ground nearer to the valley floor. In the distance, a kilometre away, Carter spotted the gravel road, the abandoned village beyond.

Carter tacked to the left, making for the fire team clustered around the outcrop to the east. Two of the guys on his fire team, Pencil and Greybeard, dashed past him as they raced back up the path to the plateau to retrieve more ammo boxes for the PKMs. The third guy on his team, the man with the pancake hat, had already dropped to a prone firing stance beside one of the boulders.

Carter deposited the boxes of 7.62 belt beside Pancake. He unclipped the walkie-talkie from his belt and switched it on, checking the batteries. Several minutes later, Pencil and Greybeard came running back down the trail, carrying two more boxes of ammo for the PKMs. They dropped down beside their machine guns and took up their firing points along the outcrop, peering through the rear-mounted iron sights at the bend in the track two hundred metres below.

Carter took up a standing position behind a flat-topped rock. He placed the walkie-talkie on top of the boulder and glanced across to the west, at the outcrop on the right flank, a hundred metres away. He saw Mansur and the guy in the yellow scarf scarpering back up the trail. To retrieve the last ammo boxes from the compound, he guessed. From his vantage point he couldn't see Vann or Hakimi, but that didn't worry him. They would be hidden behind the clump of boulders.

Carter hefted up his M4 rifle, his right hand clamped around the trigger mechanism, his left wrapped around the foregrip. Then he trained his sights on the trail below.

He had an unobstructed view of the killing zone. The patch of flat ground. He recognised the situation from his trek up the slope an hour ago. He saw the point where he'd stepped on the plywood trap, twenty metres downstream from the sharp bend in the trail. He swept his eyes across the ground, visually tracing the path as it curved round the wall of weather-beaten rock before it disappeared behind another wooded area thirty metres beyond the trail-bend. Further south, ten metres from the trap, the trail dropped off towards the treeline on the lower slope.

As he scanned the trail-bend, Carter immediately realised why Vann had chosen to split the defenders into two separate fire teams. A jumble of pine trees and mounds of rock at the edge of the footpath created a natural area of dead ground immediately below their respective positions. Any enemies who took cover to the right of the footpath would be out of sight of the shooters directly above them. Both groups therefore needed to establish a crossfire, with each team clearing the patch of dead ground on the other side of the trail.

Minutes ticked by. Carter continued to observe the flat ground leading towards the trail-bend, eyes alert for the slightest movement.

A few minutes later, in the slender gaps between the trees downstream from the kill zone, he glimpsed a loose line of figures making their way up the mountain. Four hundred metres away. Too far to pick out any distinguishing features. At least four of them. They disappeared from view as the path twisted through another area of dense forest.

He glanced at his G-Shock. One fifty in the afternoon. Almost two hours since Carter had started up the mountain. An hour since the warlord had nailed Sharza in the back of the head. Half an hour since Pencil and Greybeard had rushed into the compound to sound the alarm.

Another ten minutes or so until the first targets swept into view downslope from the trail-bend, Carter estimated.

He reached for the walkie-talkie and thumbed the push-to-talk button.

'Is everything OK at your end?' he asked Vann over the radio. 'Do you read?'

There was a long pause. Then a voice crackled out of the speaker. 'Everything's fine here,' Vann replied flatly. 'Any sign of them targets yet?'

Vann sounded slightly out of breath, Carter thought. Tension, perhaps. Nerves and adrenaline. Even the most experienced operators could suffer from it in the stressful moments before a firefight.

Carter said, 'They're on the way up. Should be coming into view of the kill zone in the next several minutes.'

'Roger that. Keep watching them, mate,' Vann said. 'Eyes peeled. We'll wait for your cue to get the ball rolling.'

He clicked off.

Carter set down the walkie-talkie.

Resumed his observation of the trail.

At two o'clock the targets briefly came into view again. A hundred metres downslope from the kill zone.

He glanced over at the three prone Afghans with the PKMs and said, softly, 'Targets are gonna be in our line of sight any minute now. Get your weapons ready but wait for me to open fire. No one starts shooting until I give the signal. Got it?'

Pencil, Pancake and Greybeard muttered their acknowledgement. He heard a chorus of metallic clacks as they tugged back the charging levers on the right side of their machine gun receivers.

Ready to open fire.

Carter assumed they were capable soldiers, at least by local standards. These guys were the pick of Hakimi's fighters. They would have been drilled on the ranges in basic shooting, weapon handling and assault drills. By Vann, or someone else from the Regiment.

Carter pulled back the handle on the side of his M4, then shunted it forward again, chambering the first round. He flipped the fire selector to semi-automatic, clicked off the safety. Tightened his left hand around the vertical foregrip.

Then he waited.

Three more minutes passed.

Carter kept his sights pinned to the point where the trail ran sharply down towards the treeline on lower ground. Any moment now, the first target would sweep into view. He rehearsed the next few minutes in his head. As soon as he had line of sight on the first target Carter would get back on the radio and alert Vann, letting him know that he was about to engage. Once all the targets had entered the kill zone, Carter would line up his sights with the rearmost fighter.

That gunshot would be the signal for the other guys on both fire teams to let rip. Vann and his guys would put down a torrent of gunfire on the enemy from their fire points around the western outcrop, while Carter's group engaged from the east. Between the two M4s and the six PKMs, they would create a lethal killing field. Their combined arcs of fire would deny the enemy areas of dead ground or cover to shelter behind.

Trapped in the narrow area of the trail-bend, the Taliban fighters would be cut to pieces before they could escape. The defenders wouldn't need to expend more than one box of ammo per PKM, leaving them with plenty of spare rounds to tackle any potential reinforcements.

But Carter wasn't thinking ahead to a second wave, or what might happen once they had routed the Taliban. He was laser-focused on surviving the next few minutes. Concentrate on the problem in front of you. Deal with the biggest obstacle first, then worry about the other stuff later.

The Regiment ethos.

Thirty seconds later, a target appeared on the trail.

Carter instinctively tensed.

He trained the rail-mounted sights on the figure below. At first he saw only the guy's head as he climbed the steep gradient leading up to the kill zone. Then the rest of his body popped into view as he reached the area of flat ground close to the U-shaped bend in the track.

The guy was Taliban. That much was immediately apparent. He wore a camo jacket, army boots, khaki trousers and ballistic helmet, and he carried an M4 rifle, practically identical to the weapon Carter was gripping. Part of the vast hoard of kit acquired by the Taliban after the frantic evacuation from Kabul. Spoils of war. From a distance, the guy could almost pass for an American infantryman.

Carter grabbed the walkie-talkie and spoke quietly into the microphone. 'I've got line of sight on the first target. As soon as the whole group reaches the kill zone, we'll open up. I'll get the ball rolling and take down the fucker to the rear. Do you read that?'

Carter listened. Silence.

He frowned at the unit.

Tried again.

'Enemies in sight, repeat enemies in sight. Do you copy? Anyone?'

He waited for a response. None came.

He tried Vann one final time, got the same dead-air response, then chucked the piece-of-shit unit aside. There was no time left to fuck about trying to fix the radio. He had to simply hope that his fire team wouldn't open up until Carter had loosed off the first shot. Fire too early, and the fighters at the back of the patrol would have a chance to retreat before they had entered into the kill zone.

The next two fighters in the line were now in sight on the trail. A thickly bearded guy in a black turban, and a third guy wearing a red skullcap. Both were packing AK-47s. They were moving in single file along the footpath, at regularly spaced intervals. A distance of two or three metres between Camo and Turban, and about the same between Turban and Skullcap. They made their way purposefully up the slope. A deliberate pace. Slower than a brisk walk, so they didn't knacker themselves out, but faster than a gentle stroll in the countryside. They weren't bothering to scan the ground in front of them and displayed none of the caution or fieldcraft of elite operators.

Camo, the lead fighter, had advanced ten metres along the flat part of the trail now. He was five or six metres away from the bend.

Carter raked his gaze back to the point where the flat ground angled down to the treeline. In the next beat, a fourth guy dressed in all black and a pair of sandals popped into sight. Two seconds later, Carter saw a fifth target. A stocky bloke with a khaki baseball cap over a mop of dark hair. The same three-metre gap between them.

Further along the path, Camo had reached the bend. In another twenty metres he would be out of sight again as the track veered up steeply to the right.

Two seconds later, a sixth figure appeared on the trail, sporting a crimson-red waistcoat over his loose-fitting clothes. Carter concentrated hard on the southern end of the track. Watching for any more targets behind Waistcoat. The gap between Waistcoat and the end of the path widened.

Three metres.

Then four.

Twenty metres further ahead, Camo had almost cleared the bend.

Carter continued observing the approach for another long beat. The gap grew wider. Five metres, then six. Still no one else appeared. At the seven-metre mark the gap was long enough for Carter to know that Waistcoat had to be the last guy in the formation. The tail-end Charlie.

Carter's throat constricted with tension. His mouth was very dry, as it always was in the moments before a contact.

Six fighters in the kill zone.

He peered down the M4 sights.

Lined up the reticule with the rearmost target.

Waistcoat.

'About to make my shot,' Carter told the Afghans in his group in an undertone. 'Start putting down rounds on the front five targets as soon as I've dropped the fucker to the rear.'

His index finger feathered the trigger. He was confident that the Taliban fighters wouldn't spot his profile among the rocks above. He had nothing shiny on him, nothing that would reflect the sun's glare and potentially give away his position.

Carter eased out a breath.

Then he squeezed the trigger.

Sixteen

Carter's M4 barked.

A gout of orange flame sparked out of the muzzle. The shot whipcracked across the warm air, shattering the peace of the valley. In the next fraction of a second the 5.56 mm bullet thumped into Waistcoat, plugging him in the head.

The other five Taliban fighters automatically froze and looked at one another. Wondering what the fuck had just happened to their comrade. Shock, mixed in with terrible panic and confusion. Two seconds ago they had been walking up the hillside. Now one of their mates was lying on the dirt with a canoe for a head.

Then everything went noisy.

The three Afghans to the left and right of Carter simultaneously opened up with their PKMs. Carter heard the familiar *duh-duh-duh* as the machine guns unleashed a murderous stream of 7.62 bullets at the trail-bend, backgrounded by the wind-chime chink of spent casings tumbling out of ejectors. Two hundred metres away, bright green tracer rounds splashed into the area around the targets before they ricocheted off the ground, shooting into the sky like bottle rockets.

Then came the heavy stuff. Sturdy rounds dating back to the Tsarist empire, discharged from brutally efficient Russian weapon systems, thumping into the compacted earth and throwing up geysers of incinerated dirt. The first rounds ripped into the frontmost target. The guy in the American military get-up. Carter saw him go down in a bloodied heap at the side of the footpath. Another five-round burst smacked into Turban. The second fighter in the column. He spasmed wildly, as if someone had just bumped him with a cattle prod. Then his bullet-riddled body went slack, and he dropped to the dirt a couple of paces behind the lead target, his rifle clattering to the ground beside him.

Half a second later, the other three fighters scattered.

They had a choice to make. The same one facing any soldiers caught in an ambush. Advance, or retreat. Move forward aggressively or fall back. Fight or flight.

Literally a life-and-death decision.

Baseball and Sandals chose to fight.

Carter saw them simultaneously bringing up their AK-47s. The muzzles flashed as they emptied rounds at the outcrops above them. A terrible idea, from a tactical viewpoint. They were in the open, on exposed ground, shooting at an enemy they couldn't see, protected by a screen of large rocks. They were shooting blindly, not bothering to aim at individual targets. Pissing bullets at the general area of the defenders and hoping for the best. Carter heard the smack of a round slapping into a rock several metres to his right. Another struck the slope somewhere below their position.

The PKMs thundered again.

The three Afghans on the machine guns beside Carter were firing in bursts of between five and ten rounds. They were feeding a serious amount of lead into the killing ground down the slope. Rounds chopped into Baseball and Sandals, puncturing flesh. Their mangled bodies fell to the dirt, like a pair of puppets after the strings had been cut.

As the guys on his fire team let rip, Carter realised that no tracer rounds had been streaming down from the western outcrop. Vann's position. He couldn't hear any gunfire coming from that side either. He didn't know why. Possibly one of the guys on Vann's team had been wounded or killed. A stray round from one of the Taliban fighters.

No time to worry about that right now.

Carter slinked his gaze back to the trail.

Ten metres behind the two dead fighters, Skullcap darted to the right, getting off the trail to seek cover. Flight winning over fight.

A rational response. Skullcap had seen the other five guys in his patrol getting torn to pieces by the PKMs. He wouldn't want to suffer the same fate.

Rounds chewed up the ground a few paces behind him as Carter's fire team rattled off another trio of bursts on the fleeing Taliban fighter. A torrent of rounds hammered into the earth, missing Skullcap by inches. A moment later the fighter threw himself forward, disappearing from sight as he reached the dead ground beneath the outcrop.

Carter gritted his teeth in frustration. His fire team had no line of sight on the fighter. Skullcap was concealed behind the clutter of trees and rocks directly below their firing position. Carter looked across to his right flank, waiting to see if anyone on Vann's team had a fix on the target yet, but their position was still quiet. Carter began to fear the worst.

He snapped his attention back to the trail-bend and raked his eyes over the ground immediately to the east of his position. A hundred metres downwind from the outcrop, Carter found what he was looking for: a loose mass of boulders strewn like rubble down the mountainside, next to the trunk of a fallen tree.

'Stop firing,' he shouted at the three guys working the PKMs. They were blasting away senselessly at the dead bodies on the footpath. 'I said hold your fucking fire!'

A moment later the PKMs stopped barking. The Afghans looked at him with quizzical expressions.

'Wait here,' Carter said. 'I'm going to cut round and drop the fucker. If you see the target pop into view again, kill him.'

Then he pushed away from the rocks.

Carter broke left, working his way around and down the gradient towards the cluster of massive rocks located midway down the slope. From there he would have a clear view of the dead ground further up the path.

By now he was sweating hard. His ears were ringing, his mouth was so dry it felt as if he'd been chewing on bales of sawdust. Carter almost lost his footing on a bed of loose shale, regained his balance and vaulted over the fallen tree before he drew level with the boulders. He dropped to a kneeling firing stance, steadied his breathing. Brought up his rifle.

A hundred metres due west, Skullcap had tucked himself close to a scattered heap of rocks, ferns and shrubs at the edge of the footpath. He had his back to the trail, staying low to hide his profile from the fire team two hundred metres above.

Carter took aim. Fired.

The bullet smashed into Skullcap's leg. He slumped backwards, writhing on the ground and screaming in agony as he clawed at his rag-order thigh. Carter squeezed off another single shot. The second round did the trick. The bullseye shot. It thumped into the target's forehead, uncorking the back of his head like a champagne bottle and painting the surrounding rocks with bright red blood and brain matter. The guy stopped screaming.

Six targets down.

Job done.

Carter retraced his steps back up the tree-studded gradient towards the eastern outcrop. Adrenaline still coursing through his veins. The snap ambush had lasted no more than twenty seconds, but it felt much longer. Any relief he might have felt at clobbering the enemy was instantly submerged beneath a wave of gnawing unease. The group on the right flank, Vann's team, had stayed out of the fight.

Something was badly wrong. He knew it.

As he reached his fire team, Carter engaged the safety on his M4 and cupped his hand to his mouth.

'Are you OK? Dave? Anyone?'

His voice echoed across the mountainside. No answer.

Carter paced quickly over to Vann's position. His heart was beating faster now. The knot of unease in his guts tightened as he swept round the edge of the outcrop.

Then he stopped dead.

He expected to find someone bleeding out. Blood all over the fucking place, field dressings, spent rounds, discarded kit.

Instead he saw nothing.

No machine guns, no Afghans.

No spent casings or bloodstains.

No Vann.

Just a patch of rocks and dirt.

Carter looked swiftly round. He scanned the path weaving up towards the plateau, shielding his eyes from the afternoon sun.

He wondered if they had started back up the path towards the compound, but he couldn't see anyone on the trail. Carter called out and pricked his ears, waiting for a response.

None came.

So maybe they were already back at the plateau. Carrying the wounded back to the compound for treatment. Except that there was no blood around the outcrop, no evidence of a maimed fighter at all. The absence of any casings was even weirder. None of the guys on Vann's fire team had discharged a round during the ambush. Why not?

Carter jogged towards the footpath. Over on the left flank Pencil, Pancake and Greybeard sprang to their feet and looked expectantly at Carter. As if waiting for a cue.

'Stay where you are,' Carter ordered them. He pointed down towards the gravel road. 'Watch that fucking roadhead. Anyone else shows up, let me know.'

He bounded back up the slope, his heart pounding savagely. He reached the plateau in another quick stride and sprinted towards the compound. As he drew nearer his eyes were drawn to the tented area to the side of the buildings. Then he stopped again.

Something like a knife sank into his bowels.

The mules were gone.

All six of them.

He knew then what had happened, what Vann had done to him, but he had to be sure. He raced over to the buildings, rushing past Sharza's corpse before he crashed through the worn timber door. The main room was empty. So was the side office. The stacks of heroin bricks were gone. Everything else had been left behind in their mad rush to escape.

Vann and the warlord had ditched him.

Carter bolted outside again, heart thrumming madly in his chest. He checked the two smaller buildings and then the cave, running around like a headless chicken. Desperately searching for any clue that Vann might have left behind.

He left the cave and swept his eyes over the plateau. He remembered seeing Mansur and Yellow Scarf running back up the trail half an hour ago. He thought back to Vann's slightly out-of-breath voice on the radio, and the knife in his stomach sank a little deeper. The bastards had been on the move for the past thirty minutes, Carter realised with a surge of bitter frustration and anger. They had bugged out of the area a few minutes after he had taken up his position to the east.

He fought back against the rage thumping between his temples and turned his mind to the problem of locating their escape route. Something Vann had told him had lodged in his brain. Something about the footpath winding down from the hideout.

This is the only route up or down the mountain.

Vann had obviously been feeding him bullshit.

So where the fuck had they gone? Carter asked himself.

He ruled out the possibility that they had retreated back down the mountain. That would take them away from the Tajik border, straight into the path of the incoming Taliban patrols. Therefore they must have fled north from the compound, heading for the meeting with the Tajik. Their contact in the smack trade. No other reason for taking the mule train with them.

Carter gazed at the vertiginous cliff-face stretching up from the far side of the plateau towards the peak. He strained his eyes, searching for any way of going up or down. Nothing. It looked impregnable.

Another dead end.

He scurried back down the trail to the eastern outcrop and ran straight over to Greybeard and the two other Afghans. They were still huddled behind the boulders, observing the roadhead. As Carter hurried over, Greybeard looked towards him and creased his features in puzzlement. Carter grabbed the man by his jacket, taking him by surprise.

'Where are they?' Carter demanded.

Greybeard reeled back and held up his hands, eyes bulged in terror. He muttered something incoherent, in a language Carter didn't understand. Carter thrust a hand in the direction of the outcrop to the west.

'Your leader has pissed off. So has my mate. They're not at the compound. So where the fuck have they gone?'

Pancake and Pencil had both spun away from the rocks. They glanced briefly at one another, a silent understanding passing between them. Then they abruptly jettisoned their machine guns and scuttled down the gradient, towards the bend in the track, running past the dead bodies slumped across the ground. Making for the distant roadhead. They had obviously understood Carter and decided to get clear of the mountain before any more Taliban fighters showed up.

Carter ignored them and shook the grey-bearded man.

'Tell me,' he growled.

The Afghan must have seen the cold fury blazing in the SAS man's eyes, because he pointed a trembling finger towards the mountain. The sheer rockface.

'But where?' Carter demanded angrily. 'Where are they? How the fuck would they have gone up there?'

Greybeard shrugged and babbled on again in his mother tongue. Carter shoved the guy aside and dashed back up the rough trail towards the plateau. He glanced back, spotted the Afghan galloping down the slope as he hurried after his two fleeing mates.

Carter swung round and started across the level ground. He beat a path towards the rockface and started examining the ground more carefully this time. Then his eyes landed on something at the edge of the copse, eight or nine metres to the left of the cave mouth.

A fresh pile of mule shit.

He jog-trotted across the plateau and followed the trail of shit for thirty metres as it led deeper into the grove of pine trees. Then Carter hit the jackpot. Amid the gloom he spotted a narrow footpath concealed by the surrounding vegetation.

Vann's getaway route.

Carter spun round and sprinted over to the compound to fetch his rucksack. He transferred the four spare M4 clips from his side pockets to the bag, along with the satphone. Then he threaded his arms through the straps, scooped up his rifle and hustled back over to the trail sneaking through the copse. He was in a mad hurry, partly because he'd allowed Vann to slip away. But also because of the ambush. The noise of the firefight would have alerted every Taliban patrol in the area, Carter knew. Reinforcements would be on their way. Within a short time the mountain would be infested with enemy fighters. Like flies on shit.

Carter knew what he had to do. Get moving, fast. *Put as much distance between myself and the Taliban as possible.*

Before I end up all over the news.

He swept past the mule droppings and picked up the trail a short distance inside the pine grove. The path ran on for a hundred metres through the woodland, twisting this way and that, before it curved steeply to the right and disappeared through a narrow crevice partially hidden between a couple of boulders the size of wrecking balls.

A secret passage.

Carter paused briefly in front of the crevice and lifted his gaze to the rockface above. From a distance, at ground level, he couldn't see the outline of the trail. None at all. It simply blended into the wall of sheer rock. A trick of the naked eye. Impossible to spot from a distance. The trail itself looked incredibly steep and narrow. No more than a metre across. An old goatherd's trail, possibly. Or a merchant track once used for transporting goods along the ancient trading routes. Wide enough for a person.

Or a mule.

He stepped through the opening and started climbing the trail as it meandered up the mountainside.

There was a precipitous drop from the edge of the path to the ground below, and Carter had to watch his footing as he continued his ascent. The ground here was barren, denuded of trees and shrubs. Nothing but boulders and scree.

After a while the track twisted round to the right. Soon Carter had lost sight of the plateau as the path zigzagged up towards the ridgeline.

He knew then with absolute certainty that Vann and Hakimi had taken off in this direction. The track would lead up towards the feature before passing down the other side and continuing north.

Towards Tajikistan.

Carter ploughed on, moving as fast as his legs could carry him. Trying to close the distance on his quarry. He guessed the ridgeline had to be something like three thousand metres high. Not a serious challenge. Not when you had spent weeks on SAS Selection climbing the Brecon Beacons with a heavy Bergen strapped to your back. Later on, after he'd earned the right to wear the beige beret, Carter had trained as an Alpine guide, learning about all aspects of mountain warfare and navigation.

Vann had done that same course years before. Both men had served in Mountain Troop in the same squadron in the Regiment. Both men had been posted as embeds.

In many ways, their careers had mirrored one another, Carter reflected.

Now I'm hunting the bastard.

The slope abruptly steepened again, and Carter sensed he was getting closer to the ridgeline. Fifteen minutes later, the path broadened and the wind suddenly picked up as he hit the ridgeline. From here Carter could see the valleys stretched out far below, veiled in a faint grey haze. Not a village in sight in any direction he cared to look.

The middle of fucking nowhere, he thought.

If I run into trouble out here, I'm done for.

He carried on for twenty metres until he reached the edge of the ridgeline. Then he looked down the far side of the mountain. The ground sloped away dramatically towards the floor of a wide valley roughly two thousand metres below. In the distance, another kilometre or so beyond the base of the mountain, the track disappeared into a heavily wooded area.

A moment later, Carter spotted the mule train, making its way north along the path leading to the forest. A distance of about three kilometres from his position. He counted six mules, accompanied by four ant-sized figures. Vann and Hakimi, plus the two other fighters from their fire group. Mansur and Yellow Scarf.

By now the smugglers had almost reached the treeline. Carter looked on as the mule train moved out of sight beyond the fringe of pine trees. Then he looked up.

Much further to the north, on the other side of the valley, the land rose up again in a series of ridgelines before fading away towards the horizon. That ground would provide the mule train with a safe passage all the way to Tajikistan, Carter realised.

He glanced quickly at his watch as he started down the other side of the mountain. Three o'clock in the afternoon. An hour since the firefight. He calculated that Vann had a fifty-minute head start on him.

There's a courier route to Tajikistan, Vann had told him back at the compound.

The roadhead, Carter thought. On the Tajikistani side of the border. Forty kilometres to the north.

That's where they'll be heading.

He was about to set off again when he glimpsed something to the south. Plumes of dust rising from the valley. Four of them. Coming from the direction of the plateau and the roadhead.

Reinforcements.

The second wave.

Heading straight for the mountain.

Shit.

Carter knew he couldn't head back now. Not an option. The Taliban would be charging up the mountain soon enough. A bigger force this time, no doubt. Anything up to twenty fighters. They would be sweeping forward aggressively, eager to avenge their six dead mates. Carter had his M4 assault rifle, five clips of ammo and the holstered Russian pistol. Against a much larger enemy formation, he wouldn't stand a chance.

There's only one thing for it, he decided.

Push on.

Keep hunting Vann.

And hope the Taliban don't catch up with me.

Seventeen

Carter plunged down the side of the mountain, picking his way along the footpath as it narrowed again. He was determined to close the gap with the mule train. But he also needed to put some serious distance between himself and the Taliban reinforcements converging on the other side of the ridgeline. A short distance further down he passed another freshly deposited lump of mule shit and his chest swelled with confidence. The beasts would leave a steady trail from here to the RV in Tajikistan. Nothing Vann could do about that. Nature in action. The droppings would make it much more difficult for Vann to shake off his pursuer. Even if Carter lost his way, he could stop and scan the ground for new piles of shit. Then resume the chase again.

As he descended towards the valley, his mind worked feverishly, calculating times and distances. Nightfall at this time of the year kicked in at seven thirty. Approximately four hours from now. At which point the temperature would rapidly plummet. High up on the mountains, exposed to the elements, it would be even worse. Carter would be freezing cold, tired and stumbling around in the darkness. Keeping up the pursuit was going to be difficult.

That was problem number one. But there was a second problem. Carter was stalking a Regiment veteran, a guy with decades of Hereford know-how ingrained into him. There was every chance that Vann might try to set up a snap ambush or plant another booby trap somewhere along the path. Nothing too elaborate. Nothing that would take a lot of time to construct. Could be something as basic as a tripwire. Take a pair of sticks, drive them into the ground at an angle to form a 'Y' and rest a fragmentation grenade on top. Ease the safety pin nearly out, thread a piece of cord through it and string it across the track at ankle height. The slightest contact would result in the tautened wire yanking the pin out of the grenade, fragging the target.

He thought, *I'll have to move cautiously. Move too fast, and I could easily miss the telltale signs of a trap.*

There was an even bigger problem, Carter knew. But he didn't want to think about that right now. He was like a boxer deep in the ninth round with his opponent, cut and disorientated, not allowing himself to think any further ahead than his next punch.

Deal with the thing right in front of you. Worry about the other stuff later.

He was working on the basis that Vann wouldn't deviate from the main footpath. The mules had five hundred kilos of heroin loaded on their backs. A massively heavy load. Vann wouldn't be able to increase his pace, and he couldn't risk going off-piste. Therefore he would have to stick to the main track, following the route across the ridgelines to the north. The most direct route to the roadhead on the other side of the border.

The slope became gentler as Carter neared the vale. He pushed on towards the wooded area a kilometre to the north of the mountain, picking out more signs left by the mule train along the way. An upturned rock struck by a mule's hoof, the slightly damp underside facing upward. A snapped twig. The lighter side of a leaf on a branch pointing up, caused by someone brushing carelessly against it. All of which confirmed his suspicion that Vann wouldn't stray from the footpath.

He checked his G-Shock again.

Four o'clock. Two hours since the firefight.

By now, the reinforcements would have arrived at the compound. They would be combing the plateau methodically, trying to figure out how the defenders had managed to slip away. Eventually, one of them would locate the trail in the pine grove. A matter of time, Carter decided.

Most of the Taliban fighters were rural guys. They had grown up in areas similar to this one, knew the lie of the land. They would instinctively grasp that there had to be a route up to the ridgeline.

Soon enough, they would start tracking him.

If they weren't doing so already.

He reached the woodland an hour later and continued slowly through the tangled undergrowth.

It would take the mule train another six hours to reach the frontier, Carter estimated. Maybe longer, given the steep nature of the terrain. Which meant Vann would have to stop for the night, if only to give the mules a chance to rest. He'd set up a lying-up point somewhere south of the border. Get off the track and put a dog-leg in. Standard Regiment tactics when you had to establish an LUP in hostile territory. Peel off to the left or right, carry on walking for two hundred metres at a ninety-degree angle from the track, then walk back on yourself for another two hundred metres until you found a suitable spot to bed down. Vann would tether the mules and post a sentry to watch over the approach. If anybody was following, he'd see them moving down the trail, taking them right past his line of sight. Then he could launch a counter ambush, catching the enemy by surprise.

That's what I would do, if I was in his boots, Carter thought.

We might have taken very different paths in our lives, but we were both taught to soldier the same way.

An hour later, Carter emerged from the dense sprawl of forest. He started up the track towards the next feature, feeling the effort in his legs, his lungs. The air began to thin as he climbed higher up the mountains, and soon Carter was struggling for breath. His skull throbbed. He felt his body beginning to flag.

The stress of the firefight, the frantic escape from the compound, the pursuit across the valley. Vann's betrayal.

The day from hell.

As he hit the next ridgeline, Carter paused to take a pull from one of the water bottles in his daysack. He took a few sips, then stashed the bottle away again. Water discipline. One of the most important rules you learned early on in the SAS. Preserve your water for as long as possible. Take no more than you needed, because you never knew when you would next find a fresh supply. The summer announcements at train stations telling people to guzzle litres of water to stay hydrated had it wrong, in Carter's opinion. Experience had taught him that the human body could survive on precious little fluid.

He closed his mind to the tiredness in his limbs and set off again. Cleared the ridgeline and scrabbled down the track towards the next feature on the map. By his estimation he had covered about twenty kilometres. Which put him about ten kilometres from the border.

The sun was beginning to sink below the horizon now, burnishing the black masses of the distant peaks.

Thirty minutes from now, I'll be in darkness.

Then my task is going to get a lot bloody harder.

As he carried on, a question prodded at the back of his mind. One that had been bugging him for the past several hours. Something Hakimi had said to Vann back at the compound.

I knew it was a mistake to remove that landmine.

Which implied that Vann had deliberately replaced the mine at some point with the early warning system. A decision that made absolutely no sense. Especially when you had the enemy breathing down your neck. *This whole area is crawling with Taliban right now.*

Taking away the landmine went against all the standard operating procedures they had been taught in the Regiment. Yet Vann had gone ahead and done it anyway. Why?

Carter shook his head.

It doesn't matter, he thought. *Not anymore.*

Vann dropped me in the shit back at the compound. Left me to take on a bunch of Taliban while he bolted with the drug stash. I'll never forgive the bastard for that.

In the first frantic minutes after Carter had bolted from the plateau, he'd considered the possibility that Vann had been taken hostage by Hakimi. Perhaps the warlord had put a gun to his head. Forced him to abandon his position and take to the hills. Maybe Vann hadn't willingly left his old mate behind. But then Carter had remembered reaching out to Vann on the walkie-talkie. His slightly breathless voice replying to Carter's question.

Everything's fine.

Vann hadn't sounded like someone talking under duress. At that moment, he had been rushing up the hidden trail with the pack mules. Leaving Carter behind to face the enemy. An action that betrayed the whole ethos of the Regiment.

Whatever bond that had once existed between them had been shattered. *Vann left me for dead*, Carter reflected bitterly. *He's a drug dealer and a bullshitter.*

He'll pay for this. I'll make fucking sure of it.

Darkness soon began to encroach on the landscape. After a while, Carter struggled to see the ground clearly in front of him. There was some ambient light from the moon, but not much. Not enough to detect signs on the ground, or tripwires, or any evidence that Vann had veered off-track to set up a snap ambush. Carter thought about reaching for the torch in his backpack, then shook his head. No. Not worth the risk. The light would advertise his position to anyone nearby.

Carter grew increasingly tired. His eyelids felt as if they had weights sewn into them. His muscles were as heavy as cement. He had a decision to make. Keep moving through the dark and risk getting killed in the process. Or bed down somewhere for the night. Hope that the trail didn't go cold.

And pray that the Taliban didn't locate him.

Pros and cons.

A gamble, whichever way you looked at it, with no sure answer. Like betting on red or black.

He decided to keep going.

I can't afford to fall any further behind the mule train.

Several minutes later, Carter felt a faint breath of wind against his cheek. The breeze quickly strengthened, whipping across the track, rustling the dead leaves underfoot and whispering through the branches of the trees. He was walking blind now, stumbling along through the grainy darkness. The wind picked up, knifing against his face, thrusting through his hair. He took another three paces forward—

Then stopped.

In front of him the ground simply ended. Beyond it was a large black shadow. Carter stared at it for a cold beat. Puzzled. He wondered if Vann had placed some kind of obstacle along the track. Or perhaps it was the opening to a cave complex. Carter pricked his ears, but he couldn't hear anything above the noise of the wind hitting the mountain.

He shucked off his rucksack and rooted around inside, feeling for the tactical field torch. He had to chance it. No choice. No other way round the shadow.

Carter popped the protective cap off the end of the torch and thumbed the switch, flicking the torch onto its lowest setting. He shone the beam over the shadow, straining his eyes and leaning forward to take a closer look at whatever was blocking the route.

Carter's heart skipped a beat.

There was nothing in front of him.

Just absolute blackness.

A void.

He dipped the beam lower, spotlighting the ground nearer to his feet, and realised with horror that he had come to the very edge of a cliff. A 2,000-metre drop to the bottom of the valley. Somewhere along the way he had wandered off the track. Another couple of paces and he would have stumbled off the cliff. Certain death.

He clicked off the torch, slapped the cap back on so its light wouldn't be seen if he accidentally turned it on again. Stuffed it into his cargo pocket. He waited until his eyes had adjusted to the immense blackness once more, then slowly backtracked away from the cliff edge and started looking for a place to lay up for the night.

Carter was snookered. His own fault. He'd been pushing it too hard. Tracking a target was almost impossible in the middle of the night. There was no way he'd be able to find the trail again, not in the darkness, not without waving a torch beam all over the place.

I'll have to bed down, he realised. *Take shelter and wait until first light before picking up the trail again.*

Unless I want to end up looking like a fucking pancake.

After twenty paces he stopped beside the base of a gnarled pine tree with a hollow shaped like a lancet window. Carter took another sip of water. He grazed on a chocolate bar from one of his ration packs, stowed the wrapper in his bag, slipped on his North Face jacket, winter gloves and woollen hat. Then he curled up beside the tree, wedging himself tight against the hollow to shelter himself against the knife-like wind. His rifle resting at his side.

His biggest fear was being discovered by the Taliban. Carter tried to reassure himself that they were unlikely to stumble upon his position. If they had pursued him north of the compound, they would be moving by torchlight, slowing their pace to a crawl. He doubted they would risk veering off the main track, not at night. As long as he stayed silent and didn't use his torch, he would be safe enough.

A gamble, maybe.

But less risky than blundering about in the dark.

Carter didn't dare use the illumination function on his watch, but he estimated that an hour had passed since last light. Eight thirty or thereabouts. Which meant the mule train had been on the move for more than eight hours. The beasts would be knackered. The smart money was on Vann stopping for the night. The guy would have probably established an LUP nine or ten kilometres short of the border, not long before nightfall. Wait until an hour before dawn, then resume the journey north to the roadhead.

He hoped.

There was always the risk that Vann might push on through the night, Carter knew. But the mules would still leave a trail of droppings in their wake. Nothing Vann could do about that. Carter was confident he could pick up their track again sooner or later.

I won't lose him, Carter vowed to himself. *No way. He's not going to get away with this.*

His eyelids were very heavy now. His brain was fogged with tiredness. His whole body craved rest. At last, several minutes later, Carter closed his eyes and fell asleep.

* * *

He awoke with a start.

Carter snapped his eyes open, his mind jolting out of its daze. It was still very dark. He had no idea how long he'd been asleep, but it couldn't have been for very long. The wind had reduced to a soft murmur. Stars pinpricked the black sky.

He heard something nearby.

Voices.

Several of them.

The tiredness fell from him like a sheet. Adrenaline surged through his veins, juicing his blood. Carter was instantly alert.

He reached for his M4 and crawled out from the lancet-shaped hollow, careful not to make a noise. He crept round to the side of the pine tree, crouched and listened.

The voices were growing louder.

Somewhere off to the right he saw a loose cluster of lights flitting in and out of sight through the gaps in the treeline.

Torches.

Shit.

The voices became more easily distinguishable, carrying clearly across the frosted night air. The figures were talking in hushed tones, whispering excitedly to one another. Carter couldn't make out their conversation, but it didn't sound like they were speaking English.

They had to be Taliban. The reinforcements. Vann wouldn't have risked using torches. An amateur mistake. Anyone using an artificial light source would be flagging their position to every other fucker in the area. Might as well paint a big target on your back.

The beams cut like searchlights through the blackness as the Taliban fighters drew nearer. Carter counted eight torch lights in total. From the sound of their voices they couldn't be far away. Twenty metres or so. Which was good news, in a way, because it meant that Carter hadn't wandered far off the main track. But also very bad news. Because in a few moments the Taliban would be dangerously close to his position.

Carter tensed his hand around the M4's polymer grip. He stilled his breath and remained motionless as the lights drew nearer. They swelled, and for an instant the voices became so clear-cut that it seemed to Carter as if they were almost on top of him. Two of them were having what sounded like a heated argument. Points of view were being exchanged. Tempers were frayed. They were clearly in disagreement over something. How much longer to continue the search, maybe.

Nobody wanted to be on a mountain on a dark cold night in the spring. Morale would start to slump the longer they went on without locating their prey. Thoughts would quickly turn from revenge to more prosaic needs. A warm bed, a brew, a slap-up meal.

There was a long pause, and then the beams shrank as the patrol crept further down the track. Carter inwardly relaxed. The threat had passed. The Taliban were moving on with their search.

I'm in the clear.

Then the lights started coming back towards him.

Eighteen

The lights grew larger. Carter sat stock-still beside the hollow, dread leaking like acid into his guts. He felt his breath trap in his throat, his muscles stiffening with fear as the lights approached. Carter couldn't be sure, but he estimated that they were no more than fifteen metres from his sheltering place now. They were getting closer.

Shit.

They've spotted my tracks.

Adrenaline flooded through Carter's body. His heart was beating so fast he thought it might explode inside his chest. He rested his index finger lightly around the M4 trigger and readied himself for the imminent possibility of a firefight. Carter had no intention of letting himself get caught by the Taliban. Better to go down fighting. Take down as many of the bastards as possible before someone cut him down.

The lights seemed very close now. Less than ten metres, perhaps. Hard to believe they hadn't seen him yet. Another step or two, and they were certain to catch sight of him in the glare of their torch lights.

Carter tensed his finger on the trigger.

A moment passed. The voices sounded impossibly loud and close in the cold stillness of the night.

Carter prepared to die.

Then, suddenly, the lights became smaller again. The agitated voices grew fainter as the patrol carried on past the hollow and headed back up the mountain slope. Carter continued watching the lights as they shrank to the size of dots. A few moments later, they vanished from sight behind the treeline, and the voices were swiftly lost to the blackness.

Carter exhaled.

They've given up the search, he thought.

They're going back home.

Thank fuck for that.

He slackened his trigger finger.

He remained crouching for a few minutes, pricking his ears, until he was certain that the patrol had moved out of sight. Then he skulked back to the hollow and curled up like an animal. He was still wired from the shot of adrenaline to his system. He closed his eyes, but sleep was impossible.

The night dragged on.

Carter stayed alert, listening for any more patrols, but the area remained quiet except for the soft mutter of the breeze hitting the side of the mountain. He tucked into a ready-to-eat meal of cold pasta and meatballs from his ration pack, gobbled down a bar of chocolate and helped himself to another mouthful of water. Carter hadn't eaten a proper cooked meal in days, not since he'd left Chile, but that didn't bother him. His body was almost immune to deprivation from the years of hard training in the Regiment. At home he often went for days at a time without eating anything. He felt like he could survive for weeks on nothing more than coffee, water and a little fruit.

A while later, he was conscious of the faintest lightening of the sky. Then came the predawn chorus of the forest, the screaming of animals and insects. Nature's alarm clock. Better than any app on a phone. Soon the pale blue fingers of sunlight were spreading across the horizon.

Carter sipped water, wished it was strong coffee, and unfolded the laminated map. He checked the route ahead of him and tried to work out where Vann was headed.

The Tajik is going to meet us at the roadhead, Hakimi had said back at the compound. *Him, and the rest of his guys.*

Tomorrow. First light.

As in, today.

Carter studied the border region directly north of his general position. A winding river formed a natural barrier between the two countries. To the north of the border, a secondary road ran along a narrow embankment sandwiched between the river and the vast mountain range further north. The only road in sight, as far as Carter could tell. Nothing above it or below. No nearby settlements.

The roadhead.

That's where Vann will be going.

In the pearl-grey dawn light he found the track easily enough. Carter simply walked away from the cliff edge at a ninety-degree angle and carried on past the trees and rocks until he hit the trail. He found the last positive sign he'd spotted the night before a few paces further back. The golden rule of tracking: only believe in what you see in front of you. Only move forward when you've found positive sign. Ignore that rule, make it up for yourself, and you were sure to get misplaced.

Carter stopped for a moment to check his watch, his breath misting in front of his mouth in the cool dawn air. Five o'clock in the morning. Carter reckoned he was three hours from the roadhead. With Vann somewhere ahead of him, accompanied by an Afghan warlord and several millions of pounds' worth of heroin.

Time to get moving.

* * *

He moved on at a steady pace down the track, looking for more positive sign, staying alert to the constant danger of running into an IED or a booby trap. As he neared the crossing point, Carter knew there was a chance his mission might be futile. Vann might well have moved clear of the roadhead by the time Carter made it across the border. There would be no way of finding him then.

I can't do anything about that.

All I can do is follow Vann's route and hope the trail hasn't gone cold.

And if you manage to find Vann? Carter asked himself.

What then?

I don't know.

He had tried not to think that far ahead during his long walk north. But now his thoughts drifted to the problem of isolating Vann. That was going to be tricky. The guy had an Afghan warlord and two of his henchmen for company. All of them were armed. Vann wouldn't give up without a fight.

Even if Carter managed to overpower Vann and eliminate the Afghans, his problems weren't over. Once he'd secured Vann he would have to put a call in to the Company. Give them the low-down on his vanishing act. The smuggling operation with Hakimi. The five hundred kilos of high-quality heroin. Carter could already predict their response.

Silence him.

Permanently.

It made no sense for either Six or the Company to want Vann taken alive. They would be desperate to avoid the scandal of a decorated ex-SAS soldier being put on trial for running smack in Afghanistan. In the ruthless logic of the foreign intelligence services, killing Vann was a small price to pay to avoid deep political embarrassment in London and Washington.

This mission is no longer a hard arrest.

This is a find-and-kill op.

I'm going to have to slot Vann. Double-tap the guy who taught me everything.

Unless he kills me first.

He shoved that bleak thought to the darkest recesses of his mind as he trudged on.

An hour later, shortly before eight o'clock in the morning, he crossed the last ridgeline before the border with Tajikistan. Carter picked his way down a rock-strewn slope until he came to a halt beside a copse a short distance from the crest. Then he scanned the terrain below.

The border.

The trail ran on for three hundred metres from the mountain down to the bank of a meandering river, no more than fifty metres wide at its narrowest point. South of the river was Afghan soil. North was Tajikistan. A secondary road ran along the southern bank. A hundred metres to the west, at Carter's eleven o'clock, a small military outpost had been built on an area of raised ground on the Afghan side of the river. The Taliban's trademark white flag hung from a pole in front of the largest building, fluttering in the gentle morning breeze.

The border looked desolate. Belts of dry ground straddled both banks. Carter had expected to see a few locals down by the river, but there wasn't a soul in sight. He saw several crumbling hovels on the far side of the river, the rusted hulk of a pickup truck. Further north the ground inclined steeply up from the bank towards a chain of low mountains dotted with trees and shrubs. At the base of the nearest mountain, a dirt road ran roughly parallel to the river.

The roadhead.

Carter felt his pulse quicken with anticipation. *I'm getting closer now.*

He took a gulp of water and observed the ground for a while. Watching for patrolling soldiers on either side of the river. Borders were typically hotbeds of military activity. But this area looked dead quiet. No soldiers, no traffic.

The ideal crossing point for smugglers.

He scanned the areas to the left and right of the Taliban outpost, looking for a way across the river. He spotted a dry stream bed at his two o'clock, five hundred metres to the east, stretching from the base of the mountain to the bank of the river.

The bed was steep-sided, Carter noticed. The product of centuries of soil erosion. Deep enough to hide an adult-sized figure from view of the guards at the outpost.

That's my route across the border.

And I'll bet Vann took the mule train the same way.

Carter took off his North Face jacket, removed his belt pouch and stuffed both items into the rucksack. Then he emptied his trouser pockets and chucked the rest of his gear into the waterproof bag: his satphone, the Russian gun knife, the tactical torch. He didn't know the depth of the river, but from where he was standing it looked fairly shallow. Waist height, perhaps. The mules had made it across, so it couldn't be too deep. Carter would get soaking wet, which would be a fucking ball ache. But he couldn't see any other concealed route across the border.

Once he had secured his kit, he set off down the mountain-side. By now the sun had risen above the peaks and he felt a warm breath of air on his face as he made his descent. He didn't feel tired, in spite of his lack of sleep and the gruelling trek north. He'd marched far greater distances during Test Week on Selection. He was still in peak physical condition. Had muscles that looked as if they had been sculpted from a block of marble, an ex-girlfriend had told him.

After two hundred metres he reached a grassy area close to the bottom of the slope. Here the mountain trail suddenly ended. He veered off to the right, moving at a semi-jogging pace, roughly following the course of the river until he reached the dried-out gully a hundred metres due south of the crossing point.

Carter worked his way down the side of the narrow channel and started walking towards the river. He stuck close to the right side of the gully, remaining in the shadows so he wouldn't be seen from the outpost. He dropped to a crouch as he reached a shallower section of the gully midway along, then straightened his back again as the stream bed deepened twenty metres further on.

Among the rocks and sticks scattered across the bed floor he picked out more mule deposits, further proof that Vann had passed through this place not long before with the mules.

I'm still on his tail, Carter thought.

I've still got a chance of catching him.

He manoeuvred down the stream bed for another hundred metres and paused briefly at the point where it opened up to a straight section of the river. Carter picked up a couple of sticks and tossed them into the water to estimate the current. He watched them drift downstream, then slid carefully down the bank, past a loose tumble of rocks, before he stopped again at the water's edge. He raised his M4 rifle above his head as he started wading across the silvery grey river.

The water was colder than he'd expected. More like a European river than a South American jungle stream. Carter edged forward, watching his footing for slippery rocks on the riverbed. He aimed for an exit point fifty metres downstream, not fighting the current, using the weight of his waterproof rucksack to let the river ease him gently along. The river quickly deepened. Soon the water had risen up to his chest, chilling his core. Carter plodded determinedly on. One foot after another. At last he made it to the opposite bank. He reached out, grabbed hold of a low-hanging branch and hauled himself out of the icy water.

He moved quickly up from the bank, shivering in his soaking wet clothes as he made for the dead ground of another dried-out gully to the north. He trudged along the stream bed for several minutes before he drew to a halt at a deeper section in the gully, a hundred metres up from the bank. Then he climbed out of his sodden cargoes and socks, replacing them with the fresh pairs he'd packed in his daysack. He laced his belt through the loops, removed the satphone, gun knife and map from the daysack and slipped them into his side pockets.

Then Carter took his M4, ejected the chambered round, eased out the clip from the mag feed and broke the rifle down into its components. He shoved the parts and the magazine into his daysack and made sure his holstered Grach was concealed beneath his shirt. From now on he would have to rely on the pistol to dig him out of trouble. He couldn't stroll around Tajikistan with an assault rifle. Not unless he was planning on spending time in a prison cell.

Carter strapped on his daysack and carried on north again, making his way up the gully towards the roadhead a kilometre away. He felt a slight sense of relief as the fear of capture or execution at the hands of the Taliban lifted from his weary shoulders.

I'm out of Afghanistan.

Thank fuck for that.

Now I've just got to deal with Vann.

After eight hundred metres he reached the point where the northern gully met the embankment rising up to the dirt road. Carter scaled the bank, calf muscles burning as he navigated the incline. He stopped at the roadside, catching his breath while he orientated himself.

The road was deserted. You could probably stand at the side of it, catch sight of a car at seven o'clock in the morning and not see another one for the next twelve hours. It was that kind of place.

The road itself looked worn down to the nub. Constructed back in the days of the Soviet Union, Carter imagined, and not repaired since. Maybe the Chinese would come along with a wad of cash in due course. Belt and Road handouts. Infrastructure and security, in exchange for surveillance-society authoritarianism.

The new way of the world.

He looked round once more but didn't see anything unusual. Nothing to suggest which way Vann and his associates had travelled.

Left or right? he thought.

This way, or that?

Heads or tails?

He chose left. A calculated guess. West was the general onward direction of travel for the heroin Vann had smuggled up from

Afghanistan. The smack route ran from Central Asia to Europe, through Russia. Travelling east made no sense. Whoever was buying the gear from Vann wouldn't want to venture further from home than necessary. West seemed the likelier bet. Towards the capital at Dushanbe, and the border with Uzbekistan.

Carter walked along the road for fifty metres, scanning the ground.

Nothing.

He moved on again. Looking for more shit, or a piece of rubbish. Anything that might have been left behind by the mule train during the transfer of the drugs from animal to vehicle. He carried on for another hundred paces and got the same result.

After four hundred metres, Carter started to think that maybe he should turn around and try his luck to the east instead. Then he caught sight of something at the side of the road. Ten paces in front of him.

A cigarette butt, next to a pile of stones.

The only piece of litter in sight.

He marched over to the tab. Bent down and picked it up by the filter tip. The cigarette was still warm, with an inch of unsmoked tobacco. It hadn't been crushed, and Carter saw no marks or disturbance on the dusty ground. Which implied that someone had flicked it out of a car window. A person on foot would have likely extinguished the cigarette under their heel. Therefore a driver or passenger. Heading west, Carter determined, because the tab had been ditched on the right side of the road.

Could be nothing, he thought. *Could be a passing truck.*

Or it could be something.

He moved on again.

After another eight hundred metres the track veered off at a ninety-degree angle from the river before snaking through a long and narrow valley. Which Carter knew from the map shuttled north for twenty-five kilometres before merging with a main metalled road. To the left, a slender gully ran alongside the secondary road on lower ground. Carter hurried along at a fast walk, following the road as it hooked round the mountainside and then opened up into the valley leading north.

Then he saw the bikes.

Four of them.

Parked on an oval-shaped patch of dirt at the edge of a steep embankment.

Two Yamahas, a couple of old Suzukis.

No sign of the owners.

Carter dropped a hand to his holstered Grach and approached cautiously.

It didn't look like a suitable location for an ambush. Too exposed, no natural cover or dead ground. He paused beside one of the motorcycles. Inspected it. The keys were still jammed in the ignition. The kickstand was down.

Two metres away, half a dozen spent bullet casings glinted under the harsh rays of the sun.

Carter paced over to the edge of the embankment, cold dread sinking its claws into his bowels. The ground fell away sharply towards a clutter of stones and dwarf shrubs along the valley floor below. A drop of maybe four or five metres. Closer to the riverbank he spotted the shell of an abandoned farmhouse, a pair of run-down shacks. The withered trunk of a dying tree.

Carter dropped his gaze.

Looked directly below the embankment.

And saw the bodies.

Nineteen

The bodies were sprawled along the bottom of the embankment. Six of them, limbs contorted at unnatural angles. Streaks of blood trickled down the slope, which told Carter the victims had been shot at the side of the road and then dumped below. Their killers had made no attempt to properly cover their tracks. Hence the motorbikes, the spent casings, the blood splashes. Their only concern had been to clear the bodies from view, so that passing drivers wouldn't spot them.

Whoever did this, Carter thought, *they were in a hurry*.

Two of the corpses were dressed in army-style camo jackets. Carter recognised their faces from the compound. Mansur and Yellow Scarf. He hadn't seen the other four guys before, but he assumed they were the owners of the bikes. The mules lay a short distance further down from the embankment, blood pooling beneath them. Whoever had shot them had probably guided the mules down before discharging single shots to their heads. Less strenuous than dragging four hundred kilos of dead animal off the side of the road.

He couldn't see Vann among the dead. Or Hakimi.

Then he spied a seventh figure partially concealed behind a large rock a few paces from the rest of the bodies. A right leg poked out from behind the boulder. Wearing camo-patterned trousers. Carter watched from the top of the embankment for several moments, but the leg didn't move. Splashes of blood trailed from the embankment to the rock. A hell of a lot of it. Whoever was wedged behind there was either dead or badly wounded, Carter decided.

He tore the Grach free from his holster and edged down the embankment, putting in a dog-leg as he approached the boulder from an angle.

Flies buzzed around the dead bodies. The air was thick with the hot stink of blood, fused with the putrid odour of voided bowels. Carter shifted past the murdered bikers and circled slowly round the boulder. Pistol raised, eyes pinned to the target. He took another step to the right. He saw the face of the guy slumped against the rock, blood disgorging from the hole in his chest, and lowered the Grach.

Jabar Hakimi had been shot twice. Once in the chest, and a matching wound to the gut. His right hand was clamped to his belly in a futile bid to stem the bleeding. His fingers were wet with blood. The warlord was still alive, just. His breathing had reduced to a shallow rasp. His face was clammy and pale. The eyes had that fading-of-the-light look that Carter had seen before, on the faces of other dying men.

Hakimi had another thirty minutes to live, he guessed.

Maybe less.

Carter holstered the Grach and knelt beside the mortally wounded warlord. Hakimi looked up at him, eyes popped wide with shock but also fear. The grim knowledge that the lifeblood was rapidly seeping from his body.

He reached out to Carter with a limp hand, mouthing a word with his cracked lips. Carter leaned in closer, straining to make out the Afghan's hoarse voice. His chest wound made a wet sucking noise every time he took in a breath.

'Water,' Hakimi croaked. 'Water. Please . . .'

Carter retrieved the half-empty bottle of water from his pack. He twisted off the screwcap, pressed the mouth to the warlord's lips. Hakimi drank greedily, fluid spilling out of the corners of his mouth and dripping from his scarred chin, until he coughed and spluttered and could drink no more. Carter set the bottle down next to his pack. Waited for the man to stop hacking his guts up.

Then he said, 'What the fuck happened?'

Hakimi licked his lips. Swallowed hard. He spoke with a great effort. 'Vann,' he rasped.

'Vann did this?' Carter repeated.

'Him . . . and the others.'

A black rage clenched around Carter's heart. He had known in his guts that this was Vann's handiwork. The realisation had dawned on him as soon as it became clear that the Ulsterman had escaped the massacre. He started to ask Hakimi why, then cut himself short.

I already know the answer, Carter thought. *Vann double-crossed the Afghans. Led them into a trap.*

He's taken the entire stash for himself.

'What others?' he growled. 'Tell me.'

'We were supposed to meet . . . the Tajiks,' Hakimi replied between ragged intakes of breath. He grimaced as another wave of pain tore through his body. 'They were supposed to wait for us to arrive. That was . . . the plan.'

Hakimi took in another gulp of air. His breathing was becoming increasingly erratic. Carter waited for him to go on. He didn't need to threaten the guy to get him to spill his guts. Hakimi had been stitched up by his partner-in-crime. He'd want to talk. In a weird way, Carter and Hakimi now found themselves on the same side.

We've both been screwed over by Vann. That means we both want the same thing.

Revenge.

'Go on,' he said.

'They crossed us,' Hakimi continued hoarsely. 'Killed my men, and the Tajiks. Took . . . everything.'

'Who?' Carter demanded.

'Vann and his friends.'

'Friends?' Carter repeated.

'Americans.'

Carter reacted with a jolt. He felt as if someone had pressed a pair of defibrillator pads to his head and flipped the shock button.

'The Americans are in on this operation?'

Hakimi gave a weak nod.

'How many?'

'Three. I saw three of them. I don't know their names.'

He started to go on, then coughed violently. Carter gave him another mouthful of water. Hakimi took a moment to recover before he spoke again.

'We have been working with them for months.'

'The Americans?'

'Yes. We bring the heroin across the border. Give it to the Americans. They had brokered a deal with the Tajiks. A big deal.'

Carter listened, his mind reeling. Hakimi went on.

'This was supposed to be the last run. We were going to make the exchange here.'

'Exchange?'

'Yes. The Americans were waiting for us here. The Tajiks too. I didn't think . . .'

The warlord clenched his eyes shut. His body convulsed with agony.

'Keep talking,' Carter said. 'Tell me what happened.'

'We began to load the drugs onto the bikes . . . made the trade. Then the Americans opened fire.'

Carter looked up at the road. He imagined Vann, Hakimi and the other guys accompanying the mule train making their way towards the RV. The Tajiks waiting for them on the side of the road. The Americans beside them in another vehicle, waiting to make the deal. Heroin to the Tajiks in exchange for money. A fairly typical exchange. Nothing out of the ordinary. There would have been no worries among Hakimi and his men. They wouldn't have suspected a thing.

Not until it went noisy.

The Americans had rushed to transfer the bricks from the mules to their vehicles. They had dumped the bodies over the side of the road and raced away from the scene. One of them would have set up an OP somewhere to the east. At a lay-by, or similar. In another vehicle. They would have been tasked with keeping an eye on the approach road, looking out for any approaching military or police patrols. Hence the cigarette butt.

'Where are they now?' he asked.

'Gone,' Hakimi replied faintly. 'Gone . . . north. With the truck. To Talbarok.'

'What truck?'

'The one the Tajiks brought here.'

'Did Vann leave with the Americans?'

'Yes.'

'What the fuck is in Talbarok?'

'The facility,' Hakimi murmured. 'The facility is there.'

'What facility?'

The warlord didn't reply. The light in his eyes was starting to go out. His breathing had reduced to a soft whisper. He was slipping in and out of consciousness.

'Talbarok . . . the facility is in Talbarok,' he repeated senselessly. 'They're going to send everything out from there.'

Carter pressed him for an exact address, but the Afghan didn't appear to have heard him. He mumbled something unintelligible, eyes dancing in their sockets. He tried to say something else, but Carter couldn't quite catch the words. He leaned in closer.

'Your friend,' Hakimi murmured.

'What about him?'

Hakimi shivered. 'Shit. So cold . . .'

Carter frowned heavily. 'What the fuck is it? Tell me.'

The warlord didn't answer. His breathing had ceased. His mouth slackened, his eyes dulled, and then his body went limp. As if someone had unplugged him from the mains.

Carter stood up, his mind frantically racing to make sense of everything the Afghan had just told him. Vann's double-cross. The Americans. The facility in Talbarok.

The Americans were narco-traffickers, he presumed. Selling heroin to the Tajiks, according to Hakimi. But who were they? How did Vann know them? And what were they doing in Tajikistan in the first place? They were a long way from home.

He had a ton of fucking questions.

There's only one person who can tell me what's really going on.

David Vann.

He took out the map from his side pocket and conducted the world's fastest map study. Talbarok was approximately a hundred kilometres north-west of the roadhead, at the southern end of a long valley shaped like a wine bottle. There was an airfield fifteen kilometres north of the town. Carter was looking at a two-hour journey from the roadhead to Talbarok.

He rooted through Hakimi's jacket pockets, fished out a leather wallet stuffed with US twenty-dollar bills. Carter jammed the cash in his pocket, stepped back from Hakimi and left him as carrion for the birds. He didn't feel bad for the warlord and his dead mates. They were drug-dealing scum.

Less than twenty-four hours ago Hakimi had been standing over Sharza's dead body, grinning sadistically. Now he'd bled to death in the arse end of Tajikistan.

I guess karma is a fucking bitch.

First things first. Get out of the area. That was Carter's immediate priority. He needed to be well clear of the roadhead by the time the next mobile patrol showed up.

Then locate Vann.

He threw on his rucksack and hastened back up the embankment to the patch of dirt straddling the roadside. He walked back over to the nearest Yamaha trail bike. It looked old, but in reasonable condition. A solidly built piece of machinery. Not the most comfortable ride in the world, but perfect for navigating back roads and mountain terrain.

Carter unscrewed the cap on the fuel tank and peeked inside. He judged it about half full. Seven or eight litres of petrol. Equivalent to around 150 kilometres. Sufficient juice to get him all the way to

Talbarok. He replaced the cap, circled round to the side of the bike, swung a leg over the saddle and seated himself. He flipped up the kickstand, twisted the engine key and flicked on the run button.

Stamped his right foot on the kick-start lever.

A few moments later, Carter steered off the dirt track. He pointed the Yamaha down the secondary road, increasing his speed as he upshifted steadily through the gears. Soon he was racing north through the steep valley towards Talbarok.

Closing in on Vann.

And the truth.

Twenty

He arrived at Talbarok at eleven thirty in the morning. Carter approached from the main road to the south, staying well under the speed limit of sixty kilometres per hour so he didn't attract any unnecessary attention from the police. There was no sign welcoming him to Talbarok. The main road simply branched off into a wide thoroughfare surrounded by neatly gridded streets, bland apartment blocks and chaotic markets, set in a broad plain of cultivated fields and grasslands. In the distance, the snow-dusted peaks of the mountains crowded the horizon.

Carter breezed down the thoroughfare for half a kilometre, grateful to be back on level ground once more after the twisty, bone-jarring ride through the mountains. The town itself was the usual modest affair, a collection of grimy restaurants, drab cafés and worn-looking public buildings. The potholed roads looked like they hadn't been repaired since the Berlin Wall came down. Carter saw a lot of big statues of the president-for-life striking various heroic poses. The only investment the place had seen in years, as far as he could tell.

He made straight for the centre of town and stopped at the corner of a small square bordered on three sides by a row of garishly lit restaurants, discount shops and a 1970s-style hotel. A marble statue of the president dominated the middle of the square. Carter parked the Yamaha at the corner of the square and glanced round. He wondered why the Americans had chosen to base themselves in the boondocks. But then he remembered the airfield to the north.

They're going to send everything out from there, Hakimi had said.

So that's what Vann is doing, Carter thought. *The bastard is working with his American partners to fly out heroin in bulk.*

This was the only sizeable settlement close to the airstrip. From here Vann and the others could load up a private jet with the smack and send it on to its final destination. Their own distribution network. Eliminate the middleman. Cut up the product on arrival and quadruple their profits.

He marched briskly across the square towards the six-storey hotel. Carter had no concrete leads on where to find Vann. Hakimi had mentioned something about a facility, but he'd offered no further details. So Carter had to attack the problem from another direction.

Look for the three Americans. His business partners.

Find them, and you'll find Vann.

They would need a place to stay in Talbarok before and after the exchange with the Tajiks, Carter figured. They'd prioritise comfort over convenience, because in his experience Americans always did. They'd want a hotel with access to Wi-Fi, decent food, air conditioning, TV, coffee, a functioning shower. At a bare minimum.

In a place the size of Talbarok, there were usually three types of establishment. A budget lodging for itinerant adventurers and backpackers, a more expensive joint in the centre of the town, and a mid-range place located somewhere on the outskirts. The Americans definitely wouldn't choose the budget option. And Carter figured they'd want to be close to the action along the main thoroughfare. Walking distance to the local amenities. Therefore the central hotel was the logical option. That was where he'd start looking.

He swept through the entrance and beat a path across the lobby to the reception desk. A sharply dressed concierge greeted Carter with a polite smile. He listened keenly as Carter asked whether they had had any American guests lately. The guy shook his head and flashed his best apologetic smile.

The concierge was sorry, he said, but they had no American guests staying with them at the moment. Hadn't received any for a while, actually. The guy sounded disappointed. Only Germans. He suggested that Carter try the Ochus Hotel across town. He might have better luck there.

Carter remounted the Yamaha and jetted north, following the directions the concierge had given him. Six minutes later, he found the Ochus Hotel. A salmon-pink building on the northern fringes of the town. Four storeys high, with sugar-white balconies fronting the street and pedimented windows. In need of obvious repairs, but architecturally more pleasing than the brutalist structure in the town centre.

A guy with a unibrow stood behind the desk, wearing a bored expression as he idly worked the computer. The place looked more like a shrine than a functioning business. Another statue of the president dominated the middle of the lobby. Paintings of the Great Leader hung from the walls. Carter saw dozens of them.

At the sound of his approaching footsteps Unibrow looked up from his screen and straightened his back. Like a soldier snapping to attention. More photographs of the president hung from the wall behind him, Carter noticed, continuing the hero-worship theme.

He said, 'English? You speak English?'

Unibrow nodded. 'Yes, yes,' he said in a thick accent. 'You need a room?'

Carter shook his head. 'I'm looking for a friend of mine.'

'Yes?'

'I think he's supposed to be meeting a few other lads. Americans. Maybe they're staying here?'

Unibrow glanced away. 'I am sorry,' he said. 'I am not permitted to give out information on our guests. Company policy.'

Carter dipped a hand into his pocket and pulled out four twenty-dollar bills. He slapped them down on the counter and said, 'This might help jog your memory.'

The concierge glanced furtively left and right and discreetly slipped the notes into his jacket pocket with the practised ease of a veteran bribe taker. 'Now that you mention it, we do have some Americans here,' he said in a lowered voice.

'How many?'

'Three. They're on the third floor.' Unibrow paused, then said, 'You did not hear this from me, OK?'

Carter said, 'These Americans. What do they look like?'

The concierge flashed a puzzled look. 'Like Americans, you know? Like you, I guess. Same height. Two of them are big guys. Very big. Like wrestlers. Like on TV.'

'What about the third guy?'

'Older.' He shrugged. 'Not so big. Not a wrestler.'

'Have they had any guests?'

'No.'

'What about my friend?' He described Vann. 'Tough-looking bloke. Blue eyes, greying hair. Beard. Late forties. Northern Irish accent. Have you seen him around here?'

'No, I am afraid not.'

'What about your colleagues? My mate would have been passing through here an hour ago. Maybe one of the cleaners saw him.'

'Sorry.' Unibrow shook his head. 'I have been on duty since seven o'clock this morning. If your friend was here, I would have seen him. We have only the Americans.'

'Where are they now?' asked Carter.

'Upstairs.' The concierge darted a quick glance towards the lift, as if he was concerned that his guests might stroll out at any moment. 'In their rooms.'

'All of them?'

'Just the big guys. The older man, him I have not seen today.'

'How long have they been staying here?'

'Three days. They are due to check out tomorrow.'

'Did they say what they're doing in town?'

Unibrow shrugged. 'I didn't ask. I guessed they were tourists. We get many visitors here now. From all over. Talbarok is the birthplace of our president,' he said proudly. 'Many people come here to learn about his life. The president himself opened the museum last year, you know.'

Carter searched the guy's face closely. 'You haven't got a clue what they're doing here? Where they might be going? Nothing at all?'

'You ask a lot of questions.'

Carter took out two more twenties from the Jabar Hakimi Life Insurance payout. The concierge glanced again at the lift, then coughed and said, 'All I know is that the two men upstairs are going out this afternoon.'

'When?'

'Two o'clock.'

'You're sure?'

'Yes. They asked me to book a car to pick them up.'

Carter looked quickly at the clock on the wall next to the portraits of the Great Leader. Six minutes to twelve. A little over two hours until their ride was due to arrive.

'Where are they going?' he asked.

'They didn't say. They just asked for a driver to collect them.'

'You didn't ask?'

'It's none of my business,' the concierge replied. 'They wanted a car, no questions asked. I did my job. That's it.'

Carter slapped down another forty bucks. He said, 'This is to keep your mouth shut. Don't say a word to the Americans, or anyone else, about me. We never had this conversation, I was never here. Got it?'

'Of course. Have a good day, sir.'

Carter about-turned and strolled out of the lobby. He made for a grimy teahouse three doors down from the hotel and took an outside table with a clear line of sight to the hotel entrance, putting him within easy reach of his Yamaha. He stowed his rucksack between his legs, ordered a glass of green tea from the gap-toothed waiter and paid the bill in dollars. Then he settled down to watch the hotel.

Carter had an innate ability to close out the noise of his own mind. It had been drilled into him during the jungle phase of Selection and sharpened in the years he'd spent at Hereford. He could shut off the pain and tiredness in his body. Like dialling down the lights on a dimmer switch. Which is what he did now. He stared at the entrance, not moving a muscle as he concentrated all of his energies on the mission in front of him.

Carter was aware that he was winging it. He had no idea where the Americans were going or what their game was. *For all I know, they might be heading out for a nice kebab.*

But I doubt it.

This had all the hallmarks of a major drug deal. Carter could almost see it mapped out in front of him. The operation to bring the heroin out of Afghanistan using the smuggling route. The double-cross of their Tajikistani partners. The onward transfer of the product from the roadhead to a private facility in Talbarok. Then the escape on a cargo jet filled with top-quality heroin and cash.

The two Americans at the hotel were the grunts, Carter reckoned. *Big guys*, the concierge had said. *Very big. Like wrestlers.* Hired muscle, probably brought in as extra firepower for the double-cross at the roadhead.

Which made the third American the boss, with Vann as his 2iC. Vann and his associate wouldn't need the muscle to accompany them for the onward journey to the airfield, Carter decided. No need. They had already done their job.

The boss would have told them to wait at the hotel while they handled the flight arrangements. Probably with orders to report to the facility later that afternoon to collect their payments. The big Americans were probably sitting upstairs right now, talking excitedly about how they were going to spend their hard-earned money. Cocaine, women, champagne. The ultimate party.

At exactly two o'clock, a late-1990s Toyota Camry turned off the main road and pulled up in front of the hotel.

A minute passed.

Then the hotel doors yawned open, and two pasty-faced figures walked out into the glare of the afternoon sun.

They were obviously American. Ex-SF. Both of them had the look. Carter recognised it in the way they carried themselves. They were tightly coiled. Slow and heavy, but capable of snapping into violent action in an instant. They wore khaki combats, dark boots and polo T-shirts so tight they were practically shrink-wrapped around their bulging biceps. Both carried small rucksacks.

They're leaving, Carter thought. *They're going to collect their money. Endex.*

Carter was already out of his chair and snatching up his rucksack as the Americans folded themselves into the back of the Camry. He paced over to the Yamaha, mounted the saddle, kick-started the engine and took off in the same direction as the taxi, heading east on the main road. He held right back, keeping a safe distance of two hundred metres from the Camry as it continued east.

Traffic was light. Carter saw delivery trucks, trolley buses, battered taxis. A few locals buzzed around on Indian-manufactured bikes. Private car ownership wasn't really a thing in Tajikistan, seemingly.

He followed the taxi as it hung a left at a T-junction and rattled north for a couple of kilometres down a two-lane road lined with neon-lit fashion stores and American-style fast-food outlets. They passed a brightly painted bus terminal in a mainly residential area on the outskirts of town. Two minutes later, the Camry dropped its speed before it angled down a bumpy side street.

Carter took the same route, nudging the Yamaha past several derelict properties.

A hundred and fifty metres away, the taxi had stopped in front of a two-storey brick building, at the end of a dilapidated industrial estate.

Carter stopped beside a derelict garage. He cut the engine on the Yamaha, dropped the footstand and dumped his backpack on the ground. Across the road a kid in a replica Argentina football jersey was kicking a leather ball against a brick wall. Carter tucked himself into the shadows of the garage and carried out a recce of the stronghold. Making a visual assessment of the target. He didn't want to walk into another one of Vann's traps.

Most of the other units in the industrial estate looked vacant. There was an old steel shipping container to one side of the estate, a couple of rubbish dumpsters overflowing with flattened cardboard boxes. Pallets and wire mesh cages.

A steel roller shutter had been lowered down over the vehicle ramp at the front of the stronghold. There was a small door to the right of the shuttered opening, and a faded business sign on the front of the building printed in some sort of Cyrillic script. Carter spotted a security camera mounted to the wall above the side door. Fluorescent lights glowed through the windows.

This must be the facility, he realised with a hot thrill of anticipation.

Vann must be inside.

I've found him.

He could guess at the set-up. The American boss would be running a front business out of the unit. Electrical goods, or a laundry service. Something unlikely to arouse any curiosity among the locals. The Americans would have brought the heroin here directly from the roadhead, for safe storage before its onward transfer to the airfield. The cash profits from the deal would be washed through a series of offshore shell companies. Carter was looking at a highly sophisticated trafficking operation. Months of planning. Huge profits.

We've been working with them for months, Hakimi had said, right before the light had gone out in his eyes.

The taxi waited outside. Engine rumbling, fumes eddying out of the exhaust. The Americans clearly weren't planning on staying in the area for longer than necessary. A couple of minutes at most. They would be keen to collect their winnings and bug out. Get on a plane, crack open the bubbly and start celebrating.

Carter focused on the building. The security camera was the biggest obstacle to a frontal assault. As soon as he approached, the occupants would have eyes on him. Anyone inside might escape before he could breach the entrance. Or reach for a gun to defend themselves, depending on how confident they were feeling.

Which led to problem number two.

He was facing an unknown number of targets. Maybe even a trap.

I've got to find out what I'm up against here.

If I go in half-cocked, I could get my fucking head blown off.

Thirty seconds later, the Muscle Brothers stepped out of the side entrance. Both of them carried small daysacks in addition to their own rucksacks. Bundles of cash, no doubt. Their slice of the heroin profits. They were laughing as they strolled back over to the Camry. Like they'd hit the jackpot. They were looking forward to hitting the casinos and the strip joints. The party of a lifetime. Wild times. As long as you didn't have a problem with getting rich off human misery.

The lights were still on inside the building.

Carter shrank back from view as the Camry rolled past, crouching behind a stack of wooden pallets next to the garage. He waited until the vehicle had turned back onto the main road before he stood up from behind his cover. Then he walked over to the kid.

'You speak English?'

The boy trapped the football under his bare foot and eyed up Carter suspiciously. 'A little.'

Carter produced a twenty-dollar bill from the roll in his pocket. 'Want to make some money, lad?'

The kid's eyes widened. Carter pointed to the stronghold, indicating the adjacent yard. A two-metre-tall wire fence enclosed a patch of bare ditch littered with rubbish, metal trolleys and pallets.

'See that yard?' The kid nodded eagerly. 'I want you to go over there, kick your ball over the fence and ask for it back. Then tell me who's inside. Can you do that?'

'Why?'

Carter gave him a sharp look. 'Do you want the money or not?'

'OK.' The kid made a grab for the note. Carter snatched his hand away. The kid shook his head. 'Money first. Then I knock.'

Carter laughed. 'I might be a foreigner, but I ain't stupid. Knock, then money.'

'OK. You wait here.'

The kid scooped up his football. A moment later, he was running off in the direction of the industrial park. He stopped just short of the yard to the right of the unit, picked up his ball and hurled it over the top of galvanised steel fence. It landed with a thud amid the clutter of garbage, bouncing on the dirt before it rolled to a halt beside a wheelie bin.

Carter quickly shifted back into the shadows of the garage. He crouched down behind the pallets, looking on from his concealed position as the kid jogged round to the front of the unit.

He felt a twinge of unease at sending in the kid to unwittingly clear the entry point. Carter knew there was a slim chance that the Muscle Brothers might have been the last to leave the building. Maybe they had rigged it up with explosives and deliberately left the lights on, ready to detonate if anyone else approached. Or someone might come out with a gun before Carter could breach the stronghold.

The kid knuckled the wooden side door.

Several moments passed.

No one answered.

The kid knocked again.

Same result.

The kid stood back. Scratched his head. For an instant Carter thought he might turn around and give up.

Then the door snicked open. Carter breathed a sigh of relief.

No booby trap.

From his vantage point 150 metres away, Carter saw a figure standing in the gloom of the doorway.

Vann.

He stared at the kid while the latter made a pleading gesture, pointing at the yard. Vann didn't seem moved. A man with bigger concerns weighing on his shoulders than a kid's football on his property. He said something to the boy, slammed the door shut behind him. The kid waited. Thirty seconds later, the door opened again. Vann handed him the ball.

The door closed.

The boy jogged back over to the garage, carrying the ball under his arm. Carter moved forward from the pallets and nodded at him. 'What's the craic, lad?'

'There is only one man inside,' the boy replied, slightly out of breath. 'He looks like you.'

'Like me?'

The boy laughed and pointed at Carter's face. 'White. But older.'

'You didn't see anyone else inside?'

'No. Just the white man and the truck.'

'A truck?' Carter frowned.

'Yes.' The kid spread his arms bear-hug wide. 'Big truck. Like this.'

Carter pressed the crisp twenty into the kid's palm. The boy clenched his fist tightly around it. Carter waved a hand in the direction of the main thoroughfare and said, 'Do me a favour. Go and get yourself a new ball or something. Get out of the area.'

'Why?'

'Just do it.'

The kid flashed a toothy grin and scampered back down the street. Carter lingered in the shadows of the building until the kid had hurried off in the direction of the main road. He shoved the rucksack behind a pile of rubble outside the garage and cast another look up and down the road, making sure he was alone before he deholstered the Grach semi-automatic concealed beneath his shirt.

He thumbed the safety on the left side of the polymer frame, keeping the pistol down at his side as he broke forward across the estate. He could feel the weight of the full clip in the Grach. Eighteen rounds of 9 x 19 mm ammunition. Ready to drop anyone who might be lurking inside the stronghold.

Carter reached the nearest unit and then increased his stride, hustling towards the stronghold from an angle to avoid being captured by the security camera. He didn't want his face showing up on anyone's monitor, not until the last possible moment.

In another six quick steps he made it to the side door leading into the stronghold. It looked sturdy. There were signs fixed to it at head height, with lots of warning symbols. Carter didn't understand the words, but he didn't need to. He got the gist of the message.

Do not enter. Trespassers beware.

Too fucking right, he thought.

He backed up a metre, giving himself space to generate plenty of momentum. He paused momentarily.

Raised his left leg.

Kicked out.

There was a sharp splintering crack as Carter drove the heel of his Gore-Tex boot at a point to the left of the scuffed handle, striking the door at its weakest part and breaking up the internal locking mechanism. The door flew back on its hinges, slapping against the internal wall.

Carter brought up his pistol.

Then he charged inside.

Twenty-One

Carter ghosted through the doorway in a blur of motion. Room clearance. Something he had done tens of thousands of times before. On the ranges at Pontrilas, on raids in Afghanistan and a bunch of other places. Breach the entry point, move forward with speed and controlled aggression. Suppress the threat on the other side of the door. Just like he'd taught the SF recruits back in Santiago.

Except this time, the target was a fellow Blade.

He swung his pistol from left to right as he moved deeper into the unit, instantly sweeping the area for threats. He found himself in a dimly lit space, ten metres wide and about twenty deep, all exposed brickwork and grey resin flooring. Fluorescent batten lights dangled from the steel rafters. Carter saw a small office cubicle built into the wall to his left, kitchenette and ablutions to the rear. A white box truck in the middle of the floor space, front cab facing the lowered roller shutter.

There was a metal workbench to the right of the truck, with a clutter of charging cables, burner phones and computer equipment laid out on the surface. Black duffel bags, three of them. Unzipped. Bricks of black tar stuffed inside. And weaponry. Carter saw a ton of hardware. Glock pistols. A Dragunov sniper rifle. AK-47 assault rifles. What looked like a GM-94 Russian grenade launcher, plus ammunition pouches filled with 43 x 30 mm thermobaric projectiles.

Vann was standing next to the workbench.

Hands at his sides. Unarmed.

Smiling.

'Hello, Geordie,' he said. 'What took you so long?'

Carter stopped dead. The gun wavered in his hand. Vann laughed and wagged a finger at him. He had changed out of his Afghan rig into regular civvies.

'You should have stayed out of this, fella,' Vann went on. 'Should have walked away when you had the chance.'

He was still smiling. A hollow sensation spread its fingers through Carter's core. Something was wrong, he knew.

Very wrong.

'Too late now, of course,' Vann added. 'Fucking shame, that. But then you never were very good at taking advice, were you, Geordie?'

Carter felt an intense pressure building between his temples. He kept his pistol trained on Vann's centre mass. The smirk on the guy's face widened. He didn't look surprised to see Carter. The opposite, in fact.

Like he'd expected Carter to come crashing through the door at that precise moment.

'Put the gun down, son,' a voice drawled.

It came from Carter's nine o'clock.

A voice he'd heard somewhere before.

American.

Carter looked past his shoulder.

A silver-haired man with a heavily lined face and pale blue eyes stood in front of the cubicle doorway. He was dressed in a black T-shirt, stone-grey trousers and dark hiking boots, and he gripped a Glock 17 pistol in his right hand.

The dark mouth of the barrel aimed squarely at Carter. Trained at a spot between his eyes.

Carter felt his guts turn to ice.

Bill Ramsey grinned and said, 'Hell, son. You ought to see the look on your face right now. Frigging priceless.'

Carter stared at the ex-CIA director speechlessly. The pressure between his temples became steadily more intense. Invisible vice jaws clamped around his skull.

Bill Ramsey.

The man who had presented Carter with the Medal of Honor several months ago. The president's most trusted confidant.

What the fuck is he doing here?

'I won't ask you a third time,' Ramsey said in his languid Southern accent. 'Lose the piece. Do it nice and slow.'

'Do as he says, Geordie,' said Vann. 'Don't be a fucking idiot.'

Carter ground his teeth in anger. He hated to admit it, but Vann was right. Two against one. Shite odds. Vann was less than arm's length from the hardware laid out on the workbench. Carter could take down one of them, but not both.

The moment I open fire, I'm a dead man.

Very slowly, Carter lowered himself to a kneeling position and placed the Grach on the floor. Bill Ramsey's knife-edge-thin lips parted into a smile.

'Attaboy.'

He kept the Glock fixed on Carter while Vann stepped forward and picked up the Grach. The Ulsterman straightened up and set the weapon down on the workbench, out of Carter's reach.

'What the fuck's going on?' Carter said, flicking his gaze from Ramsey to Vann and back again.

Vann sidestepped the question and said, 'I tried to keep you out of all this. Remember that. I gave you the chance to fuck off back home, and you didn't take it. None of this is my fault.'

Carter shook his head. He tried to think clearly. To make sense of the situation. Couldn't. All the wiring in his brain had been scrambled.

'What the fuck is he doing here?' he demanded, indicating Ramsey.

Vann said, 'Bill is my business partner, fella. We've been working together for a while now.'

Carter stared disbelievingly at the former CIA man.

'Got to hand it to you,' Ramsey droned on. 'You're one stubborn son of a bitch. When I got the call to say you were approaching this place, hell, I almost spat out my coffee.' He glanced at Vann and grinned. 'Guess you were right. Your friend hasn't got the good sense to know when to quit.'

The words floored Carter. 'You've been tracking me?'

'Every step of the way.' Ramsey laughed and dipped the Glock 17, pointing the barrel at Carter's side pocket. 'The satphone. In case you're wondering how we did it. There's a tracking device in the battery pack. We've had eyes on you since you landed in Uzbekistan.'

The realisation didn't dawn on Carter. It punched him in the face. He thought back to the briefing. Santiago. Chile. Only a few days ago, but it felt like it predated the Big Bang. He remembered Mike Mullins's serious expression as he handed Carter the satphone.

Whatever happens, do not lose this phone.

He said, anxiously, 'Mullins. He set me up.'

Ramsey nodded. 'Mike tipped us off that Langley was sending someone out on a search mission. I asked him to plant a bug on the satphone. A precautionary measure. Just in case you managed to locate David. But we didn't think you'd get very far. Not this far, certainly.'

'Jesus,' Carter said. 'Jesus Christ.'

Vann gave a snarl of contempt. 'Get over it, you daft cunt. That tracker helped to save your life.'

'What the fuck do you mean?'

'Mullins told me about your movements,' Vann explained. 'Gave me time to replace that landmine on the trail with the light bulb. If it wasn't for me, you would have been blown to bits.'

Several things fell into place. 'That's why you took out the landmine? Because you knew I was coming?'

'If it was anyone else, I wouldn't have bothered,' Vann said. 'But I didn't want to see you get hurt. That's why I did it. I saved you, mate.'

'Bullshit.' Rage flamed inside Carter's chest, burning the back of his throat. 'You left us for dead back there. Them Afghans could have wiped out the lot of us.'

Vann laughed. 'I seriously fucking doubt it. I helped train you, didn't I? I've seen you in action. I knew you wouldn't have any problems dealing with a few poor-quality Taliban.'

'Of course, we hoped that David would lose you in the mountains,' Ramsey cut in. 'That would have been better for all concerned. We could have avoided all of this unpleasantness.'

Something didn't make sense to Carter. He turned to Ramsey. 'Why would you get involved in trafficking gear? You used to run the CIA, for Chrissakes. You can't be short of a few quid.'

Ramsey looked over at Vann. The two of them shared a look and promptly erupted in fits of hysterical laughter. Carter glared angrily at them.

'This isn't about the money,' Ramsey said. 'You couldn't be more wrong about that, son.'

Carter snorted his contempt. 'Fuck off. You've been selling smack to the Tajiks. Then you decided to rip them off. Take the drugs and the money for yourselves. Hakimi told me everything. He spilled his guts, right before he bled out.'

'Half right. We've got an arrangement with the Tajiks. Or at least, we did. But not for money.'

Ramsey smiled. There was a gloating look in his eyes that unnerved Carter.

'We were trading it for something else,' he added. 'Something much more valuable, in fact.'

Carter looked askance at Vann. 'What the fuck is he talking about?'

'See for yourself,' Ramsey said.

He indicated the back of the truck with his Glock. An amused expression crossed his smooth features.

'Go on, boy. Take a look. Then you'll understand.'

Carter moved warily round to the rear of the wagon. The back door had been rolled up, he noticed. Five army-green trunks had been loaded into the cargo space, each one housing a waterproof metal container about the size and shape of a beer keg, sheathed in a protective carry case. An Alice frame had been securely fastened to each pack, complete with shoulder straps and back pads for easy transportation.

Ramsey was grinning with excitement. 'You know what these are, right?'

Carter felt a chill crawl down his spine.

He had seen similar models to the containers in front of him. SADMs. Special Atomic Demolition Munitions. Otherwise known as backpack nukes. Portable weapons, developed by the US military at the height of the Cold War and designed to be carried to the target location on the back of a parachutist or infantryman. They could even be detonated underwater to destroy enemy shipping facilities.

Each metal casing housed a small nuclear warhead, Carter knew. A one-kiloton yield. Equivalent to a thousand tons of TNT. Small in comparison to the strategic nukes, but still powerful enough to destroy a football stadium-sized area.

He was looking at the Russian equivalent to the SADM. There were subtle differences in the design and function, but essentially the same destructive capacity.

Tens of thousands of deaths per bomb.

Whole sections of a city annihilated.

'Beautiful, aren't they?' said Ramsey. 'Kind of poetic, in a way.'

'Jesus,' Carter said.

'Three tonnes of heroin,' said Ramsey. 'In exchange for five backpack nukes. That was the price the Tajiks set.'

Carter rounded on the two men. 'You got these from the Tajiks?'

'They have a guy in Moscow,' Vann said. 'Very well connected. He was supplying the bombs.'

Ramsey said, 'The Russians lost a bunch of these things when the Soviet Union collapsed. Ninety-seven, according to the intelligence reports, although the true figure is probably much higher. A few of them eventually turned up in some weird places. One oligarch kept a backpack on display in his dacha in St Petersburg. Another guy had been storing one in his leaking basement. Said he'd kept it as a memento. But most of them were never found.

'The Tajik came into possession of these units eight months ago. Don't ask me how. Our guy reached out to his associates. Told them to put the feelers out. See if any parties might be interested in a sale. Terrorist groups, the Taliban. That's how we heard about the hardware. The Tajik gangsters handled the negotiations. It was a swift deal. Nukes are a buyer's market. The Tajiks asked for fifty per cent of the product as a down payment, the other fifty on successful delivery. We completed the exchange at the road-head this morning. A beautiful moment. You should have been there to see it.'

'I saw enough,' Carter snarled. 'I saw them bodies.'

'It had to be done. The Tajiks, Hakimi. Those guys knew too much. Leaving them to walk away free? Hell, that was a risk we couldn't take. You see where I'm coming from. Right?'

Carter stared at the American and tried to assemble the fragmented thoughts in his head.

Heroin for nukes. The straight swap made sense. It avoided the problem of cash. The number-one obstacle for anyone involved in the drug business. Smuggling gear into a country was a relatively risk-free undertaking. The big issue was getting the money out again. Money always left a trail. Everything had to be rinsed clean. Which took a lot of time and effort and expense. By insisting on a direct trade, both parties avoided the hassle of dealing with hard currency.

'This is what you've been doing in-country all this time?' he asked Vann. 'Smuggling gear so you could buy nukes?'

'It didn't start out that way,' Vann replied. 'I was originally sent in to train the rebels.' He cocked his head at Ramsey. 'Bill was working the other end of the operation.'

'The National Alliance needed weaponry,' Ramsey explained. 'They were up against a serious military force, ably supported by Pakistan and China. It was clear they'd need more than a few AK-47s to have any chance of success. My job was to supply the hardware. David would train the rebels. Show them how to work it. RPGs, small arms and so on. And Stingers.'

Carter's eyebrows lifted in surprise and puzzlement. FIM-92 Stingers were easily transportable surface-to-air missile launchers. In the right hands, you could bring down almost anything with them. Choppers, aircraft, drones.

For a brief moment he wondered why the Afghan rebels needed anti-aircraft weapon systems. But then he recalled what Mullins and Ortega had told him about the fleet of Black Hawk helicopters. Spoils of war, they had said. Seized by the Taliban in the wake of the withdrawal from Afghanistan.

He thought about the Chinese-supplied drones.

The support from Russia.

Ramsey said, 'The initial plan was to target the Taliban by providing limited assistance to the rebels. That was Langley's idea. A small-scale insurgency. Minimum risk. But a few of us were pushing to widen the net.'

'Meaning?'

'We wanted to go after Chinese targets inside Afghanistan. Civilian aircraft, ferrying engineers and geologists to and from the mining sites, the factories. We argued that disrupting Beijing's operations was the best way to destabilise the Taliban. Force the Chinese to pull out. Isolate the regime in Kabul. Deprive them of allies.'

Carter remembered something Sharza had told him.

The Chinese are opening mines now.

They want the Taliban to guarantee the safety of their workers.

'What did Langley say?' he asked.

He wanted to keep Ramsey talking, letting the American warm to his theme. Buying himself time to figure out an escape plan.

Somehow I've got to get the fuck out of here.

'The Company vetoed the plan.' Ramsey sniffed. 'POTUS himself weighed in on it. Told them not to do anything that would piss off Beijing. Around this time, the CCP had started making noises about recapturing Taiwan by force. The president dismissed it as more of the same old sabre-rattling bullshit from Zhongnanhai. But I read the intelligence reports. I could see that the Chinese president was determined to go the distance this time. Full-scale amphibious assault. The biggest in history. A million men. It'd make the Normandy landings look like a beach party. That's when we decided to pursue a different strategy.'

Ramsey was bragging now, eyes shining with feverish intent. Carter swallowed nervously. He knew there was only one possible reason why Ramsey would be telling him this stuff. But his mind really didn't want to go there.

Ramsey went on. 'We knew the Taiwanese wouldn't be able to withstand an all-out invasion. Support from our side would be strictly limited in the interests of avoiding a full-blown nuclear confrontation. Sure, we might threaten the Beijing elite with sanctions, but that would be the extent of it. So we figured we needed a new type of deterrence. The kind that would make them think twice before they messed with anyone again.'

He gave a chilling smile. Carter felt a quivering in his chest.

Ramsey said, 'There's a private jet coming in today. Landing at the airfield north of here. Wheels up in sixty minutes. The nukes are being transported to Taiwan. We've got friends on the ground over there. People we can trust. Folk who are determined to resist the Chinese menace at all costs, even if it means sacrificing their own lives.'

Carter didn't want to ask the question. But he asked it anyway. He had to know for absolutely sure.

'What are you going to do with them?'

'We'll deploy the nukes at pre-designated sites around the country before the Chinese invasion,' Ramsey said. 'At strategic airheads and harbours. Any forward operating base the Chinese are planning to establish. When the attacking forces land, we'll detonate them remotely. Right in the path of the enemy. And, by God, teach them a lesson they won't live long enough to forget.'

Twenty-Two

For several seconds Carter couldn't speak. He struggled to breathe. Felt as if someone had been piling stone slabs on his chest. The throbbing between his temples returned with a vengeance.

'You can't,' he said at last. 'You bloody can't. Christ, you're talking about setting off nukes on a densely populated island. It's fucking madness.'

Even as the words left his mouth, Carter could hardly believe it was true. Then he saw the arrogant expression in Ramsey's eyes, and he knew the American was deadly serious.

Ramsey said, 'I'll tell you what's madness. Doing nothing while our enemies in the East gain strength. And don't give me any of that crap about sanctions and aid packages. We both know that's nonsense. Political virtue-signalling. Gestures of support without having to commit serious manpower. Shine the colours of a country's flag on the wall of a public building, add an icon to your social media profile. Tell your followers you stand with the people of Ukraine against tyranny. You can't manufacture victory out of a meme.

'We've been weak for too long,' Ramsey continued. 'We squandered the peace dividend at the end of the Cold War. We indulged ourselves, contributed to our own our moral and spiritual decline, while all the time our enemies grew stronger. You have no idea how much time I spent arguing that we needed to prepare for the next great war, that the Chinese needed to be destroyed. That Armageddon was coming. But nobody wanted to know. Heads in the damn sand. All the pointy heads knew best. Thought we were invincible. Now China smells weakness. They believe we're afraid, you see. They think we don't want to go down into the trenches. Well, some of us are ready for the fight. We're ready to make a stand. To do what must be done.'

Carter fought to ignore the growing pressure in his ears. He was dazed. Disorientated. 'Does the Company know about this? Six?'

Ramsey chuckled. 'Take a wild guess.'

'But you must have had help. Something this big.'

'There are people sympathetic to our point of view,' Ramsey conceded. 'People inside the Establishment who have grown tired of pretending to look the other way instead of countering Chinese aggression. True believers.'

'People like Mullins, you mean.'

'He's one of them. There are others, too. In the Pentagon and elsewhere. Decent God-fearing men and women who understand what is at stake.' He gave a lopsided smile. 'We're something of an endangered species these days. But you probably know all about that, being a soldier.'

Carter was still stalling for time. He couldn't see any way out of his predicament. Ramsey had the Glock 17 aimed at him. Vann stood another metre away, a similar-looking pistol tucked into a holster clipped to his belt. There was another door to the rear of the unit, ten metres back from the box truck. Carter briefly considered knocking down Ramsey and making a run for it. But no. He'd never reach the door in time. Vann would drop him long before he could make his escape.

'What makes you think the Chinese will even invade?' he challenged. 'It could be another bluff.'

'Like Ukraine, you mean?' Ramsey snorted derisively. 'The Russia analysts kept telling us that the Kremlin wasn't serious about invading their neighbours. The cost would be too great, they said. It would be economic and political suicide. Then they went ahead and did it anyway. Yesterday the experts were right. Today they're wrong. We're living in a new world, son. The old rules don't apply anymore. All bets are off.'

'We wouldn't let them take Taiwan,' Carter insisted. 'There'd be a global backlash. We'd have to act.'

Ramsey shook his head. 'I know the president. Better than pretty much anyone, in fact. He's a callous sonofabitch. Nothing like the decent family-man image he projected on the campaign trail. The Russians could drop a tactical nuke on Latvia or Estonia, hell, even Germany, and our guy wouldn't lift a goddamn finger. Believe me, when the bombs start falling on Taipei, he won't dare respond militarily. So it's down to us.

'If we can inflict fifty per cent casualties on the Chinese forces, it would spell the end for the invasion. Not even the Communist Party could absorb losses that big. Troops would be withdrawn. The Chinese president would have to resign. The next leader would be anxious not to repeat the same mistake as their predecessors. We'd tame Beijing for a generation, maybe longer.'

Carter looked at him in dismay. 'You're talking about killing hundreds of thousands of people.'

'This is the only way to win. This is about nothing less than the survival of the Christian world.'

Bloody hell, Carter thought. *This guy is starting to sound like a TV evangelist.*

'God spoke to me, you know,' Ramsey carried on, softly. 'He came to me in a vision. Told me that this was the great mission of my life. I had been chosen, He said. To stop the menace from the East from destroying our way of life.'

He spoke in an eerily calm voice. Detached. Carter listened in dismay as he continued.

'It's right there in the Bible, you know. Book of Revelations. You should read it. China is the Devil incarnate. God has chosen a few of us as His righteous soldiers, to prevent the forces of evil from being unleashed on our land. This right here,' he added, waving his gun at the nukes. 'This is the wrath of the Lord.'

His face was a picture of serenity. The guy was fucking insane, Carter realised. *He really thinks the big bloke upstairs is telling him to detonate a load of bombs for the greater good.*

Ramsey was so wrapped up in his own twisted orthodoxy Carter knew he didn't stand a chance of getting through to him. He switched his appeal to Vann.

'This is murder, Dave. Mass murder.'

Vann shrugged. 'It is what it is, mate.'

'Are you telling me you're happy to go along with this shite?'

'It's China,' Vann said. 'Totalitarian dictatorship. Frankly I couldn't give a toss what happens over there. Makes no difference to me.'

'Then why are you working with Ramsey?'

'Money, Geordie. Plain and simple. Bill offered me top dollar to help out with the smuggling side of the operation. Two million, plus half the heroin stash to flog once we get out of here.'

Carter swivelled his eyes back to Ramsey. 'You're getting paid for this?'

'Of course. An operation as big as this requires substantial investment.' He smiled again. 'Thankfully, our friends back home have been generous. Very generous indeed. They understand that we're fighting a war against the enemies of Christ.'

Ramsey glanced at his watch. The guy was beginning to lose interest. Which was bad news, Carter realised. He was running out of time.

'What about the other two lads? The ones I saw leaving this place just now? Are they in on it as well?'

Ramsey shook his head. 'They're ex-Delta. Door-kickers. Hired guns, brought in for a specific operation. They're in the dark. Me and David, we're the ones calling the shots.'

Carter looked towards his old mucker. 'You can't do this. This isn't right. Surely you can see that?'

Which drew a throated laugh from Vann.

'I was shat on by the Regiment, Geordie. I'm a long way past giving a toss about right and wrong.'

Carter tried again. 'Two million dollars won't be any good to you. Not if you've got to spend the rest of your life on the run.'

'It won't come to that,' Ramsey interjected. 'We've covered our tracks. No fingerprints. No one will link the nukes to us.'

Carter shook his head fiercely. 'You can't trust this bloke,' he said to Vann. 'He's already double-crossed the Tajiks. What makes you think he won't do the same to you?'

'I'll take my chances,' Vann replied flatly. 'Bill and his mates have promised to take care of me. An appointment with one of the big arms manufacturers. Good money. Big house somewhere in the country. A lot better than seeing out my days in Hereford, waiting for the phone to ring. That's for fucking sure.'

Ramsey cleared his throat and said, irritably, 'We've wasted enough time. Let's wrap things up. We're in the air in fifty minutes.' He nodded at Vann. 'Kill him.'

Vann did a double take. 'Wait. Who said anything about slotting him?'

'He's your problem,' Ramsey replied. 'You failed to take care of him before, across the border. This is your mess. Time to clear it up.'

Carter felt the blood draining from his head to his feet.

'Don't,' he said. 'Jesus, Dave. Don't do it.'

There was the slightest flicker of hesitation in Vann's expression. A struggle played out on his face. Inner torment. Caught between his loyalty to an old Blade and his orders. He turned to Ramsey.

'We could tie him up instead. Slap a pair of plasticuffs on him and dump him in the office. We'll be in the air long before anyone rescues him. Less messy.'

Ramsey said, 'Can't do it. This asshole could cause a lot of trouble for us down the line. For you as well. Sorry, son, but he needs to die. That's just the way it is.'

Vann still hesitated.

'Don't do this, mate,' Carter pleaded. 'For fuck's sake, we're both Regiment.'

Vann's face hardened. A cold look clouded his faded eyes. 'I fucking told you, Geordie. I told you to stay away, didn't I? But you didn't listen.'

He sounded like a guy trying to silence the voices raging in his head. Tamping down the doubts.

'Get on with it, man,' Ramsey ranted impatiently. 'Drop him. Don't you want to get paid?'

Vann still hesitated.

Carter stood rooted to the spot, the breath freezing in his veins.

He was out of options. No escape.

Then he heard the throated roar of a car engine.

Twenty-Three

The growl came from Carter's six o'clock. From somewhere beyond the front of the industrial unit. What sounded like a pack of approaching racing cars. Carter heard at least two of them. Getting louder as they cannoned towards the stronghold. Followed in the next moment by the scream of car tyres skidding across the asphalt, vehicles jerking to a halt. The thud of car doors slamming shut. Voices shouting at one another.

The temperature in the room went sub-zero.

Vann glanced over at the workbench. The laptop screen. Carter looked in the same direction. So did Ramsey. The main window displayed a live video feed in high-res colour. Carter recognised the scene at once. The front of the estate.

Two black Mercedes-Benz G-Wagons had stopped outside the stronghold, 63 AMGs. Chrome-edged SUVs with side exhaust pipes and wheels big enough to fit a monster truck. They were maybe seventy metres from the entrance. Figures were pouring out of the sides of both wagons.

Eight of them.

All armed with AK-47s.

On the screen, five of the gunmen peeled off from the main group and started scurrying down the side of the building. Moving round to the rear.

'The Tajiks,' hissed Ramsey. 'Shit. They're on to us.'

Vann shook his head in disbelief. 'Not fucking possible. They don't know about this place. They've never been here before.'

Ramsey shot him an accusing look. His face was white with rage. 'They must have followed your man here. This is all your fault, you fool.'

Vann glared darkly at him. Then he nodded at Carter. 'Geordie, use the GM-94. Take them fuckers coming round the back. We'll deal with the three guys at the front. Move.'

There was no time to lose. No time to think.

Carter knew he had no choice but to fight with Vann and Ramsey. The Tajiks were unlikely to distinguish between Carter and his two captors. They had rocked up for one purpose. To avenge their murdered friends.

If they overrun this place, they won't spare me.

Fight, or die.

Vann was already springing into action as the words left his mouth. He raced over to the workbench. Chucked one of the AK-47s at Ramsey and grabbed a second rifle for himself. Then they sprinted off towards the windows either side of the lowered roller shutter.

At the same time Carter snatched up the Russian grenade launcher, plus a pouch of three 43 x 30 mm thermobaric rounds. Otherwise known as the lung-suckers. Principally designed for use in room-to-room combat, because the rounds produced almost no fragmentation. They packed enough of a punch to shred a lightly armoured vehicle, by generating extreme levels of heat and overpressure. The resulting explosion consumed all the oxygen in the air, creating a deadly vacuum that could suck a person's lungs out or rupture their vitals.

Carter picked up his Grach, jammed it into his pancake holster, then dashed across the unit towards the door at the rear. Behind him, the thunderlike crack of gunfire split the air as Vann and Ramsey started firing through the windows at the three gangsters attacking the front of the stronghold. The glass panes exploded in a torrent of broken shards. At once the enemy started returning fire. Bullets whipped through the openings, striking against the front cab of the truck and slapping into the brickwork, chewing up the mortar.

One round struck the fire extinguisher bracketed to the rear wall. A cloud of white hissed out of the pressurised container in a furious spray, coating the wall in foam. Carter hurried past it, hit the back door and wrenched it open. The door opened out to an asphalt yard about half the size of a basketball court, enclosed on three sides by larger warehouse buildings. There was a skip piled high with debris at his two o'clock, fourteen metres away. A forklift truck next to a stack of pallets at his twelve.

Carter dropped to a kneeling firing position half in, half out of the doorway. Using the frame to protect himself from any enemy incoming. He dumped the ammo pouch beside the door frame and worked quickly to load the GM-94. He'd used the grenade launcher a few times before on the ranges at Pontrilas. Foreign weapon familiarisation. An important part of every Regiment man's tool kit. The ability to pick up almost any weapon and know how to operate it without wasting valuable time.

He prised open the top cover on the mag tube and took out a round from the ammo pouch. Slipped the grenade into the tube situated above the pump-action barrel. Closed the cover again. Flipped up the aiming sights. Pulled back the slider and shunted it forward.

Carter trained the weapon at the corner of the building to his right. In the same breath, three mobsters surged into view.

Two of the guys were running ahead of their mate. A short pot-bellied bloke in a black-and-green tracksuit, and a shaven-headed guy dressed in a pair of acid-wash jeans and a shiny blue shirt. A third Tajik in a grey hoodie lagged a couple of metres behind the 1980s tribute act. All three of them were aiming their AK-47s at the doorway as they scurried forward across the exposed ground.

A moment later, their muzzles flamed.

Bullets zipped through the air, whizzing several inches above Carter. The door frame behind him erupted in a shower of splinters. Other rounds smacked into the wall, spitting out clouds of hot dust. Carter held his nerve. He didn't panic. The key to winning a firefight.

Any idiot can fire a gun from behind cover. But at some point, if you want to kill the other guy, you're going to have to expose yourself. In that situation, the person who wins is the one who has the balls to stay calm and take a well-aimed shot.

Carter made a millisecond assessment of his opponents. His soldier's eyes quantum-processing their gaits, their firing stances, their tactical awareness. He could see that these guys were badly trained. They were running straight towards him, pissing bullets, spraying from the hip, not even bothering to aim at Carter. Hoping for a successful outcome in that situation was like a football player taking a penalty kick blindfolded. The odds of Carter getting clipped by these amateurs were a million to one.

Tracksuit and Acid Wash were twelve metres from him now. Hoodie was maybe a metre behind, closing the distance on his friends. Combat FOMO. He was desperate to join in the killing.

A couple of metres behind him, the other two gangsters had come tearing round the corner. One man wore a leather biker jacket; his mate was sporting a black beanie and a shiny puffer coat.

Carter calmly aimed the GM-94 up at an angle. He steadied his breathing. Lined up the launcher sights with the three nearest mobsters barrelling towards him. He wasn't worried about firing the weapon at such short range. You could pop a thermobaric grenade at a target ten metres away without risk of injury.

In the next second, he squeezed the trigger.

The GM-94 had a hell of a kick on it. Carter felt the recoil shuddering through his body as the round popped out of the barrel. There was a stunning flash as the grenade struck the ground two inches to the side of the skip. An ear-shattering bang ripped through the air. Smoke gushed into the afternoon sky.

The three mobsters were shredded. The destructive power of a thermobaric round in action. You didn't need to hit the target. Stick it anywhere in the three-metre kill radius, and the pressure wave and the vacuum would take care of the rest.

Three enemies down.

Two to go.

The first bang got the attention of the two gangsters to the rear of the dead guys. Carter glimpsed them in his peripheral vision, breaking across the open ground, running for cover behind the forklift at his twelve o'clock. Their survival instincts had taken over. No one wanted to be on exposed ground when they were on the receiving end of a grenade launcher. Getting behind something solid was suddenly their top priority in life.

Carter fetched another grenade from the pouch and slid it into the tube. More bullets spattered the door frame around him as the two guys behind the forklift popped up from cover and opened fire. Two rounds thudded into the door frame no more than six inches to Carter's right. He felt the whoosh of hot air as another bullet zipped overhead. The gangsters couldn't aim for shit. Carter felt like they could have shot at him all day without hitting the target.

He aimed at the forklift.

Lobbed another grenade.

The gangsters made no attempt to relocate. They had four thousand kilograms of metal separating them from the soldier in the doorway. They felt they were safe.

They were wrong.

The round struck the forklift side-on. The two mobsters hunkered down behind it let out demented screams of agony. The guy in the puffer coat staggered away from the kill zone, blood streaming out of his ears and eyes. Mouth hanging open in unspeakable agony.

Carter ditched the grenade launcher and tore his Grach pistol free from his holster as he rushed forward to finish the job. Puffer had sunk to his hands and knees on the ground a couple of metres from the forklift, coughing up a gout of blood. The effect of the pressure wave massacring his vitals. Turning them to relish while leaving the shell of his body intact.

The Tajik grasped Carter's intentions as the latter closed in on him. He raised a trembling hand in a futile effort to protect his face and made a deep moaning sound in the back of his throat. Begging for mercy, maybe. Carter didn't know. He wasn't a linguist.

He double-tapped the mobster at point-blank range. Painting the asphalt a new shade of brain red. Then he hooked round to the side of the forklift. Ready to dispatch the other guy.

Biker Jacket was sprawled on the ground with his head turned inside out. All his facial cavities had exploded. The shock wave had distorted his features. Like a badly drawn approximation of a face. Somehow, he was still drawing breath. An inhuman groan escaped from the torn hole that had once been the guy's mouth. Carter gave him the good news with two quick rounds to his fucked-up face.

Take that, you prick. And don't ever mess with the SAS.

He ran across to the skip to engage the other three mobsters before they could recover. He shouldn't have bothered. All three of them were dead. They had been caught in the grenade's three-metre kill radius. The shell had decimated their bodies. Blood was leaking out of their eyes, their noses, their mouths, their ears.

No more than a minute had passed since the mobsters had debussed from their G-Wagons. Carter's ears were ringing. He was dimly aware that the shooting from the front end of the building had ceased. Vann and Ramsey had walloped the three remaining mobsters.

Eight dead. Textbook military defence.

Almost over.

But not quite.

Now I've got to finish off the other fuckers.

He reholstered the Grach, stooped down and seized the AK-47 lying next to Tracksuit's disfigured corpse. Carter thumbed the mag release catch and checked the clip. Making sure he had enough ammo for the two remaining targets inside the unit. Steel-jacketed 7.62 x 39 mm rounds gleamed dully in the magazine.

Two-thirds full. Twenty bullets or so.

Good enough.

He popped the clip back into the mag well. Pushed the fire selector lever in the down position. Semi-auto firing mode.

Then he started for the rear doorway.

Time to sort out Vann and Ramsey.

Carter cautiously approached the stronghold. He moved at a slow walk, wooden buttstock flush against his shoulder, the AK-47's front and rear sights fixed on the entry point fifteen metres away. Several seconds had passed since he'd last heard gunfire coming from the other side of the stronghold. There was a chance he might be walking into a snap ambush. Ramsey and Vann might be lying in wait for him inside. Behind the truck, perhaps. Weapons trained on the back door. Ready to empty rounds into Carter as soon as he appeared in the entrance.

He would have to neutralise Vann. There was no question about that, not anymore. The guy had passed the point of no return. Any residual sympathy Carter had felt for his old mentor had been blown away as soon as he'd laid eyes on the backpack nukes.

Hundreds of thousands of casualties. Mass destruction.

And the end of the world, possibly. Once the Chinese realised who had been culpable – an inevitability, no matter how careful Ramsey had been – they wouldn't hesitate to hit back with unimaginable force.

Greed had driven Vann to a very dark place. There was a price to pay for that. *We might both be former Para Reg*, Carter thought, *but I'm not the same as Vann. I'm not the same as him at all.*

He was ten metres from the entry point when he heard a distinctive sound.

The whirr of an electric motor.

Somewhere inside the building, an engine puttered into life.

Carter felt an icy pang of dread.

He broke into a run. Caution thrown to the wind. In a few manic beats he dashed through the entrance and looked towards the front end of the stronghold. The shutter roller door had been raised. Daylight was streaming in through the opening, flooding the interior space.

The box truck was screaming down the vehicle ramp.

Racing towards the main road.

Carter levelled his weapon with the back of the vehicle. No time to properly aim. He gave three quick pulls of the trigger, pointing the AK in the general area of the tyres. Disable the truck before it could make its getaway. There was no danger of triggering the nukes, Carter knew. They were enclosed in bulletproof protective containers to keep them safe during transit.

Two of the bullets landed short, thwacking into the asphalt several inches behind the rearmost tyres. The third round ricocheted off the rear sliding door.

The engine growled. The truck rapidly gained speed. There was a jolting shudder as it ran over the dead body of a Tajik gangster before it ploughed on past the two stationary G-Wagons, leaving the mobster's ragged corpse behind it in a tangle of bloodied limbs.

Carter loosed off a fourth round at the departing vehicle. A desperation shot. The bullet struck the rear licence plate as the truck pulled clear of the stronghold.

After a hundred and fifty metres, the truck abruptly slowed, brake lights flaring in the greying afternoon light. A tongue of bright flame licked out of the passenger's side window. Rounds sparked against the Yamaha, riddling the fuel tank.

Carter watched his ride go up in smoke as the truck sped off again. A few moments later, it reached the main road and slewed to the right, dropping out of sight.

There was no time to fuck about. Carter instantly knew what he had to do.

There's a private jet coming in today, Vann had said.

Them nukes are being transported to Taiwan.

The small airfield, he realised. Fifteen kilometres due north of Talbarok. The only airstrip anywhere in the vicinity of the town.

That's where the bastards were going.

He ditched the AK-47 and raced out through the garage door, chopping his stride as he sprinted madly towards the bodies sprawled on the ground twenty metres in front of the stronghold.

Vann had shot up his Yamaha in the hopes of stalling Carter. But he could still give chase in one of the G-Wagons.

Find the keys. Get on the main road.

If I floor it, I've still got a chance to catch Vann and Ramsey before they can ferry the nukes to the airfield.

He dropped down beside the guy who'd been flattened by the truck and started padding down his mutilated corpse. Carter checked his jacket pockets, his trousers. He found nothing. The guy was just a bag of crushed bones and squidgy flesh.

Carter hotfooted it over to the other two gangsters. Thoroughly searched both of them. He found a crocodile-skin wallet, a couple of burner phones, clips of cash, flavoured gum, Russian-branded cigarette packets, cheap lighters.

But no key fob.

Shit.

He ran back through the stronghold. Heart drumming inside his chest. Carter bolted out of the rear doorway and hurried towards the two dead guys at his twelve o'clock. He checked Puffer first. The guy was a million different kinds of fucked up. Blood dribbled out of his nostrils. His ribs had been pulverised, his eyeballs blown out of their sockets. His skin looked like bruised fruit. Within moments Carter's hands were lacquered in blood. He still found nothing. He turned his attention to Biker Jacket, moving fast as he rooted through his coat and trouser pockets. He located the shattered remnants of a key fob in the Tajik's inside pocket. Smashed apart by the sheer force of the pressure wave.

No good.

Carter got up again. Ran over to the other three guys lying face-down beside the debris-filled skip.

Whole minutes had passed since the truck had bombed out of the industrial estate. Right now Vann and Ramsey would be racing towards the airfield, putting crucial distance between themselves and Carter. Every extra second increased their advantage.

Carter finally hit paydirt on Tracksuit's body. He pulled out a sleek-looking key fob from the guy's blood-soaked joggers. The fob was smeared with blood. Carter wiped it down on the tracksuit sleeve, shot to his feet and flew back through the rear entrance into the stronghold. He halted briefly beside the workbench and picked up the Dragunov sniper rifle. Figured he'd need something with more accuracy and range than an AK-47 or the broken-down M4 rifle in his rucksack.

The Dragunov was chambered for the 7.62 mm Russian, a bigger round than the 5.56 mm used by the M4. Which basically translated to more stopping power. That could prove useful, if he needed to blow the truck tyres, or put some rounds into the side of the private jet.

I'm going up against an ex-Blade and a retired US Delta operator, Carter thought. *Both of them armed with assault rifles.*

I'm going to need all the help I can get.

He slung the Dragunov tactical carry-strap over his shoulder, muzzle pointing up. Scooped up a couple of mags of spare ammunition for the rifle, ten bullets to a clip. Tucked them into his side pockets, then legged it out of the unit through the busted front door. Carter bustled over to the two G-Wagons parked seventy metres away. He stopped a dozen paces from them and tapped the unlock button on the Benz key fob. The vehicle on the left flashed and clicked.

Get fucking moving, the voice in Carter's head urged.

He shoved the Dragunov into the back of the G-Wagon, jogged round to the front and dived behind the wheel. The interior was all luxury leather stitching and ambient lighting and polished aluminium. Carter stabbed the start button. The engine rumbled. The dash display lit up. The fuel indicator arrow was near the full mark. Some sort of bass-heavy Russian rap music thumped out of the internal speakers. Carter muted it.

He shifted the stick into Drive and U-turned in the middle of the asphalt patch until the front end of the G-Wagon was facing the main road. Then Carter mashed the pedal, and the twin-turbo V8 engine emitted a deep roar as he motored away from the industrial estate.

He pulled up after 150 metres. Next to the garage and the shot-up Yamaha. Carter hopped out of the wagon and retrieved the rucksack he'd stowed behind the mound of rubble. He pulled out the satphone, threw it aside and tossed the pack into the back seat, next to the Dragunov rifle.

In the distance, the mechanical wail of police sirens pierced the air.

Cops.

The sound of the gunfire and the GM-94 rounds would have travelled for miles, Carter knew.

Another minute, and the police will be all over this place.

Time to get the fuck out of here.

Carter vaulted back into the driving seat. He gunned the G-Wagon and hurtled towards the main road, wrenching the steering wheel hard to the right as he reached the T-junction. The vehicle lurched heavily, two and a half tons of metal fishtailing across the tarmac, tyres squealing, motorbikes swerving to avoid him, taxi horns blaring. Carter wrestled with the wheel, straightened out, put his foot to the pedal again.

The wagon shot forward. Zero to sixty in under five seconds.

Thirty seconds later, Carter was bulleting north out of Talbarok.

Speeding towards the airfield.

Twenty-Four

Carter bulleted north on a ramrod-straight road for six kilometres. Foot to the pedal, white-knuckled hands gripping the wheel. Driven by a compulsive determination to stop Vann once and for all. Vann, and Bill Ramsey. The man who heard God whispering in his ear, telling him to blow up tens of thousands of civilians to prevent the Armageddon. Hard to believe that a guy like that had once been in charge of the CIA, Carter reflected. Had spent the past three years stalking the corridors of the White House, advising the president, setting the agenda on China.

Then again, maybe not.

As he closed in on the airfield, Carter kept glancing at the dashboard clock. Two fifty-nine. By his calculation he was eight kilometres from his destination. Eleven or twelve minutes out. Four or perhaps five minutes behind the truck. Valuable time had been lost searching the slotted Tajiks. But Vann and Ramsey would be unlikely to be moving at top speed towards the airfield, Carter thought. Partly because of the appalling state of the roads in Tajikistan. But also because they had five nuclear warheads rattling around in the back of the truck. Minds would be concentrated. Nobody wanted an accident in transit. Carter felt confident he could close the gap before they reached the airfield.

Put a couple of bursts in the tyres with the Dragunov.

Disable the vehicle.

Then drop Vann and Ramsey.

He bowled on for another kilometre before he hit a T-junction beside a truck stop.

Then his plan went to shit.

There were no road signs on the approach to the T. Nothing to indicate which way to go for the airfield. No signs at all.

Fuck.

Carter pumped the brakes and pulled over. He had to waste more precious minutes digging the map out from his rucksack and orientating himself. He found the route, took off again, made the right turn at the T, and then stamped down on the accelerator as he nosed the G-Wagon down a rough-hewn road. The route took him past a ruined landscape of dust-brown valleys and desolate fields. In the distance, he saw steep mountains, snow-covered peaks like neatly filed teeth. He saw no signs of habitation anywhere, no villages or petrol stations or market stalls. Just a vast expanse of nothingness.

The emptiest place in the world.

Five minutes out from the airfield.

Not long to go now.

Almost there.

Christ, it's gonna be fucking close.

He pushed the G-Wagon as fast as it would go, desperate to make up the lost ground on Vann and Ramsey. The engine sounded its beast-like roar as the speedometer upticked above a hundred per. Carter felt the shudder in his bones as the SUV lurched over crater-deep potholes. At the same time he scanned the horizon. He was three minutes from the airfield now, but there was still no sign of the truck ahead. Which could only mean one thing, he knew. The truck had already arrived at the airstrip.

I've still got time, Carter told himself.

The jet would need to refuel before take-off, he reasoned. A long-haul flight to Taiwan. It would take a few minutes to unload the backpack nukes and transfer them to the private jet. There would have to be pre-flight checks. All of that. It would be incredibly tight, but there was still a chance he could make it.

Sixty seconds later, he crossed a concrete girder bridge over a narrow river, and then he caught sight of the airfield, four hundred metres to the north, separated from the road by a wide dirt field. The airfield was situated at the bottom of a narrow valley, surrounded by a flimsy chain-link fence, with steep scree-covered mountains on either side of the vale.

From his map study Carter knew that the single airstrip ran for about two kilometres on a north-east to south-west axis. Long enough to land a medium-sized jet. Built at the request of the domestic elite, Carter presumed. The president and his family would need a decent runway to fly in and out of the country on their private jollies.

A hundred metres further west he noticed that a section of the chain-link fence had been smashed apart. Tyre tracks ran through the dirt, stretching from the roadside to the breach in the perimeter, before they carried on again towards the north-eastern end of the runway two kilometres away. Carter knew then that Ramsey and Vann had gone off-road, crashing through the fence and cutting across the dirt field. Shaving off valuable seconds in their mad rush to make their getaway.

At the far end of the strip Carter descried a mid-sized jet, a white truck parked up beside it. He gripped the wheel even tighter and felt a hot surge of anticipation in his chest.

They're still here. Thank Christ.

I'm still in the game.

He willed the G-Wagon on, pushing the engine hard as the road skirted in a clockwise direction around the edge of the airfield for several hundred metres. He hit the turn-off for the entrance, hung a sharp right and arrowed the vehicle east down the narrow access road.

There was no security presence at the airfield, no checkpoint or guardhouse. Just a gap in the chain-link fence leading to the tarmac apron at the far end of the access road.

Carter pelted past the entry point and stuck to the access road for four hundred metres. He highballed past the parking lot and stomped on the brakes just before he reached the row of sheds and hangars on the western fringes of the apron, skidding to a halt ten metres from the nearest shed. He sprang the side handle and dived out of the Benz, boots thudding against the asphalt. Scooted round to the rear door, popped it open and took out the Dragunov. Then he dashed towards the apron.

Carter was running on fumes now. He'd been pushing himself to the very limits of his endurance for almost two days, with virtually no sleep and hardly any sustenance. His muscles ached with tiredness, every cell in his body craved rest, but none of that mattered now. This was it.

Win or lose.

Do or fucking die.

He heard the blood rushing in his ears, felt his heart hammering inside his chest. Carter spurred his exhausted body forward. Summoning his inner reserves of strength for one last effort.

Keep moving.

Hurry.

Whatever happens, I've got to stop that jet from leaving.

He hit the south-eastern corner of the apron in two brisk strides and stepped out of cover from behind the nearest shed. In front of him was a tarmac stand the size of two football pitches. On the left, at his eleven o'clock, stood a line of low aircraft buildings. Hangars and run-down sheds and workshops. In one hangar he saw a bunch of maintenance equipment: air stands, tyre dollies, aviation tools, the exposed innards of a disembodied turbofan engine.

A fire tender had been parked up in a large carport outside the next hangar, along with a four-wheeled snow plough and several other vehicles. North of the apron was an air traffic control tower and a fuel dump.

Carter assumed there would be a skeleton crew at the airfield. A couple of guys in the tower, maybe a few mechanics in the hangars working on one of the jets, but he doubted they would get involved once the rounds started flying.

He dropped into a prone firing position on the ground to the immediate right of the nearest shed. Carter lowered the bipod clamped to the underside of the barrel, propping the legs on the asphalt. He placed his cheek against the leather cushion fixed to the top of the stock, yanked the cocking handle to chamber the first round of 7.62 Russian. Then he peered down the PSO-1 4 x 24 telescopic sights fixed to the mounted rail. The floating reticule had a bunch of markings and lines to help the shooter correctly estimate things like range to the target, bullet drop and windage.

Carter lined up the cross hairs with the Learjet parked on the edge of the runway six hundred metres to the north-east, at his one o'clock.

He was looking at the front end of the aircraft. On the left side of the fuselage the airstair was in the lowered position, although Carter's view was partially obscured by the cockpit. The truck was parked eight or nine metres from the bottom of the airstair, at the edge of the runway. Ramsey was pacing urgently beside the vehicle, phone glued to his ear, pausing mid-stride to check his watch.

Carter searched the area again. He couldn't see Vann anywhere. In the main cabin, maybe. Loading one of the nukes. He considered taking a shot at Ramsey, but instantly ruled it out. He didn't want to alert Vann and give him another chance to escape. Better to wait until he had sight of both targets.

Vann's not getting away this time. Not a fucking chance.

Carter checked the cockpit. One of the pilots was looking down at the flight plan. He wouldn't see Carter, not at this distance. The guy would be preoccupied with running through the checks prior to take-off. The co-pilot's seat was empty.

Probably at the back of the jet, thought Carter. *Helping to secure the nukes. A two-man job to make sure they're strapped into place. You don't want one of those things rolling down the aisle mid-flight.*

Carter couldn't shoot the pilot. The cockpit glass was roughly two inches thick. A 7.62 round would deflect off the surface. Like throwing a rock at a tank. If he had a .50 calibre rifle, nailing the pilot might have been an option. But not now.

So he waited.

Bided his time.

One chance to get this right.

Three seconds later, a figure emerged from the cabin.

Carter didn't get a clear look at him until he had cleared the treads at the bottom of the airstair. Then he saw it was Vann. He watched as Vann started towards the rear of the stationary truck, moving at a brisk trot. A man in a powerful hurry.

Ramsey was still on the phone. He made no attempt to help Vann cart the nukes aboard the cabin. Grunt work. He didn't strike Carter as the kind of guy who liked to roll up his sleeves and muck in. Guys like Ramsey always left the heavy lifting to their subordinates.

Carter kept the optics trained on the truck.

He looked on as Vann grabbed another backpack nuke from the back of the truck. The last one. He set it down on the runway, then hopped into the front of the truck and steered it over to the side of the runway, putting it well clear of the Learjet. He jumped out again and jogged back over to Ramsey and the last nuke.

Carter tensed his finger on the Dragunov trigger.

As soon as he'd dropped Vann, he would turn his attention to Ramsey. Carter would have to clip the guy before he had a chance to run for cover or escape.

Once they were both out of the picture Carter could rush forward and secure the backpack nukes at gunpoint. He doubted the aircraft crew would put up much resistance. Then he'd use one of their phones to put a call in to Vauxhall Bridge.

Tell them what the fuck had been going on.

In the next second, Vann stooped down to pick up the drum-shaped nuclear backpack. Ramsey stood close by and lowered his phone. He said something to Vann. Had to shout to make himself heard above the constant whine of the jet engines and the low rumble of the truck. They hadn't noticed Carter. Hadn't even glanced back towards the apron. No reason why they should. They were preoccupied with getting out of the country.

Vann stopped and looked up at Ramsey. He shouted something back at the American. There was lots of energetic hand-waving and gesturing from both parties. Vann seemed pissed off. He started jabbing a finger at Ramsey. An argument over the money, perhaps. Terms of payment. Perhaps Vann felt he was entitled to a sizeable bonus.

Carter exhaled, relaxing his muscles as he aimed for Vann's centre mass. The body shot. At a distance of six hundred metres you had to go for the biggest target to give yourself the best possible chance of a kill. A chest wound worked just as well as a head shot, in Carter's experience.

He pulled the trigger.

Heard a click.

Nothing happened.

Shit.

Stoppage.

Carter lifted the lever and pulled it back, ejecting the 7.62 round. He pushed the handle forward and down again, chambering the next bullet from the box mag. Looked down the sights and refocused on Vann's torso. Vann was still standing beside the truck, continuing his heated exchange with Ramsey.

He squeezed the trigger.

Click.

Same result.

He recocked the weapon a second time, panic and confusion quickly spreading through his body. Carter jerked his head back from the sights. He looked down at the last ejected round. The percussion cap on the base of the bullet hadn't been struck by the rifle's firing pin. Therefore not a stoppage, but a defective pin. Doctored by someone, or just plain fucked. Either way, it didn't matter.

The Dragunov was knackered.

Carter tried to think. The Grach was no good for anything other than close-range shooting. He could rush back to the G-Wagon and retrieve the M4 components from his backpack, but there was no time to reassemble the weapon. Even if he did manage to piece it together before the jet took off, the M4 wouldn't be very effective, not at a range of six hundred metres.

I'm fucked, Carter thought bitterly. *No way of stopping these bastards from getting away.*

Then he heard a crack.

Twenty-Five

Carter looked up.

Six hundred metres away, Vann was slumped on the ground next to the backpack nuke.

Ramsey stood over him. Pistol in his right hand.

Carter frantically looked through the Dragunov sights again, centring the reticule on Vann. He couldn't see where the guy had been shot, not at this distance, but one look at his motionless body told him that the guy was dead. Head shot, he supposed. Clean and efficient.

We've covered our tracks, Ramsey had boasted at the stronghold. *No fingerprints. No one will link the nukes to us.*

Vann had been a fool to trust his American partner. Now he'd paid the ultimate price.

Carter watched helplessly through the sights as Ramsey shoved his pistol back into the waistband of his trousers. He snatched up the last backpack nuke by the shoulder straps and lugged it over to the airstair, stepping around Vann's lifeless corpse. As he hustled up the treads, he began shouting at the pilots at the top of his voice.

Get moving. We're out of here.

Carter saw him disappear inside the cabin. Then the airstair retracted, the cabin door sealed shut, and the steady machine-like drone of the engines boomed louder as the Learjet made its final preparations before take-off.

Carter looked around despairingly.

The whine of the jet engines rose to a high-pitched crescendo. He had only a few more seconds before the jet would start tearing down the runway.

I've come this far. I can't fucking lose. Not here.

Not today.

His gaze instantly settled on the bright orange snow plough. An idea took split-second shape in his mind. Maybe a chance in ten it would work. But he had to try.

One last desperate roll of the dice.

Carter bolted upright. He left the Dragunov on the asphalt and raced over to the carport sixty metres away, lungs burning with the effort.

Hurry up.

He tugged open the door on the side of the snow plough and clambered up into the main cab. The key was already wedged in the ignition. Carter twisted it to the right.

The engine didn't start.

Carter cursed in bitter frustration. More broken equipment. He was beginning to take this shit personally.

By now the whirr of the jet engines was deafening.

He had seconds until the Learjet started rolling forward.

Carter turned the key to the start position again. There was an agonising pause as the diesel engine coughed noisily, spewing out black smoke from the exhaust. Then it sputtered into life.

I'm in business.

Carter strapped on his seat belt, because in another twenty seconds it might save his life. He shoved the vehicle into gear, hit the accelerator and started rolling forward across the ground towards the Learjet, six hundred metres from his position.

As the plough gathered momentum Carter worked the hydraulic lever on the right-hand side of the seat, lifting the blade off the ground by about a metre or so. He would have to wait to raise the bucket the rest of the way up until the last possible second before he collided with the aircraft. Otherwise he would be driving blind.

The vehicle picked up pace as Carter cranked up through the gears, climbing to a speed of fifty kilometres per hour. Fast enough to generate the necessary force for what he had in mind. The plough engine screamed, drowning out the incessant whine of the jet. In another few metres he broke clear of the asphalt and Carter struggled to control the plough as it jounced and rocked over the irrigation ditches parallel with the taxiway.

Four hundred metres from the Learjet.

Carter hit the taxiway with a jolt. He drove right across it, crashed through a sign, then looked up again and saw that the jet had started rolling forward along the runway.

Making its escape.

No, you fucking don't, pal, Carter thought.

He made an instantaneous calculation, based on speed and distance, and adjusted the vehicle so that the half-raised blade was pointing at a spot on the runway approximately three hundred metres south of the Learjet's current position. A rough guess, but the best he could do under the circumstances. He had one chance to hit the aircraft and stop Ramsey from getting airborne.

To the north-east, the jet carried on down the airstrip. Moving faster now. Two hundred metres from Carter. He had to constantly alter the vehicle's path, compensating for the increase in speed as the aircraft surged down the runway. Like targeting a fast-flying bird. You had to follow through the bird, aiming a couple of metres ahead before pulling the trigger, so that the bird flew into the shot. This was the same principle. But much higher stakes.

The ground became bumpier as Carter cleared the taxiway and steered over the rough ground. A hundred and fifty metres to the target. The pilots must have spotted him by now. No way they could have missed him, not at this distance. But they hadn't slowed down. Which meant they were gambling on racing ahead of the plough before it could collide with the aircraft. They were playing the world's most dangerous game of chicken.

Carter had resigned himself to the fact that this was a suicide mission. The chances of him walking away from a direct collision with a moving jet were virtually nil. But he was out of options, and time, and luck. He had a choice between letting Ramsey escape, and hoping that someone else sorted the problem later down the line, or stopping him right now.

No kind of a choice at all.

Carter didn't believe in letting other people fix shit. A question of personal responsibility. The way he looked at it, you could do something right, or do nothing at all. Which was just as bad as doing wrong.

Lives depended on the outcome of this face-off on the runway. If that meant having to sacrifice himself, so be it.

In another fifty metres Carter steered onto the runway, bull-dozing through the row of marker lights. He was less than forty metres from the jet now. The aircraft was shooting along at well over a hundred kilometres per hour, the pilots flooring it in their sheer desperation to avoid the snow plough. Carter made a final correction to his trajectory and steeled himself.

He didn't think the nukes would detonate on impact. It would take more than a violent jolt to trigger them.

He hoped.

In the final few seconds before contact, Carter pulled hard again on the hydraulic lever, lifting the blade up so that it reached the same height as the front of the Learjet. The bucket now fully blocked his view but that didn't matter. He knew he was going to hit the aircraft. Impact was inevitable.

He wondered if kamikaze pilots had felt like this, in the moments before they slammed into a battleship.

His body tensed. Carter braced himself.

The plough rammed into the cockpit at a forty-five-degree angle, shearing off the front end in a shriek of twisted metal and engine-screech.

Carter had just enough time to see the Learjet spinning off its axis, tipping over onto its left wing. Then the force of the collision threw him forward. His head slammed against the dashboard.

Carter saw white for the briefest moment. A jarring pain ripped through his skull, and then his world went sideways as the plough tipped heavily onto its right side. There was an incessant din of shattering glass, metal scraping against metal, the squeal of burning rubber and the high-pitched scream of a damaged engine. The cab shook violently, throwing Carter from side to side, and he felt sure that he was going to die.

The plough engine cut out.

Carter opened his eyes.

Alive, he realised.

Christ, I'm still alive.

He was conscious of something in the air. The unmistakable smell of avgas, pissing out of the ruptured Learjet tanks. A second later, he felt a searing wave of heat through the cabin's spider-cracked windscreen as the aircraft caught fire.

Some primitive survival instinct seized hold of Carter. A voice in the lizard part of his brain spoke up, shouting at him above the scream of the engines.

Get out of the cab. Right fucking now.

Carter shook glass fragments from his head and reached for the driver's side door. Which was now facing skyward. He desperately flung the door open, pushing it up, like a trapped crewman forcing open a submarine hatch.

The flames quickly spread as Carter crawled out of the over-turned vehicle. He tumbled down to the ground, scraped himself off the glass-sprinkled asphalt and hurried away from the aircraft.

He was twenty metres away when the jet burst into flames with a furious roar. The heat scorched the back of his neck; he staggered on for several paces, then paused to glance back at the blazing wreckage.

Apricot flames engulfed the canted Learjet. Smoke spewed up from the fuselage, billowing into the afternoon sky. There was debris all over the ground. Twisted bits of metal, lengths of electrical wiring, shattered flight instruments. Amid the carnage,

Carter spotted the severed torso of one of the pilots, cooking in the glow of the flames. The plough blade had cleaved his body in half.

He spied a flicker of movement beyond the flames. Carter shielded his eyes against the intense heat and smoke and saw Ramsey limping away from the aircraft. Carrying a black duffel bag in his right hand. The guy struggled on for another three or four metres before he collapsed.

Carter slowly approached the stricken American. Blood-splashed fingers fumbled for the Grach in his holster. He stopped beside Ramsey. The latter peeled his face away from the asphalt and rolled onto his back as he gazed up at Carter. He was in a seriously bad way. His clothes had been singed. His flesh had been badly burned. The left side of his face looked like someone had taken a blowtorch to it.

Ramsey read the intention in Carter's eyes. His face, or what was left of it, went pale with fear.

'No,' he gasped. 'No.'

'Yes,' Carter said.

He shoved the tip of the Grach barrel against Ramsey's blistered forehead. His eyes were wide with terror. He let out a final pleading moan before Carter blew his brains out.

Carter turned away from the dead American. He shuffled back down the runway towards the control tower.

A million different nerve endings flared in his body. His skull felt as if it had been split down the middle with a battleaxe. He'd lost a couple of front teeth. A bruise the size of a grapefruit throbbed painfully on his temple.

It hurt like fuck to breathe, and he could feel the blood oozing out of a deep wound on his scalp. But otherwise he seemed OK. No serious internal damage. Nothing that wouldn't heal eventually.

Bad, but could have been a fuck of a lot worse.

He stopped at the edge of the airstrip and paused briefly as he looked back at Vann. At the man he'd once admired, now sprawled on an airfield in Tajikistan with a hole in his head. Carter half expected some profound meaning to occur to him, but none did.

The control tower was six hundred metres away, but it felt more like six miles. His legs were heavy with fatigue, every muscle in his body ached abominably. Like the end of Test Week. It took a great will of effort to stumble through the door and climb the stairs to the control room.

One last thing to do.

He briefly wondered what would happen once he reported this to Six. There would be a frantic effort to cover their tracks. That would be Vauxhall Bridge's first priority. A clean-up crew would be dispatched to the airfield urgently. Local assets. The nukes would be seized. Witnesses paid off. The skeleton crew at the airfield was in for an unexpected bonus.

There would be a debrief once he'd returned home. Six would want to go over his story in forensic detail. The Company probably wouldn't get involved. They'd be busy cleaning up in-house. Mullins, and Ortega, and whoever else was involved in Ramsey's deranged plot. But the hawks would use it to their advantage. There would be some difficult conversations in the Oval Office. Uncomfortable truths would be presented to the president. A week or two from now the White House would send a fleet to the South China Sea. Training exercise. Back channels would be opened with Beijing. Warnings issued. Nothing specific, nothing overtly hostile, but with just enough meat on the bones to persuade the CCP that they were serious.

You really don't want to call our bluff on this one. Trust us, you don't want to go there.

No one would thank Carter for his efforts. There would be no gong, no handshake from the head shed. That was for fucking sure.

He reached the top of the stairs, pulled the Grach on the crew working the tower and told them he needed to use a phone. None of them apparently understood him. They simply stood looking at the bloodied Englishman with expressions of shock and terror. Eventually one of them got the message and directed him to a console with a keyboard and a bunch of monitors and a Cisco phone.

Carter picked up the receiver and punched in a UK number from memory. An emergency contact number at Vauxhall Bridge. For assets in the field.

The phone rang twice. A female operator answered in a polite businesslike voice and gave the name of a generic data solutions business, one of several fronts used by Six.

'How may I direct your call, sir?'

'Department Nineteen,' Carter said.

'Please hold.'

There was a beat of dead air, followed by a burst of cheery hold music. Some upbeat 1980s pop song. Carter listened to it for several moments while he watched the aircraft burn through the slanted tower windows.

Then someone picked up.

'Yes?' the voice asked.

'This is Carter,' came the reply. 'They're all dead.'

EPILOGUE

Hereford, UK

Four days later, Carter sat at the end of a long table in a windowless briefing room at the Regiment camp in Credenhill. There were several such rooms at SAS headquarters: bland, sparsely furnished, with no electronic devices permitted inside, ideal for secure meetings.

He had been summoned by the Regiment ops officer to the camp earlier that morning. Three days after his return to Hereford. Carter had been kicking his heels at home since he'd left Tajikistan, reading and recovering from the injuries he'd sustained at the airfield attack. His own form of decompression. There had been an initial debrief at the British Embassy in Dushanbe in the immediate aftermath of his phone call. But Carter knew there would be a follow-up at some point once he was back home. Inevitable, given the sensitivity of the mission. When the ops officer had called him with orders to report to base, he knew exactly what was going on.

Four people sat around the table in front of Carter, their features starkly lit by the ceiling panel lights.

Peter Hardcastle, the CO of 22 SAS, was a stern man, a career Rupert who despised Carter for his freelance attitude. It was an open secret that he'd wanted Carter out of the Regiment ever since the Mali siege.

Next to Hardcastle sat a smooth-faced man in his late fifties with piercing blue eyes. Eliot Lebrun was a senior Six officer, an old China hand, with an accent redolent of old money and French aristocratic roots. Part of the Old Etonian dynasty that still liked to think it ruled Six, but increasingly found itself on the back foot.

To Lebrun's right was another Six officer, Philippa Beck. She was dark-haired, with mouse-like features, small but fierce, a forty-something Northern lass with a fondness for strong ale and rugby league. Carter had liked her from the moment they had first met.

The fourth person was a chubby guy in an ill-fitting suit and a Tory-blue tie, mid-forties, with a prominent bald patch. James Gregory was a former Colonel in the Grenadier Guards, and one of the up-and-coming figures in the Foreign Office. He had a permanent frown etched across his brow, and the restless energy, limitless ego and naked ruthlessness of a man who had his eyes on one day becoming Defence Secretary.

Carter had worked with Gregory, Beck and Lebrun on various jobs in the past. They had been waiting for him in the briefing room when he'd arrived at the camp. Lebrun did most of the talking. He greeted Carter with a pleasant smile and feigned concern for his injuries, then asked him to talk through his story one more time.

Hardcastle made no attempt to hide his displeasure with Carter. He spent most of the meeting glaring at him in silent contempt.

'. . . and that's when I decided to crash the plough into the jet,' Carter said, finishing his account.

'A rather risky move, don't you think?' Lebrun asked. 'Could have easily turned out rather badly for you.'

Carter shrugged. 'I had no option. It was the only way I could see to stop them taking off.'

'Why not let them get away?' Gregory wondered out loud. 'You could have made a note of the tail number and called it in to us. Our chaps would have been able to track them down sooner or later. Hell of a lot less messy, wouldn't you say?'

'I had to make a decision,' Carter said. 'I couldn't take the risk.'

'Seems sensible enough to me,' Beck said in her strong Lancastrian accent. 'There's no guarantee we would have caught them in time. Ramsey might have cached the weapons before we could locate them.'

Gregory muttered something under his breath.

'Go on,' Lebrun said.

Carter said, 'After the crash, I neutralised Ramsey. That was it. I walked away, called it in to your lot. End of.'

'What about Vann?' asked Gregory. 'Did you go over to check his body?'

Carter realised the others were staring at him intently.

'No need,' he replied. 'I saw him go down. He was dead. I figured Ramsey had shot him in the head.'

'But you couldn't be sure?'

'A plane full of nukes was on fire,' Carter replied tetchily. 'I didn't plan on sticking around the scene for long.' He frowned. 'What the fuck's going on? Why are you asking me all of this stuff?'

Lebrun and Beck exchanged a look. Gregory coughed and shifted uncomfortably. Hardcastle sat with intertwined hands, glowering at Carter like he was something he'd scraped off the sole of his boot.

Lebrun said, 'After your call our friends at the Company sent in some of their local assets to secure the airfield. It had to be the Americans because we didn't have any assets of our own in the area. They found the plane and the snow plough, in exactly the condition you described. They found Ramsey, and the two pilots. But there was no sign of your chum.'

Carter flinched in shock. He felt something cold running down his spine. 'No.'

'Also missing, a duffel bag filled with heroin, if we are to believe your version of events,' Lebrun continued.

Gregory gave him a long, searching look. 'I don't suppose you'd know anything about that, would you?'

'Of course not.'

'Still.' The Foreign Office man spread his hands. 'It looks rather convenient, wouldn't you say? Your friend vanishing without explanation, plus the drugs.'

Carter shook his head. 'I don't understand. Vann was right fucking there. He went down. I saw him.'

Lebrun slipped on a pair of rimless glasses and consulted his scribbled notes in front of him. 'Let's be specific, shall we? You told us that Vann was killed by a shot to the head.'

'Aye. That's right.'

'But you can't possibly be sure, can you? Not from a distance of six hundred metres.' He looked up from his notes. 'Unless you wish to volunteer some other explanation to us?'

Carter glowered at the Six officer but just about managed to bite his tongue.

Don't give them the satisfaction. They're trying to needle you, that's all.

Keep a level head.

Hardcastle had been silent throughout the briefing. Now he leaned forward and shot Carter a look so hard you could have crushed rocks with it.

'This is far from the only disconcerting aspect to this mission, Geordie,' he said.

Carter frowned. 'Not sure what you mean, boss.'

'Aren't you?' Hardcastle snorted. 'Let me lay it out for you, then. We've got a CIA agent dead on a runway in Tajikistan with a gunshot wound to the head. We've got two American contractors working as pilots, who were also found dead on the same runway. We've got a badly damaged private jet, not to mention the body of a former Coalition interpreter who appears to have been shot in the head at point-blank range. One of our most valuable assets in-country. Last seen in your company, I understand.'

Carter felt his face flushing with anger. 'You're not suggesting I had anything to do with the guy's death. I told you, Hakimi killed him. I saw it happen.'

'Perhaps all of that is true,' Lebrun replied diplomatically. 'But you must admit, it's not a good look. There's a trail of destruction that seems to have followed you from Afghanistan to Tajikistan.'

'I was just doing my job,' Carter hit back. 'I had no choice.'

'Your job?' Hardcastle repeated tetchily. 'You were given orders to locate Vann and bring him in, Geordie. Now he's missing, and you've fed us a highly colourful tale of Vann going rogue and getting involved in the heroin trade.'

'It's all true, boss. Every word of it.' Carter struggled to keep the rage out of his voice.

'Don't be ridiculous,' Hardcastle thundered. 'I know David Vann very well. I know his character. Are you trying to tell me that a highly regarded former member of the SAS is now a drug smuggler? Do you think I'm fucking thick, Geordie?'

He stared defiantly at Carter, almost daring him to respond. Carter looked back at his CO. And suddenly understood what was happening.

This is a bloody stitch-up. They're trying to cover their tracks. Vann's going to be rehabilitated. Orders from above, probably.

They don't want a public scandal blowing up in their faces.

'Well?' Hardcastle snapped.

'No, boss,' he muttered.

'There's also the question of the portable nuclear bombs,' Gregory put in. 'The, ah, backpack nukes, as you refer to them in your statement, I believe.'

Carter nodded. 'Aye, what about them?'

'You're not seriously suggesting these things exist, are you? This is a nonsense story, man. Fantasy material. Belongs on a conspiracy website.'

'If you don't believe me, ask the Company,' Carter said. 'They'll have removed the nukes from the jet by now.'

Gregory smoothed his Tory-blue tie and flashed a thin smile. 'We have asked them already. They have assured us that no such weapons were discovered at the airfield. We've also independently contacted some of our Russian sources to clarify whether such bombs were developed during the Cold War. They have confirmed to us privately that they cannot. They are adamant that they would know about it, if indeed the Soviets had ever embarked on such a programme.'

Carter knew at once what had happened. As soon as the alarm had been raised the Americans had swept into the airfield and seized the bombs, disposing of the evidence before anyone else could get hold of them. Langley would have quietly disposed of the nukes and shared only the very sanitised version of events with their friends at MI6.

'You can cover up this shit as much as you want,' Carter said. 'But I know what I saw. I know what was there. If you're worried about me spilling my guts, forget it. As far as I'm concerned, it stays with me.'

'Absolutely no idea what you're talking about, old chap.'

'Any more questions?' Lebrun looked round the room. Then he laced his fingers and offered Carter an insincere smile. 'I think we're just about done here. You're free to leave, Carter.'

'What about my next posting, boss?' Carter directed the question to his CO. Who looked at him with his expression contorted into a scowl.

'You've got two years left,' Hardcastle said. 'I was minded to send you on another posting overseas to see out your contract, but now I hear that you battered the son of some general in Chile. So you can bloody well forget about anything like that. No, you'll be seeing out your contract at home.'

There was a wicked gleam in the CO's eyes. Carter felt his heart sink. He shook his head furiously. 'What am I supposed to do for the next two years, then?'

'Sit in the pub, for all I care. Get pissed and tell old war stories. Hang out at the local bookies. Learn a new language. Honestly, I couldn't give two shits what you do. But you won't be setting foot in the camp ever again. I don't want you anywhere near this fucking place, d'you hear? No roll call, no turning up unannounced.'

Carter's mouth hung open. He stared at his CO in stunned silence. 'What for?'

'You're a liability,' Hardcastle said icily. 'We sent you out to do a straightforward search-and-rescue op, and you turned it into a bloodbath. Moreover, you've provided knowingly untruthful statements in an attempt to mask your incompetence by slandering Vann and Ramsey. This is totally unacceptable behaviour.'

This was all part of the big Six cover-up, Carter realised bitterly.

Keep me out of the Hereford loop. Blackball me. Trash my reputation. Make sure no one at Hereford wants to touch me with a barge pole. That way, if I ever go public with my claims, they'll brand me an embittered fantasist with zero credibility.

This is the end of my Regiment career.

Lebrun said, 'One more thing.'

Carter turned to the MI6 man and waited for him to continue. Lebrun looked him hard in the eye and smiled coldly.

'If any of these, ah, outrageous rumours should ever reach the public domain, we will hold you personally responsible,' he said. 'At that point, we'll tell the Americans who killed Ramsey. We wouldn't want you to face a murder charge. Would we . . .?'

If you enjoyed *Outcast*,
why not join the
CHRIS RYAN READERS' CLUB?

Keep reading for a letter from the author . . .

Hello!

Thank you for picking up *Outcast*.

In the years since I began writing fiction, the nature of modern warfare has changed dramatically. During the long conflicts in the Middle East, the guys in 22 SAS conducted a lot of door-kicking operations, going out on multiple raids each night to apprehend targets and working closely with their American counterparts in Delta Force and SEAL Team Six. Now the West is facing a new threat from authoritarian regimes equipped with vast military resources and skilled in the arts of disinformation. The spectre of nuclear catastrophe has become a possibility once more, as recent events in Ukraine have sadly shown.

One of the reasons I wanted to write *Outcast* is to illustrate what role the Regiment might have in this new dynamic. Despite their differences, both Carter and Vann operate in the 'grey space' of the battlefield: training up foreign resistance forces, securing the passage of weaponry into war zones, gathering intelligence on the strength and disposition of enemy forces and extracting key figures from hotspots. This kind of work is going to be increasingly important for the SAS going forward. But it also brings new risks for the guys involved. What if a soldier goes missing, or gets captured? How would the British government react to that situation? Those questions gave me the initial idea for *Outcast*. Ultimately, this is a story about the potential consequences of sending in men to operate alone behind enemy lines, without support.

If you would like to hear more about my books, you can visit **bit.ly/ChrisRyanClub** where you can become part of the Chris Ryan Readers' Club. It only takes a few moments to sign up, and there are no catches or costs.

Bonnier Books UK will keep your data private and confidential, and it will never be passed on to a third party. We won't spam you with loads of emails, just get in touch now and again with news about my books, and you can unsubscribe any time you want.

And if you would like to get involved in a wider conversation about my books, please do review *Outcast* on Amazon, on Goodreads, on any other e-store, on your own blog and social media accounts, or talk about it with friends, family or reader groups! Sharing your thoughts helps other readers, and I always enjoy hearing about what people experience from my writing.

Thank you again for reading *Outcast*.

All the best,

Chris Ryan